ACTS OF LOVE

Talulah Riley is an actress, writer, director, and the co-founder and COO of Forge, a mobile app for the scheduling of hourly workers in retail. As an actress she has appeared in numerous feature films and television productions, and in the West End. *Acts of Love* is her first novel.

ACTS OF LOVE

TALULAH RILEY

HODDER &
STOUGHTON

First published in Great Britain in 2016 by Hodder & Stoughton
An Hachette UK company

1

Copyright © Talulah Riley 2016

The right of Talulah Riley to be identified as the
Author of the Work has been asserted by her in accordance
with the Copyright, Designs and Patents Act 1988.

A CIP catalogue record for this title is available from the British Library

Hardback ISBN 978 1 473 63790 0
Trade Paperback ISBN 978 1 473 63787 0

Typeset in Guardi by Palimpsest Book Production Ltd, Falkirk, Stirlingshire

Printed and bound in Great Britain by Clays Ltd, St Ives plc

Hodder & Stoughton policy is to use papers that are natural, renewable and
recyclable products and made from wood grown in sustainable forests. The
logging and manufacturing processes are expected to conform to the
environmental regulations of the country of origin.

Hodder & Stoughton Ltd
Carmelite House
50 Victoria Embankment
London EC4Y 0DZ

www.hodder.co.uk

For Sarah Carvosso

1

In her face, Bernadette St John had all the necessary symmetry, all the youthful indicators and hyper-feminine features so revered by the opposite sex. But these delights masked a mind riddled with a poisonous bigotry: a profound and very real contempt for men that extended beyond anything reasonable or healthy. It was a prejudice formed slowly, over years of disappointment.

This defeat was as much a part of her as her arresting face, with its pointed chin, retroussé profile, and high cheekbones. Her eyes were hazel; copper-coloured in some lights, witch-green in others, rarely just brown. No man who looked in those eyes ever guessed at the hostile feeling behind them; instead, most were left with an impression of a genial sensuality, a soft femininity, the promise of an understanding love.

She was used to arriving at parties alone, and only slightly afraid of it, but on the evening of Tim Bazier's annual Christmas drinks, her usually stoic persona betrayed definite signs of unease. She was nauseous. The thin material of her dress, what little there was of it, clung coldly to the sweat that had formed across her back and under her arms. Most disconcertingly of all, tears were threating to form behind mascara-clad lashes.

Bernadette, unfortunately, believed herself to be in love with the host of the party, who was too diffident and unassertive for practical romancing. Her belief though was quite unshakeable, and her misandry extended to every man except this one.

Of course, Bernadette was not born into the world with a fully formed pathology; as with all deviants, there were reasons for her prejudice, a narrative that could go some way to excusing her contempt. Her father had been very handsome, tall and dark, and charming when it suited him, but equally malicious when the mood struck.

He had a habit of making profoundly unsettling and under-mining remarks that could shift Bernadette's whole reality. He would say to his wife and daughter, 'The only reason you are emancipated as women is because men in the West have decided it should be so. But we could change our minds at any moment. Most of the world is not like this! Remember, you are dependent on the benevolence of men.' Or he would tell Bernadette that her lovely mother was a whore, that 'all women are whores. It just depends whether you take them on a short-term or long-term lease.'

The abuse was insidious and constant, and it would have been difficult to escape such an overbearing environment unscathed, but Bernadette was a precocious infant, with her sire's stubbornness, and once she realised that her father's beliefs were not absolute truths and could be questioned, she turned her back on him. She knew empirically that the words he chose to describe her mother – 'ungrateful', 'demanding', 'complaining dependant' – were not accurate.

'But Daddy, I'm your dependant too,' she pointed out, once he had explained the word to her.

Her father had laughed heartily and drawn her on to his lap. 'You get right down to it, don't you? You know where your bread is buttered! Worried you're as expendable as your mother, eh? Well, don't worry. There's always more leniency for the pups. As long as you're a good girl. You belong entirely to me, you see.'

As an antidote to her unfortunate beginnings, she immersed herself in fictional romance and prospered, finding friends and heroes between the covers of books. Her inner monologue was framed by Victorian fiction, and her habits and speech became a peculiar mix of the old-fashioned and poetic and the unashamedly forward-thinking, with a healthy disregard for the patriarchy. She might have been tempted to be a supporter of the archaic regime, which seemed quite benign in Arthurian legend, but she knew from real-world experience that it was a dangerous and unstable thing.

She developed a romantic ideal of what a man should be from fictional characters, which were more often than not created by women, and gave her an impractical expectation of romantic love. It was this divide between reality and fiction that contributed to her misandry as an adult; she had placed all her childhood faith in an ideal, and men continually fell short.

Bernadette had chosen to drive herself to the house party, rather than be driven, as the latter presupposed irresponsibility. She was frequently irresponsible, but always prepared for her better self to triumph. But as she pulled up to the valet stand, and gazed morosely at the large Brentwood house, which was luminous with festive cheer, intoxication seemed suddenly inevitable.

There was always the option of driving on and avoiding the evening altogether, but a number of cars had formed a line behind her, and the young Mexican valet was hovering hopefully by her door. She emerged, and flashed him a quick, apologetic grin as he handed her a pink ticket, thanking him in her most pronounced English accent. There was a definite advantage to having an English accent in Los Angeles, and Bernadette was keen to flaunt her distinction. It added at least twenty points to her perceived IQ, and she could relax in conversation, knowing that her imperious tone was tantamount to actual knowledge and experience in the ears of her listeners. Unless they were wise enough to know better (and few people were), at first glance it was easy to mistake Bernadette for a young trustafarian, a struggling actress or, worst of all, a model. She moved with a Saturnian grace, startled as easily as a colt, and her wide eyes, which slanted slightly at the corners, looked as clear and trusting as a child's. It was a constant battle to be taken seriously, but the accent helped a little.

Tripping slightly on the uneven tarmac (damn LA and its poorly maintained surface structures!), and disguising the stumble as a jaunty hop, she passed in front of her car and smiled quite flirtatiously at the line of uniformed valets. This, to Bernadette, practically equated to a good deed, and she strode onwards with new purpose, buoyed by the happy knowledge of having done a selfless thing.

The house was large and beautiful in the dark, set back from the road behind high hedges. It was exactly the sort of place

Bernadette would like to call home. New England in style, kitsch and pretty, with a well-planted garden and welcoming porch, it appeared to be a beacon of domestic felicity, and signalled everything she equated with a well-lived life. Tim Bazier was no less attractive than his house, a blonde-haired, blue-eyed, straightforward man, lean and tall. Bernadette had wanted him instantly, from the first moment of their acquaintance. Before he spoke, she had correctly divined his superior nature, and her thieving, broken heart hungered for his subjection.

He was, in fact, the only man Bernadette was currently capable of admiring, the only man beyond reproach in appearance, behaviour and consequence. She had never been allowed close enough to find fault, and it was this remoteness, his lofty content-ment, that allowed her so-called love to flourish unchecked. Tim was a shining ray of light in Bernadette's dark, man-hating world. With all other men, at the slightest sign of weakness, the merest hint of an innocuous moral failing, she extrapolated to the worst conclusion, and labelled them monsters. It was a matter of self-preservation.

Tim, however, seemed to have jumped from the pages of her beloved romantic novels, so steadfast and unassuming was he – it was as if he had been pulled from her childhood's imagin-ation into the real world, and was finally with her as a real-life companion.

She remembered the first time she had seen him, the way he had looked up as she entered his office, how young he had seemed for a man in his thirties, so boyish and kind. And he was wearing glasses! Who actually wore glasses any more? His wonky grin and the bashful way he stood to take her hand were absolutely the most heart-wrenching gestures she had ever seen, and her breath caught in her chest painfully. 'So,' he had said, 'you're the Man Whisperer.'

She had wanted him then as she had never wanted anything before. It was a rapacious need, a strength of feeling that seemed to explain her very existence. It was unaccountable and unexpected and thoroughly beyond her comprehension, a heady chemical rush that overpowered every other impulse. It was a relief, in fact, to believe that there might be one redeeming male.

Tim was unlike the others because he didn't use the fact that she was a woman against her. He seemed completely disinterested in her as a woman, almost oblivious to the wide chasm between them. He treated her as a friend and fellow human, and asked nothing of her. Equally, he didn't make allowances for her – Bernadette had long ago learned to use her seductive charms to gain favour and preference, but Tim had rebuffed every advance she had ever made with gentle redirection and good humour. It was intoxicating.

He had been the first to coin her moniker, 'The Man Whisperer' – and what an enterprising suggestion! To address her as such at their initial meeting, to use that as his opener, so respectfully and with so much polish, appealed directly to her feminine pride. It defined a power she had as yet left unnamed, and excused the sexuality she had a hard time controlling. Bernadette quietly imagined his love and forgiveness, as evidenced in that one sentence, and couldn't have found more comfort had he been a priest explaining the promise of resurrection.

The party was already in full swing. Through bright windows Bernadette could see people moving around, laughing and talking, as waiters offered trays of dinky holiday-themed canapés. A Bing Crosby track wafted out from the open front door, which was bedecked with an evergreen wreath and a big red bow.

Mounting the faux-rickety wooden steps, having successfully crossed the cobbled driveway in extremely high heels, Bernadette wondered where in the house Tim would be, and her body tensed in anticipation. She remembered that she felt sick.

The Christmas party was the perfect place to make known her true feelings, because what was more romantic than Christmas? When she had received the invitation in November, she had had an uncanny, premonition-like feeling that something extraordinary would occur. Tim had told her very pointedly that he looked forward to her attendance.

Almost as soon as she entered the house, she saw him. He was standing with his back to her, talking to a couple she didn't know, and miraculously his blonde head bobbed and nodded under an audacious bunch of mistletoe that had been pinned to a low archway. She took a shaky step towards him, mentally planning dialogue, and deciding whether to kiss him on both cheeks, or to try and accidentally-on-purpose catch the corner of his mouth. The mistletoe surely offered a whole world of kissing potential. But before she could reach him, she felt small, gentle hands on her waist, and, turning, was caught in a sincere hug, a tight, clinging embrace that communicated genuine friendship.

'Elizabeth! How lovely to see you,' Bernadette lied. She tried not to freeze in the other woman's arms, tried to ease away without signalling her distaste.

Elizabeth Wentworth was Tim's girlfriend, and the thorn in Bernadette's side. Elizabeth was exactly the type of good-hearted, guileless female that Bernadette refused to believe existed. She was convinced that behind the front of sweet-tempered liberality lurked a cynicism even darker than her own.

Elizabeth was looking up at Bernadette, nodding and smiling as though she had been asked a question that required a yes answer. Tim's attraction to Elizabeth was a source of infinite puzzlement. She was not particularly pretty, nor especially smart; she didn't light up a room, she'd never been known to crack a joke, and she never put a foot wrong. When Bernadette looked at her, phrases like 'bookish and plain' and 'solid and dependable' sprang to mind. Elizabeth was thirty-three, of average height and average weight, never wore make-up, and always dressed appropriately. She was the type of person Bernadette occasionally wished she herself could be, conspicuous only by her inimitable ordinariness.

'Come and say hello to Tim,' Elizabeth said. 'He'll be so happy to see you.'

To Bernadette's horror, Elizabeth linked arms with her, and chaperoned her towards Tim and the mistletoe. Catching their approach out of the corner of his eye, he excused himself from the conversation, and turned with a smile. Bernadette couldn't stop herself from smiling back like a fool, and felt the familiar hot chemical rush.

Tim was undoubtedly the most sublime and perfect person to ever grace the planet. He was over six foot and gangly, slim-built and angular, and his hair fell in a sandy mop across his forehead. He never wore cologne, but always smelt freshly washed, like soap.

'Hello, Bernie,' he said, and hugged her. She pressed herself into his embrace, whilst trying to make it look informal. 'It's not a party without you,' he continued. 'You look fantastic.' He stood back to admire her dress, holding her left hand and smiling in appreciation of the effort she had made. Bernadette felt an almost imperceptible squeeze of his fingers around hers as he dropped her hand.

'Thanks,' she managed. 'You look fantastic too.'

Tim always appeared shiny bright and perfect, but particularly so that evening. He was wearing a red plaid shirt – a cool, comfy plaid, Bernadette was pleased to note, not a weird lumberjack one – which seemed appropriately festive in a Hogmanay-ish sort of way. His jeans were not fashionable and he was sporting a pair of dark blue Toms. He always looked like he was ready for some type of outdoorsy adventure, even at formal events or business meetings. Bernadette had him pegged as a hiking/biking/save-the-world-by-recycling type.

Elizabeth had stood silent and approving for the exchange, clearly waiting for her turn to speak. There was an uncharacteristic air of expectation around her as she smiled up at Bernadette. 'I think there'll be a lot of people here you already know,' she began, 'but there's someone I'd really love to introduce you to!' She exchanged a blushing glance with Tim, who rolled his eyes in a humorous way and grinned his lopsided grin. 'A friend of mine from medical school,' she added.

Elizabeth was a doctor at Cedars-Sinai, specialising in livers, or kidneys, or some other organ that made Bernadette think of urine. The last person in the world she wanted to meet was some do-gooder, mortality-obsessed workaholic who smelt of cheap cleaning fluid and latex gloves. She gave a visible shudder. 'Well, I'd really like a drink first,' she said, turning to Tim with a please-save-me face.

'Sure!' Elizabeth fluttered. 'You know your way around, right? There's a bar out back. Do you want me to show you?'

Bernadette bristled at Elizabeth playing hostess in Tim's house. It seemed quite ridiculous, given that they'd only been dating for a year. Tim had been Bernadette's literary manager for three years, which, chronologically at least, was a more substantial relationship. 'No, I'm fine. I have been here before,' she said, pointedly.

Bernadette moved through the house, observing the other party guests and making a note of any women who were better-looking than her. It was an ingrained habit on entering a room, or any new place. She looked first for men she might love (there never were any, as men were bastards), and second for any threateningly beautiful girls (there were always far too many).

Bernadette's father had been very particular about the way his daughter should look. He had an eye for detail, and her physical flaws had seemed to genuinely hurt his feelings, her gawkiness an affront to his superior genes. He used to take a ruler and measure the symmetry of her facial features down to the millimetre. She would stand in front of him in her gingham school dress and white socks, shifting in subdued discomfort from foot to foot as he measured her face and recorded the results in a notebook. 'What a waste!' he would sigh. 'I only married your idiot mother because I thought she'd produce decent-looking offspring, and now look at this! Thirty-four millimetres! Preposterous! And the ratios are all wrong!' Then he would ruffle her hair in a kindly, paternal fashion and say, 'Let's hope you have a little of my wit, at least, to distinguish you from the other unattractive girls. Poor little poppet.' Bernadette had been disappointed to learn that she wasn't beautiful. She wanted to be worthy of a literary romance in order to encounter a man more loving than her father, and all her favourite heroines were described as being impossibly, otherworldly attractive.

As an adult, she had received enough compliments on her appearance to counter her father's low opinion, but she still disliked being defined by her looks either way, and didn't feel secure enough to be able to withstand honest competition. She spent her life surreptitiously checking out legs and boobs and butts, with more vigour than a horny adolescent boy.

It was a typical LA house party, full of agents and clients, financiers, hipsters, artists and philanthropists. Bernadette slunk around alone, nervous and disdainful, always keeping a watchful eye out for Tim. The apprehension of seeing him, the dread of an evening spent lovelorn in his company, had given way to a more practical, scheming instinct. Her overactive mind began to concoct numerous plans for the night ahead. Being in Tim's house was too good an opportunity to miss, after all, and something positive had to come from the tedium of the party. Perhaps she could feign sleepiness and slip off to his bedroom, or encourage him to dance with her in the moonlight. At the very least, she could corner him under the mistletoe, which seemed to hang at every doorway, taunting her with plump pearls of promise.

They were unsophisticated plans, but then Bernadette was entirely juvenile in her self-centred pursuit of love. Real love must be possible, because people had written about it – and made it sound so wonderful in the writing! All really was fair in love and war; love itself was often war, and made otherwise inadmissible behaviour entirely noble. And love was a concept

that didn't need to be too closely examined: *wanting* was enough
of a definition. Bernadette had learnt, from prior, painful experience, that men took what they wanted. She would be no passive
female, destined to put her own desires aside. She would pursue
her whims at any cost.

She found the bar out on the back deck, stepping from the
warmth of the house and marvelling, as she still frequently did,
at LA's Mediterranean climate. The smell of oiled pine rose
from the boards under her feet, and mingled with lavender and
quince from the thicket bordering the ample garden. Fairy lights
strung around lemon trees provided a drowsy and romantic
half-light, along with hanging lanterns in an arbour, three crackling fire pits, and the pinpricks of cell phones, whose owners
preferred virtual life.

She ordered a lychee martini, which the unemployed-actor
bartender insisted on dusting liberally with ground cinnamon.
She downed it and immediately ordered another. The bartender
winked at her, and she bristled at his impertinence.

As she stood at the bar, drinking alone, a pleasant-faced man
about her own age approached and smiled. 'Hey,' he said. 'How's
it going?'

'I'm sorry, I don't speak American,' she reproved haughtily,
and left him to think on his mistake.

When she was younger, Bernadette would smile welcomingly
at unknown men who approached her, and would happily engage
in friendly conversation, treating them as fellow human souls,
and secretly hoping to find a romantic hero. She had put so
much faith and trust in the concept of one exceptional male.
These men would be kind, jovial and complimentary, but when
she politely declined their romantic advances, the mask of kind-

ness would slip, and underneath would be anger. She had experienced too often the shock of a pleasant conversation turning violent, of a seemingly normal man becoming a frightening opponent. It reminded her strongly of her father's double nature. No longer did she smile when men approached her.

House parties always made Bernadette feel slightly wretched, but she never dared refuse an invitation for fear of dying alone. Generally, every attempt at having an interesting, exciting night out turned out to be an exercise in self-loathing and despair. No one ever behaved as she wished them to, and she was never able to rise to the standard she set herself.

Yet there still remained the dim and secret hope that something wonderful would happen at a party. Nothing wonderful was likely to happen in everyday life, but the dark rooms, the heightened atmosphere, the libations, the strangers . . . Bernadette could be convinced that unusual and brilliant things did sometimes occur at parties. Someone might fall madly in love with her, or save her life in some other way. It had never happened to date, but she was unwilling to let go of the fantasy. And Bernadette lived for fantasy.

She wandered around the garden in large circles, trying to look like she had friends in some other area of the party anxiously awaiting her return. She had no one to talk to, nothing to say for herself, even if she did have an audience, and her feet were already extremely sore.

It was then that she witnessed the pleasant-faced man from the bar being rejected by a no-good piece of baggage in her early twenties. The man had only given a friendly salutation, but the girl had rolled her eyes and turned away with a sneer.

It looked wrong to Bernadette, and she suddenly regretted her earlier behaviour, ashamed of her own violent dismissiveness. Besides, she had a constitutional abhorrence of any man being snubbed by any woman other than herself, and an even greater desire to protect the innocent. With this boy suddenly framed as a victim in Bernadette's eyes, she felt a sudden rush of warmth for him, and a desire to show him he was not alone. She strode over to resolve the situation.

'Darling!' she said, loud enough for the other woman to hear, taking the startled young man by the hand.

He stared at her in consternation. 'I—' he began, but Bernadette cut him off.

'Don't say it! I know. I know your family will never accept me. I can't even bear to think about it!'

'I—'

'I still wear the ring you gave me,' she went on, warming to her part, and flashing the large sapphire ring that she always wore.

She kissed him warmly on the cheek, and he responded somewhat, putting his hand to her waist. She surreptitiously slapped it away. 'I'll always love you,' she gasped, then trotted off towards the house. Turning back, she saw him gazing after her, incredulous, and the mean girl swooping in on her new friend, suddenly all smiles.

Bernadette circled through the house, hoping to catch a glimpse of Tim. She settled in the sitting room, where groups of guests chattered loudly. It was a large room, comfortably furnished, and not at all showy. The well-worn sofas and the handsome oak sideboard had an old-money, East Coast feel. The ornaments were mostly books and houseplants. Festive bunting and poinsettias acknowledged the season, red-and-green exclamations of merriness in the otherwise decorous space.

Amid the chaotic milieu, Bernadette became aware, by some animal sense, by the prickling of the hairs on the back of her neck, that someone was staring at her. She turned her head and saw the provoker.

A man stood alone by the pine-cone-studded mantelpiece. He refused to drop his gaze, even as she stared back at him. There was something challenging in his look; it seemed too intimate and knowing. Bernadette was half pleased that she had so clearly taken his fancy in some way, but he was also giving her the uncomfortable feeling that her skimpy dress was, in fact, not chic, but slutty. She surreptitiously tried to tug the hemline down a couple of inches, and was rewarded with a far too perceptive smirk.

She was displeased, yet compulsively intrigued. He seemed to be in his mid-thirties, and was immensely tall and broad. She had never seen a man with as much breadth to him; his shoulders were as wide as anything, and even through his suit he appeared to be all muscle. It was obscene almost, for a man of that physicality to be standing in a well-tailored suit. The dark material was pulled over strong arms and long thighs: a most incongruous fashion, saved from disaster by something dangerous in his arrogant posture that defied convention and forbade censure. His face looked as though it were cut from stone, his expression unchanging as he slowly moved his focus from Bernadette's short skirt to her face, only his eyes flashing with wickedness and mirth as he again lowered his gaze to run his eyes slowly up and down her legs.

She was so busy trying to muster up further indignation that she failed to notice Tim, who had come to stand next to her. 'Good-looking, isn't he?' he asked, nodding in the direction of the giant.

'Not my type,' she said quickly.

'Do you have a type, Bernie?' he asked, quietly.

This was the kind of exchange that Bernadette could never quite interpret to her satisfaction. Tim didn't truly flirt with her, but he often said things that seemed filled with additional meaning, and when he did, he always looked at her in such a sad way, as if she had done wrong and he wanted to put her right. He was watching her closely and, she was sure of it, with longing. She didn't understand him at all. If he wanted her, why didn't he just say something? Why did he have to make it all seem so melancholy, so serious?

He smiled sadly over at the stranger, who was now inexplicably deep in conversation with Elizabeth. Tim gently placed his hand in the small of Bernadette's back and leant down to speak in her ear. 'Come with me,' he said.

She thrilled at his touch, and for a wild moment believed that he was leading her away to some dark corner of his house, to his bedroom, anywhere he could have her alone. Her heady excitement was short-lived, as he guided her not to some private lair, but across the room to the mantelpiece, where Elizabeth stood with the hulking unknown.

'Bernadette, this is my friend, the guy I was telling you about.' Elizabeth smiled eagerly. The friend raised his left eyebrow slightly at her words, and Bernadette's stomach tightened with frustration. It wasn't right to introduce a man that way, to announce that you had been discussing him. It sounded like they had been plotting a female attack. In this instance,

16

Bernadette believed Elizabeth to be stupid, rather than intentionally bitchy, but she glared at her anyway. 'Oh? I don't remember . . .' She trailed off, trying to sound cool and unconcerned.

'From medical school!' Elizabeth clarified, nodding desperately.

The bastard's mouth was twitching up at the corners. 'I noticed you from across the room,' he said, politely.

Bernadette started slightly at his accent, which was completely unique. His voice was low and soft, with the most idiosyncratic inflection she had ever heard. It had a transatlantic sound, though seemed neither American nor English. His lips hardly moved as he spoke, and his voice seemed disconnected from his body, as though he were a lazy ventriloquist.

'Yes,' she replied, quite stunned that Elizabeth and the treacherous Tim had forced her into conversation with this oddity. Tim was still looking at her with that same wistful hunger. She wanted to grab him by the shoulders and shake him hard.

Elizabeth made some vague excuse about having to see to the music, and taking Tim firmly by the arm, she moved away, leaving Bernadette alone with the brute. She felt quite dwarfed by the bulk of him. He seemed to be built on a different scale to everything else, and he was studying her as a wolf might appraise a lamb before gobbling it up.

'Elizabeth speaks very highly of you,' he drawled.

She couldn't help the derisive snort that escaped her. 'I really don't know her that well,' she said, dismissively.

He cocked his eyebrow again, and his mouth hardened into a tight line, in clear disapproval of her tone. 'You could do a lot worse than Elizabeth for a friend. She's a fine woman.'

Bernadette blinked at him incredulously. His description of Elizabeth made it sound as if he were talking about a horse, or some other piece of livestock. 'Yes. She's very nice,' she demurred, looking around for some means of escape.

His left eyebrow gave another shrug, and he looked bored suddenly, as though she had abruptly lost all appeal.

She considered her options. Clearly the man was a swine, but at least standing near him, engaged in banal conversation, was better than circling the party alone.

Elizabeth had obviously set up this encounter in the hope that it might lead to something, and the idea that Tim and Elizabeth would quiz him about her later decided his fate: she would leave a good impression.

'I'm sorry, I didn't catch your name,' she said, smiling at him winningly, and giving her best bedroom eyes.

'Radley Blake,' was the answer. The name stirred in her subconscious a little, and she wondered if Tim had mentioned him before.

'I'm Bernadette St John.' She stepped closer and offered her hand. He took it, engulfing it in his massive palm.

He said nothing, just stared at her. It felt very much like he was now waiting for her to leave.

'How long have you known Elizabeth?' she tried.

'Over a decade. I think she mentioned that we met at medical school?'

Bernadette was just about to answer when he added, 'I read your articles occasionally, in *Squire* magazine. They're very good. They have an air of studied neurosis that I find appealing. Being a medical man.'

Bernadette was justly proud of her work for *Squire* magazine, where she wrote under the pseudonym of 'The Man Whisperer'. It was one of the first jobs Tim had found for her, and here was this Radley Blake character mocking her work and openly laughing at her. She wasn't quite sure how to respond, until he continued airily, 'I sometimes think you should interview me. I'm sure I'd enjoy your particular line of questioning.'

'Well,' she said, 'you would be the first *doctor* I've ever interviewed. Usually I profile politicians, royalty, heads of state, globally successful entrepreneurs . . . You would make a fascinating change, I'm sure.'

He nodded his head curtly in acknowledgement of her thinly veiled aggression and regarded her anew, a smirk still dancing round the edge of his mouth. They stared at one another in silence, and she noticed how very dark his eyes were, like pools of melted chocolate, flecked with caramel.

'Tell me,' he said, finally, 'what were you thinking about when you were standing over that side of the room? You had such an expression on your face.'

It seemed an impertinent question, though by now she expected no less from the conceited Radley Blake. She wondered what expression had played across her face, to have so caught his attention. She had probably been thinking of Tim, since that was what she most often thought about, but there was no way she was going to own as much to Elizabeth's particular friend.

'I was thinking . . . I was probably worrying about the US becoming increasingly isolated in the Middle East.'

He looked at her as though trying to assess whether or not she was being serious. There were several moments of silence, in which she tried to arrange her countenance into a placid and inoffensive mask, the face of a concerned citizen of the world. And then he laughed, abruptly. A guffaw of genuine enjoyment that creased his features and made his eyes shine.

'What do you think of Tim?' she asked, desperately trying to change the subject.

He answered readily, and seemed to be enjoying her company once more. 'He's a decent enough sort of man. But I worry he's not good enough for Elizabeth.'

Bernadette felt her mouth drop open several inches and she shook her head in bewilderment. Tim was better than Elizabeth in every single way: better-looking, more successful, more intelligent.

'Are you in love with her?' The question fell from her lips before she could stop it.

Radley Blake gave a cynical laugh, very different from the first hearty peal. 'A woman like Elizabeth would no sooner be with a man like me than she would sprout wings and fly to the moon,' he said, gazing stormily around the room as if to lay eyes on her.

Bernadette was flabbergasted. She just could not understand Elizabeth's appeal. 'I think Tim is a wonderful man,' she said, emphatically.

He smiled, a cold, uncivil sneer, his red upper lip curling slightly to show a flash of brilliant white teeth. She felt, for the first time, the full force of his fierce gaze as they locked eyes. 'I'm sure you do.'

She knew then that he knew, without a doubt. Somehow, in the few moments they had been talking, Radley Blake had magically surmised her feelings for Tim. And he was making it perfectly clear that he thought her despicable.

At that instant, the pleasant-faced man from the bar appeared, smiling genially, with every intention of engaging them in conversation. But as he opened his mouth to speak, Bernadette immediately raised her hand and pointed a warning finger at him. 'You. No,' she said. 'Go away.'

The poor soul shut his mouth, exchanged a confused look with Radley Blake, and then crab-stepped awkwardly away.

'You're quite amusing,' said Radley, smirking still.

'And you're not,' she said. 'I don't know what you were suggesting by that last comment, but I don't think it's appropriate. Please excuse me.' She tossed her head rather dramatically, turned on her heel, and wiggled away as fast as her dress and shoes would allow.

Elizabeth ambushed Bernadette as soon as she set foot in the dining room, a rectangular space with a fourteen-seat table, a sideboard, and a slew of Christmassy paraphernalia, including a porcelain nativity scene with a thimble-sized baby Jesus. A few of the more antisocial guests had gathered, clumped in small groups against the boundary of the room like proverbial wallflowers.

'Isn't Radley awesome?' she asked, beaming with pride. 'I didn't want to put you on the spot, but he's just moved to LA and I can't help thinking that you two would hit it off. He's got the same amazing zest for life that you do.'

'He's fascinating,' Bernadette agreed, seeing Tim approach. Elizabeth turned her grin on her boyfriend.

'She likes him!' she giggled triumphantly.

'Did his billions win you over, then, Bernie?' Tim asked gently.

'What billions?'

'Bernie, come on! That's *the* Radley Blake. Please tell me you know who he is? One of the most successful entrepreneurs of our generation?'

'Oh, she doesn't care about that,' cried Elizabeth, piqued on Bernadette's behalf.

'You said he was a doctor!' Bernadette turned reproachful eyes on Elizabeth.

'Oh no! We met in medical school, but he dropped out to start Clarion Molecular. He developed the technology to sequence individual full genomes. He's a genius!' Elizabeth explained, with an almost religious fervour.

'Lizzie was convinced that you two would be all over each other tonight. I, selfishly, thought there could be an interview in it, at least. He's notoriously reticent about talking to the press, but I'm pretty sure you could work your Man Whispering charms. It would be quite a triumph to get an in-depth with him,' Tim said, grinning.

Bernadette felt somewhat weak, trying to replay her conversation with Radley Blake in her head.

'What did you guys talk about?' asked Elizabeth.

'Um, mostly about the Middle East.'

Elizabeth nodded earnestly, and Tim laughed. He touched his girlfriend lightly on the cheek.

'Lizzie, I'm going to give the speech now.'

'Now?' she said, blushing. 'Okay.'

Tim took quick strides into the main room. Elizabeth grabbed Bernadette's arm and pulled her along after him. 'Come on, Bernie!' she smiled. 'Let's get to the front.'

Tim asked people for quiet, the music was turned off by some invisible power, and a crowd formed obediently around him. Guests who weren't lucky enough to be in the room itself jostled in archways and doorways, necks craning to get a good view. Expensively attired, high-maintenance women with coiffed hair and carefully made-up faces towered above their dates on platform heels. Young bohemian girls in Chloé shorts and vintage blouses, their sun-kissed locks falling in tousled waves over their shoulders, were giggling in groups, their arms about each other's waists. The men were in jeans and sports coats, or suits-with-no-tie. Everyone tried to suppress the merry chatter with shushes and yells, to control their mirth to a level where Tim might be heard. He was beaming round at the happy throng, a glass of wine raised and the usual twinkle of human kindness in his eyes.

Bernadette glanced towards Radley Blake, still standing impassively by the fireplace. 'He doesn't *look* like a genius,' she muttered bitterly.

'Friends, family,' Tim began, 'Elizabeth and I are thrilled that you could join us for a little holiday celebration.' He beckoned Elizabeth over, and she went to stand next to him, tucking herself under his shoulder. Bernadette felt a familiar surge of injustice. Everyone whooped and cheered. She tried to catch Tim's eye, but he wasn't looking in her direction.

'It's been a great year, in so many ways. I've been very lucky. Made it through the LA marathon – only just! Thank you to everyone who supported me, sponsored me, and put up with me. I finally got to go to the Galapagos – if you haven't seen the pictures, you will! I have amazing clients, who make my job a dream . . .'

Here he nodded vaguely in Bernadette's direction, and she flashed her best smile in return.

'. . . and most importantly of all, I found Lizzie.'

He looked down at Elizabeth, and she gazed up at him with the most sincere and trusting expression in her pale-blue eyes. Never did a simple-hearted woman have love written so plainly across her face. It made Bernadette feel slightly sick. Elizabeth reminded her of a pet Labrador she had had as a little girl in England. It used to have the same docile, untroubled look.

'We're so happy to be able to announce our engagement!'

Bernadette's manner did not visibly change, and anyone who was watching her would simply think it a little strange that she did not move at all, that she was as still and beautiful as a petrified rose. Her lips grew white and her breathing shallow, but it would have taken a keen observer to notice such things. For Bernadette, all sound had receded in a giant whoosh to nothing but a blurred background murmur, and she could hear blood from her heart thudding in her ears. Dark splotches had formed in front of her eyes, and she blinked rapidly to try and rid herself of the blindness. She felt faint and dizzy, and the other people in the room were so far away. It seemed as if she would be entirely alone if she fell, that no one would care or even notice.

But Radley Blake was staring at her. She couldn't faint. She'd never fainted before in her life; she wasn't the swooning type. He bowed slightly, the tiniest of nods in her direction. He was mocking her again, mocking her misery. She was so confused by his behaviour that she managed to snatch a little gulp of air. She took deep breaths, and became more sensible of her environment. People were cheering as Tim and Elizabeth kissed. It was too much to endure, and the strange fog of misery threatened to engulf her entirely. She shut her eyes and succumbed to it.

Suddenly, strong arms encircled her, and Radley Blake half guided, half carried her outside, pushing through the blithe multitude. The back deck was quite clear, as people were still trying to get close to Tim and his fortunate fiancée, everyone wanting to be the first to offer congratulations.

Radley seated her, somewhat roughly, on a low deckchair. 'Wait here,' he said. 'You'll be fine.' He returned a few moments later with an iced glass and placed it in her hand. 'Drink this.'

'What is it?' she asked, eyeballing the clear liquid with mistrust.

'It's water.'

'Oh.' She took several girlish sips and then, overcome with a sudden thirst, gulped down the rest of it. The fresh air and the water did go some way to making her feel better, and she looked gratefully at Radley.

'It will pass, you know,' he said. 'Whatever you're feeling right now. I promise. There will be a time when you don't feel it.'

She was in no mood to engage in meaningful conversation with a stranger. She needed room to think, to make sense of what had happened, to process the enormity of it. Adrenalin had given way to fatigue, but her boisterous nature would not allow her to admit defeat in front of a man, and she raised dark eyebrows in playful mockery. 'My unwelcome saviour. Do you often drag women from crowded rooms like that, without their consent? I was fine, you know.'

He smiled suddenly. 'Liar. You were about to keel over.'

She smiled at him in turn, and tilted her head in coquettish fashion. 'You're amazingly presumptuous. You can have absolutely no idea what I'm feeling. If you did, you would know to leave me alone.' Here her head dropped a little, and her breathing threatened to quicken again. She was too tired to go on flirting after all. 'Please leave me alone,' she said, turning large, sad eyes upon him.

He got up immediately, and was gone so suddenly she wondered if she had imagined him. It was unusual for someone to match her in erratic behaviour, but he had vanished, abandoning her with all the force of his previous concerned regard. She half wished she hadn't asked him to leave.

The next few hours passed in a blur. She continued to hydrate herself, but with drinks much stronger than water. Her fertile mind was working at speed, as her reaction times became slower. She briefly flirted with the idea of tearing off all her clothes, writhing on the wooden decking and screaming in primal agony in front of the other guests, not caring what anyone thought of her, consumed only by her thwarted passion in a Heathcliff-like rage. But such demonstrations were hard to recover from.

It seemed absolutely wrong. How could Tim and Elizabeth be engaged? They'd only been dating a year.

She comforted herself with the fact that an engagement was not marriage. Lots of engagements got called off, or dragged on for years and years. The usual selfish optimism, the belief that life would eventually work out exactly the way she wanted it – because hadn't it always before? – rose to the surface, and she began to feel almost cheerful. Anything could happen over the course of an engagement! Elizabeth could contract some horrible chronic disease from being around her sick patients. Or Tim could come to his bloody senses. He loved her, she knew he did; she had a very keen intuition for such things.

The party had thinned out. Bernadette sat alone on an outdoor couch, by a low fire pit. She stared into the hypnotic flames, wishing with all her heart, and with no sense of guilt, that Elizabeth would die or disappear. Without realising it, she was emitting a low moan, a sort of wounded animal noise, like a dying calf.

Elizabeth sat down next to her and worriedly took her hand. 'Bernie!' she cried. 'Are you okay?'

Bernadette had managed to avoid Elizabeth and Tim since the engagement announcement. She didn't think she could humanly stand Elizabeth's gloating. 'No,' she said, miserably. 'No, I'm not okay.'

'Are you sick? Can I get you anything? Do you want some Tylenol?'

'I need to speak to Tim,' she found herself saying. Her speech was slurred and she listed to one side, slumping against the concerned Elizabeth.

'Sure! I'll get him.'

'I need to speak to him privately. Alone. It's private. It's very private.'

'Oh, *hon*!' cried Elizabeth, stroking her hand. 'I wish I could help. You look *awful*!'

Bernadette turned a cranky eye upon Elizabeth and arched an eyebrow. 'Private,' she slurred again. 'I must.'

'Of course,' responded Elizabeth, gently and very serious. Bernadette wondered if it was the voice she used with her patients. 'Whatever it is, Tim can help. Go through to the guest room. Do you know where it is?'

Bernadette listened carefully to Elizabeth's instructions, nodding her head, her shoulders so hunched her forehead was parallel to the ground. 'Wait for him there,' Elizabeth finished. 'I'll send him through to you.'

Bernadette quietly opened the door to the guest room and closed it behind her, the latch clicking discreetly into place. It was a large and comfortable room at the side of the house, with French doors leading out to the garden. The doors stood open, and a soft, warm breeze gently puffed the sheer drapes back and forth in a mesmeric dance. She felt like she was in some kind of a dream. Tim was being sent to her, and she had to do something, say something, to forever seal their fate. The problem was, she wasn't entirely sure what to do. She felt a sudden wave of cinnamon-tinged nausea, and fear gripped her. She thought about running away through the open French doors and never coming back.

She sat shakily on the edge of the bed, trying to steady her physical self and steel her bothersome nerves. She wondered how long she would have to wait before Tim arrived. He seemed to be taking his time about it, considering that Elizabeth had rushed off to find him in a state likely to communicate an emergency.

The bed was quite comfortable. She pondered lying across it provocatively. Her bronzed legs would look very nice stretched out over the crisp white linen. She could prop herself up on one elbow, facing the door, and scoop her hair over one shoulder. It would make a striking picture.

She knew that Tim desired her. They had spent years exchanging arch emails, and they lingered for hours over business lunches. Bernadette had always related to him, in full Technicolor detail, the behavior of various men who had tried to woo her. But throughout she was always waiting, always fully expecting, that one day, when he gathered the courage, he would – in some romantic way – declare his true and deeper feelings.

Tim had a gentleness and sensitivity that was missing in other men. He was non-threatening and non-sexual, and gave the impression that he would do right in any situation. It was his goodness that Bernadette most admired. She herself was too world-weary to be good, but Tim made her feel good by association.

His engagement to Elizabeth must be nothing more than an error in communication. Bernadette should have made explicit her love for him; there was no way he would choose to marry a bland, unattractive, middle-aged nobody when he could have her instead. She just had to let him know that it was him she truly wanted.

She looked up as Tim entered the room. She had not had a chance to arrange herself over the bed, and instead of coming across as a seductive siren, she must have looked to Tim like a frightened girl, perched awkwardly, gazing at him with troubled eyes. Whatever he saw, it was enough to make him shut the door carefully behind him.

'What's wrong, Bernie?' he asked kindly, keeping near the door. 'Have you had too much to drink?'

She was briefly annoyed at his unromantic question, but fear got the better of her, and when she opened her mouth, she was unable to speak. Abandoned by words, she opened her arms helplessly, like a child asking to be carried. Concerned, Tim crossed to her, sat next to her on the bed and hugged her to him. It was all the encouragement she needed, and she breathed in deep, luxuriating in his clean, soapy smell.

'What's wrong?' he asked. 'Has something happened?'

She pulled back to face him. 'Yes,' she whispered, tragically. 'Yes, something has happened.'

'What is it? You can tell me.'

'I'm in love with you.'

It was as if a shock of electricity passed through him, and he jolted back so suddenly, the bed bounced beneath them. His expression half incredulous, he looked at her as though she were an exotic wonder of a female, the likes of which he had never seen before, and for a moment she felt like singing with joy. But then she noticed the pain in his eyes, the torment etched in the lines of his face, and a cold fear gripped her. It had been a relief to say it, finally, and she felt the giddying rush of a secret shared. Telling him had been inevitable – given her open nature, it could be no other way – but what did not necessarily follow was that her declaration should find a warm welcome. The unpredictable, unknowable nature of men frightened her. In her imagination he had been receptive, but in reality he was not behaving as she wished. He wasn't doing what the heroes in the romance novels did.

He gave a small, tense laugh. 'You're kidding, Bernie, right? Very funny.' He was speaking politely, as if she were a stranger to him, but worse, he was moving away from her slowly, as though she were mad or threatening, a wild creature about to strike a fatal blow.

'Don't, Tim, please don't. You know I'm not joking. I love you. I love you so much.'

His body slumped, and she noticed for the first time the greying hairs around his temple. He took both her hands gently in his. 'I didn't mean to hurt you.'

'Then don't! Don't hurt me. It's so easy not to hurt me.' She leaned forward to kiss him, but he pulled away.

'I'm engaged to Elizabeth.'

Bernadette's breath was coming in ragged gasps, her chest rising and falling with a too-quick rhythm. 'Can you honestly tell me,' she said, her eyes boring into his, 'that you don't want me?'

The rosy blush that spread from his neck to his ears silently announced his defeat. 'I can't tell you that,' he said miserably. 'Of course I want you. You're so young, and vital – and beautiful.'

She moved to kiss him again, but her lips had barely touched his before he sprang up alarmed and started pacing the room. 'I can't, Bernie, I can't,' he said, stricken.

She took the pacing as a good sign; she could feel her victory close at hand. Bizarrely, at that moment she hallucinated Elizabeth's pasty face staring at her placidly, those mild blue eyes blank and unknowing. She pushed the thought firmly from her mind, with no stirring of conscience.

She slowly removed her high heels, lay back on the bed and rested her head against the pillow. 'You *can*,' she murmured, Lolita-like. He stopped pacing and stared at her in consternation. 'I can't bear to be without you, Tim. I've loved you from the very first day, truly. I want to be with you. Every single piece of me loves every little part of you. I want to marry you, and have a whole parcel of babies!'

She could feel actual tears welling in her eyes, which was alarming. Tim looked as though he might cry too. He sat next to her on the bed again and began to stroke her leg, near her knee. Her breath caught in anticipation, and she waited for his hand to move upwards, over her thigh. She smiled at him encouragingly. But his hand stayed at her knee, and she realised that his touch was not designed to stir her passion, but was more soothing, the touch of a mother comforting a small child. Bernadette thought of her own mother, and of how much she would disapprove of this drunken behaviour, and her heart ached.

'You – you do want me,' she said, faltering. 'You do.'

'Yes, I do, Bernie. But I'll never be able to have you.'

'Why?' she cried, petulantly.

'Because I care about you too much. And I care about myself, enough to be sensible. And I mean, you're . . . you're kind of crazy!'

'That doesn't make any sense,' she said, sitting up in displeasure. 'I want to be with you. Always.'

'Please don't,' he groaned. 'Don't say any more. You'll regret it. You'll hate me for letting you talk.' He stopped, and gasped with nervous laughter at the sight of her face. 'Oh Bernie, you look so fierce. You'd be too much for me. You'd be bored with me after a week.'

She disliked his laughter, but sensed a glimmer of opportunity in his last comment. 'Is that what you think?' she said, swiftly, tenderly. 'That I'd tire of you, my darling? I never would. You're the only person in the whole world that I love, Tim. You're the only man I trust to be good to me.'

'I love Elizabeth,' he said, unable to look her in the eyes.

Bernadette stiffened, a calm, icy feeling numbing her heart. She knew that feeling in herself – it was the moment before the breaking storm, the calm of a clear mind before her fury would be unleashed in a primitive, uncontrollable temper. 'You just said you wanted me.'

'I shouldn't have said that. I'm engaged. I shouldn't have said it.'

32

And now her rage broke, the spite and anger flowing unchecked, her body trembling with the effort. 'No, you shouldn't have said it, if you won't act on it. You've always known how I felt about you. Why flirt with me? Why all the sighs, and the secret bloody hand squeezes, and the longing looks, and the incessant emails? Why do it? You're just like all the others, and I thought – I really thought – that you were a *good* man. The only good man.'

'I didn't think it was that serious to you, Bernie. I mean, you're the Man Whisperer; that's what you do! You flirt this way with everyone.'

'Don't you dare throw that back at me,' she cried. 'You were the one who *made* me the Man Whisperer! I don't care for anyone but you. I actively despise any man that isn't you.'

His head drooped pathetically and his blush was as deep as she'd ever seen it. He was distraught, but she couldn't stop. She knew, in fairness, that he had never consciously crossed the line of a bantering friendship, although he had given a thousand subtle signals of his longing. But she couldn't be fair. The humiliation of rejection was bitter and unusual, and she was horrified with herself. To be thwarted by Elizabeth was a loathsome thought, and her own behaviour, her idiocy and lack of control, hurt most of all.

'How can you prefer her to me?' she demanded angrily. 'Tell me how! I'm younger and better-looking! I have more wit!'

The look on Tim's face would haunt her until the day she died. He was as blank as a piece of white paper, the emotion suddenly drained from his face. She had repulsed him, frightened him, shocked him, and he was gone from her for ever.

'Don't speak like that,' he said.

Talulah Riley

'You have no right to tell me what to do!' she exclaimed, and before she could think, she had raised her right hand to slap him across the cheek. She caught herself halfway, and managed to hold back from hitting him with full force, but still followed through with a half-hearted gesture. The pathetic action was worse, even, than a full-on slap, but it still sounded horribly loud in the otherwise empty room. Bernadette winced on contact, while Tim remained impassive. She withdrew her fingers as though she had been burnt, and her rage collapsed immediately into quiet. 'I'm sorry,' she whispered.

Tim held her by the shoulders. His grip was firm, but his eyes were still blank and emotionless. 'No, Bernie, I'm sorry.' He sighed, removed his glasses and rubbed at his cheek. He looked so cute and boyish that she wanted to cry; she felt weak with guilt and shame. 'I'm going to go back to Elizabeth and tell her that you had too much to drink. Please, let's pretend this never happened. I value our working relationship. And I really do care about you.'

Before she could reply, he hugged her to him, kissed the top of her head firmly and left the bedroom, shutting the door behind him.

She collapsed on the bed, her mind in a whirl. The shame was too much to bear, to be passed over for Elizabeth, the most boring and unattractive woman on the planet. Bernadette squeezed her eyes tight shut, clenched her fists, curled her toes and prayed with every ounce of her being for the wretched feeling to go away. Nothing could be worse than this.

'It's true,' said a voice from the garden. 'You would be bored with him after a week.'

She started upright, her eyes springing open in fear. There,

34

framed in the open French doorway, the dark mass of him flanked by the billowing white linen drapes, stood Radley Blake.

'How . . . how long have you been there?' she asked, her mouth dry.

He gave a sharp laugh. 'Long enough. I was out here exploring the garden and saw you come in. I initially thought you'd come to find me. But alas!'

'Why didn't you say anything?'

'And miss all the fun? Tell me, do you know what melodrama means?'

She could feel the bile rising in her throat. All excess emotion – and Bernadette had an abundance of emotion – now focused on the man standing taunting her.

'How dare you . . .' she began.

'Now, now, don't get me wrong. I admire you, I do. Tim should thank his lucky stars for a girl with your – what was it? – youth, and vitality, and beauty.'

'Fuck you!'

'Ah, none of that! What happened to the eloquent vixen of a moment ago? I should like to see if you can find the negative of the pretty drivel you just spouted. Come at *me* with that tongue and see how I take it. I'll be much more receptive than the last fellow, I assure you.' Unlike his former lazy drawl, his words were now spitfire quick and made her head hurt. He held out his hands in cruel parody, opening his arms wide in the way she had first motioned for Tim to join her on the bed.

'You're not real,' she said firmly, standing up. 'You're a figment of my imagination. This is all a dream.'

'I promise you, I'm as real as you are, and equally human. We are the same, you and I.'

He confused her. She couldn't read him at all. She had to escape this silver-tongued phantasm. She was in an agony of humiliation, but at least she never had to see him again. 'I'm leaving,' she said wearily, making for the bedroom door. 'If you ever mention this to anyone, I'll curse you for a thousand years.'

'I believe in the power of your witchcraft,' he said, swiftly crossing the room and blocking her planned exit.

'Let me pass. If you don't move, I'll scream.'

He gently placed his massive palm over her mouth and planted a kiss on the back of his own hand, so that she could feel his warm breath on her face. 'Go ahead and scream.' It was carefully played as a non-threatening antic, but was still too bold for her taste. The man was somewhat polarising, although his breath had stilled her. The intimate warmth on her cheek felt like a colt puffing sweet, molasses-scented air through its nostrils, a friendly and innocent gesture.

'Let me take you home,' he said.

'No way,' she shuddered, shaking her head. 'You've got the wrong idea about me. I don't just throw myself at any man . . .' Here a little sob escaped her, and entirely overcome, she began to cry.

'What makes you think I'd want you? I'm trying to be a Good Samaritan. What was it you called me – your unwelcome saviour? Besides, do you really want to head out of here alone, and risk running into Tim or Elizabeth? Much better that you're too ill to be seen. Let me carry you out, and spirit you away in my car.'

His words were creepy, but his eyes seemed kind. 'I don't need to be rescued,' she said, through her tears.

He rolled his eyes and scooped her easily into his arms.

Evidently he was as strong as his muscled frame suggested. 'Come along, young lady,' he smiled. 'Shut your eyes and pretend to be in an alcohol-induced coma.'

'I'm not drunk.'

'Of course you're not.'

'And don't call me "young lady". That's so condescending.'

'And here I was, being polite. I can think of much worse names for you, I assure you.'

She glared at him, prepared to retaliate, but something in the twitch of his mouth stopped her. She chose the only sensible course of action. She shut her eyes, and leant her head against his ridiculously broad shoulder.

2

The following morning, Bernadette awoke from the bliss of her
dead slumber to a raging headache and a nagging guilt. Self-
reproach was unusual, and she spent a moment trying to frame
the feeling, taking into account the fact that her body was heavy
with sadness, her eyes stinging and puffy, her limbs listless and
her mind slow.

Then she remembered that Tim was engaged. A moment
later, she remembered her manic confession, and several
moments after that, she remembered Radley Blake. She sat up
slowly, straight-backed, like a beautiful zombie rising from a
shallow grave. With horror, she remembered everything.

He had carried her swiftly from the guest room, whilst she had
kept her eyes shut tight, hoping against hope that they wouldn't
run into anyone.

'Elizabeth!' Radley hissed a warning, and she felt him come
to a stop, and Elizabeth's voice near her head.

'Is she okay?'

'She's passed out drunk,' Radley replied. 'She mustn't drive. I'm going to drop her home.'

'Can't she stay here? I can take care of her!' Elizabeth's gentle fingers brushed a strand of hair back from Bernadette's face. Bernadette hated women who played to men. She heard Tim's voice join the group, and her heart leapt as her stomach lurched.

'What's going on?'

'I found her in the guest bathroom, passed out,' Radley said, with full conviction. Bernadette started working frantically backwards in her head, wondering if it was believable that such a short time after her passionate dalliance with Tim, she should be found senseless on the floor of the WC. Luckily, Tim seemed to buy it. He agreed with Radley that it would be better if she were delivered home, rather than spending the night in Elizabeth's care.

'Don't you just love her, Rad?' Elizabeth asked. 'She's so cute! And such a good heart.'

Bernadette could feel them all staring at her face. She was terrified that they would discover that she was, in fact, not unconscious, but wide awake and fuming. She considered adding in a little snore for dramatic effect, but doubted her ability to pull it off convincingly.

'She's a delicate china doll,' said Radley. Bernadette wanted to kick him, but that too would have given the game away.

'I could never think of a match for you,' Elizabeth went on. 'But when I met her, I just knew! She has the same feel as you – absolutely honest, with no side to her. A kind of raw honesty, and so smart.'

Bernadette wondered what Tim was doing during this

39

exchange. Was he wishing he had kissed her? Was he jealous to see her in Radley's arms?

'Well, you know me better than anyone, Lizzie,' Radley said, in an unnecessarily soppy voice.

Bernadette thought of his remark from earlier in the evening, how a woman like Elizabeth would never choose to be with a man like him. She felt a grudging respect for Radley Blake. She could never admire a man that someone like Elizabeth would actively choose to be with – no man other than Tim.

They managed to make it out to the valet stand without any further incident. 'Keep your eyes shut,' he instructed. Happy now to be directed, Bernadette did what she was told, and felt the unusual and dizzying sensation of being placed in the back of a large sedan by a stranger with an unknown motive. He managed to lay her across the back seat, her head by the far-side door, her feet near the open passenger door.

'Nice shoes,' he said provocatively, flicking her left heel.

She opened her eyes to glare at him, just in time to see him apparently climbing in on top of her. She struggled to sit up, but he pushed her gently back down.

'They might be looking out the window,' he said, clearly enjoying himself, his arms braced on either side of her body. 'I only wanted your valet ticket. Where on your person might it be? Mick can follow us in your car.'

'Who's Mick?' she demanded.

'I'm Mick,' said a nasal voice from the driver's seat. She turned to see a stocky guy in a chauffeur's uniform staring at her in resignation. He seemed unsurprised at her appearance on his back seat. Meekly she fished out the pink ticket from her evening bag, and handed it directly to him. 'Thanks, Mick,' she croaked.

'Uh-huh,' was his only response.

Radley replaced Mick in the front seat, and finally they were off. Bernadette sat up almost immediately when they were out of view of the house, her head spinning a little.

'Where do you live?' he asked.

She gave him her address, and he tapped it dexterously into the navigation system. His hands were large, like a manual labourer's, but he had incongruously nimble fingers.

'Now go to sleep,' he said. 'Oh, but before you do, I'm taking you to dinner tomorrow night.'

'No way,' she said, shaking her head vehemently.

'Why not? Your beloved Tim isn't going to be wining and dining you, so I don't see why I shouldn't have an evening of your company.'

Horror of horrors! She began to cry again, not loudly, but several tears rolled down her cheeks, and she snuffled a bit to prevent her nose from running.

'I'm sorry,' he said, quite kindly. 'It was wrong of me to tease you so soon. Here, let me make it up to you – I'll take you out to dinner tomorrow night!'

'No!' she cried, loudly and piteously.

'Why not?' he asked, baffled. Clearly he was not used to being refused.

'Because – because you're mean!' she wailed. And then she hiccoughed.

'Mean?' he said, flabbergasted, as if he didn't grasp the concept. 'You think I'm *mean*?'

'Yes.'

'Well so are you, you heartless vixen. What I witnessed tonight was hardly generous, was it?'

'I'm in love with him. Love. You know? The only thing in life worth having, the most important part of anyone's existence, the impossible dream?'

'Oh, spare me.'

They drove for several miles in silence, the dead air broken only by the occasional direction from the satellite system, delivered in a computerised female voice, and the click, click, click of the indicator.

As she drifted off into sleep, drooling slightly on the comfortable leather interior, Bernadette reviewed the evening. It certainly had the outward appearance of failure. She had declared her love to Tim, only to be rejected, and had insulted Radley Blake, an excellent interview prospect. But she knew only too well that things couldn't be judged purely by their looks, and that truth often hid in the less conspicuous detail. For example, no man would offer to drive a drunk woman home, would take the care that Radley Blake was taking with her, unless he was truly attracted to her – so all was not lost there.

Bernadette had less of a professional interest in Radley than a personal one. She always allowed her personal life to take precedence. Success at work had come easily, so she valued it little, whereas her single-minded pursuit of Tim was proving to be more challenging. Fate seemed to be signalling to her. Here was a handsome, intelligent billionaire who was obviously enamoured with her and was Elizabeth's long-time friend. He would be the perfect vehicle for planting the seed of jealousy in Tim's heart. Bernadette grasped just how impressive jealousy could be as a means of motivating affection; she herself suffered agonising pangs any time she witnessed Tim with Elizabeth. If Tim were to believe that she and Radley were an item, if she could flaunt another man's good fortune and show Tim exactly what he had passed up, she could drive him crazy. It was an ancient routine, but it worked. She wanted him unsettled and green-eyed and hurt. 'Okay,' she mumbled out loud. 'I'll have dinner with you.'

She peeked at Radley's face in the driver's mirror. He looked a little surprised at her drastic change of heart, or perhaps he was just surprised that she was awake. She saw his eyebrows rise quickly, his eyes widen, and he opened his mouth to say something, but shut it again. He seemed pleased.

'Dinner,' she repeated. 'Tomorrow night. Eight o'clock.'

Bernadette was used to dealing with hangovers. She had a robustness of constitution that belied her delicate frame. But she idled away the day in bed regardless, writing scraps of poetry, surfing the internet and eating ice cream. She lived in a spacious, high-ceilinged apartment in Santa Monica. Nearly every room had a view of the ocean, and she lived her life with the windows wide open. She lived alone, of course.

A large portion of the day was spent in researching Radley Blake. He was, by all accounts, some kind of genius, and the company he had created, Clarion Molecular, was the most advanced biotech firm in the world. There was a surprising lack of direct press coverage. It was easy to find quotes *about* him, but there were very few sound bites that could actually be attributed to the man himself. On YouTube she found a video of a lecture he had given at Oxford University. She admired his skill at public speaking; he was witty and concise, and delivered a vast amount of information in a palatable way. He was clearly immensely knowledgeable, yet kept his subject accessible and entertaining. He was too charming, for a scientist.

At seven o'clock, she began a careful toilette. She rubbed Moroccan oil in her hair, coconut oil on her skin, and applied her make-up with the skill of a true artisan. She opted for a smoky eye and a nude lip; a lot of men found lipstick (especially scarlet – her favourite!) to be threatening. She needed to appear ethereal and demure, to counter the impression of the night before. Dressed in soft leather trousers, with high-heeled suede boots and a grey cashmere sweater, she was artfully styled as an urban angel, an empyrean fashion plate with no high-grade thoughts in her head. The look was incredibly tactile. She had allowed her hair to dry naturally, and it framed her face in loose waves.

At eight o'clock sharp, Radley Blake was at the door of her apartment. He seemed impressed by the vision that greeted him, as she smiled a shy welcome and let him kiss her on the cheek.

'I thought you'd have forgotten,' he said simply. 'I wasn't sure you were cognisant when you agreed to this.'

She laughed a musical laugh. 'I'm looking forward to it, actually. You know, I'm just terrible at handling alcohol. I was a beast last night. This gives me a chance to show you that I'm not always that way.' She flashed a dazzling grin, and he looked at her shrewdly, his eyes twinkling.

'I don't know that you're all that different.'

She felt herself bridle testily. Everything this man said was a confrontation, designed to provoke. She laughed again, airily. 'Well, shall we head out?'

He gestured gallantly for her to pass him. 'Certainly, if you're not going to invite me in.'

She grabbed her silver clutch bag from a low table and strode out into the hallway. She went to push the elevator button, but Radley leapt in front of her and made a great show of pressing it first. 'Allow me,' he said, with a flourish and a low bow. He put his hands to his face and pretended to curl an invisible Victorian moustache.

'Why are you behaving like a cartoon villain?' she asked, crossly.

He laughed, a surprisingly youthful laugh that made his eyes crease in a friendly way, so that he looked almost attractive. 'I don't know,' he grinned. 'It's just something you bring out in me. I keep seeing you as you were last night, displayed on that bed – "I want to marry you and have a whole parcel of babies!" It was exquisite. You bring out the theatrical in me. I'm not usually like this.'

'You know,' she said, trying desperately to control her feelings of dislike, 'you put on this whole gentlemanly act, but the sign of true manners is not making the other person feel uncomfortable, not highlighting the other person's faults or . . . or faux pas.'

'No one could make you feel uncomfortable,' he said, as they entered the lift. 'You have skin as thick as a rhinoceros's hide. Besides . . .' the doors closed and he took a step towards her, standing disconcertingly close, looking down at her from his great height, 'you have no faults.'

Bernadette gulped, made her eyelashes flutter, gazed at his mouth with her very best wanton expression, and then glanced demurely up into his eyes, expecting to see him smitten. Instead, he was struggling with silent laughter.

'And if you're going to put on such a great act, then why

shouldn't I?' he finished, removing himself to one wall of the elevator, leaning against it and laughing outright.

Bernadette was used to having complete control in one-on-one social situations. It was quite disconcerting to be faced with Radley Blake, the genius, who seemed to have an almost omniscient understanding of her character, who had seen her at her very worst, her most vulnerable and exposed, and was choosing to use that against her. This was why she hated men – they couldn't *feel*. They had no empathy. They didn't operate on any human level.

'Consider yourself privileged,' he went on. 'I'm never usually this cheerful. I'm quite a sombre sort of person usually. My friends wouldn't recognise me.'

'You have friends?' she asked sweetly, as they arrived at the lobby.

The balmy evening air was a pleasant relief from the confines of the elevator, and Bernadette studied Radley as he ambled leisurely towards the waiting sedan. He was actually quite hand-some, in an enigmatic, intelligent sort of way, though she much preferred Tim's clean-looking, fresh-faced energy. Radley looked tortured and brooding, where Tim was joyful and bright. A sigh escaped her as she thought of Tim. It was time to redouble her efforts with Blake. Despite his intentional tormenting, he was taking her to dinner, which had to mean something. A man in Radley Blake's position couldn't afford to waste his time being kind or sociable, and if he had chosen to spend an evening with her, it must be because he had something serious in mind.

Mick was standing by the sedan. He opened the back door

as she approached, and she slid on to the seat with a mumbled 'Thanks, Mick.'

'Uh-huh,' was his only response.

Radley joined her in the back, and she was overtaken by an irrepressible desire to cuddle up against him. He looked so vast and comfortable, and his body was so large next to her own. She fortunately managed to restrain herself, and busied herself with looking out of the dark window, hating her feminine weakness. Despite loathing all men (except Tim), she found something in their physicality incredibly compelling. Her body wished to seek refuge in the arms of a burly male, even as her mind cried out his unworthiness.

The restaurant was one she had never been to, a small Italian place, near the beach. They sat at an outside table in a pretty courtyard, lit only by candlelight and the glow from the moon and the city. Even Bernadette began to relax a little under its spell. The maître d' seemed overly delighted to see Radley, and they had soon ordered a range of dishes, and an excellent wine.

Bernadette flirted manfully, with plenty of giggling and hair-tossing, to which Radley responded elegantly. He too was clearly an accomplished flirt, and on an abstract level she admired his technique and wordplay. It was rare to be faced with such a skilled opponent.

After a while, he fixed her with a steely gaze. 'Enough of the pleasantries,' he said. 'I know you remember that I was lucky enough to get a glimpse of the real you last night, and you're far more interesting than this insipid display would suggest. Thank God for eavesdropping!'

'Are you never going to forget that?' she asked.

'Never.' He leant back confidently in his chair, balanced in a precarious fashion, and she had the overwhelming desire to kick the legs out from under him.

'Tell me about yourself,' he said. 'I'm intrigued to know your history. There must be a reason you're the way you are.'

Bernadette looked down at her hands, unnerved, and began to fiddle with her sapphire ring. It was always discomfiting to learn that people found her behaviour abnormal. She wondered what she had done to give herself away.

'Is that an engagement ring?' asked Radley, pointing to her fidgeting fingers.

She nodded. 'My father gave it to my mother. He left when I was nine.'

'Oh,' said Radley, softly.

Bernadette detected too much feeling in the little word, and she looked up sharply. 'Oh, come on, nothing dramatic about it. Everyone has daddy issues.'

'No,' said Radley, shaking his head and looking at her kindly. 'They don't, actually.'

She scowled at him. 'I don't want to tell you about myself,' she said. 'I don't like to be interrogated over dinner.'

'Says the journalist!' he laughed. 'I don't know about interrogation. I was just going to proceed with a loose question-and-answer format, in the style of general conversation. We don't have to talk about anything too personal, if you're not up for it, but it will be a dull evening if we can't ask things of one another.'

'All right,' she said, resting her elbows on the table and her chin on her clasped hands, staring at him in what she hoped was a sexy but intimidating way. 'I have a question.'

She paused for dramatic effect, and he laughed again. 'I'm breathless with anticipation.'

'What do you want from me?' The words came out more serious-sounding than she had intended, with a rising inflection that was pure and unforced, and she realised that the authenticity must be due to a genuine desire to know his answer.

'Ah, now we're getting down to it.' He righted himself in his chair and took a contemplative sip of wine. 'Well, not a puff piece, obviously.'

'I'm sorry?'

'Sorry, I'm not suggesting that you write puff pieces, at all. In fact I know you don't. But that's what's always put me off before, you know? Ideally, I would want someone who would report facts, accurately. I can't stand creative non-fiction, this current obsession with new journalism. But failing an impartial reporter, I'd like someone who wouldn't go with the obvious story, at least. And your perspective is always unique. I prefer negative feedback to inappropriate positive enforcement. I really want nothing other than to put myself entirely at your mercy. I like your work.'

'You want me to interview you?'

'Yes please.'

'You mean this isn't – this isn't a date?' she asked, before having a chance to gather her thoughts.

He looked at her, puzzled. 'A date? No. No, I didn't intend for this to be a date.'

'Why not?' she demanded, fiercely.

'Why would I ask someone out on a date when they, ridiculously, think they're in love with someone else? That would be foolish. And I am no fool.'

'Yes, but . . .' Bernadette stared at him in confusion.

'Yes, but . . . you're open to persuasion? Your heart could be tempted elsewhere?' He smiled.

'No!' she said, angrily. 'I could never be tempted by anyone. There *is* no one else. You couldn't possibly begin to understand the way I feel about Tim.'

'In that case,' he said, leaning back and folding his arms across his chest, as if he had just announced checkmate, 'if that is true, if you are so wonderfully loyal, why would you accept this "date" with me?'

She had no answer for him and floundered, hating him and hating herself in equal measure. He wagged his finger at her, like an adult telling off a small child. 'See this?' he said. 'This is the finger of disapproval. It's pointed in your direction.'

'Please don't be so fucking condescending,' she said.

'You're an absolute menace, woman. But I see you. Everything you think is written plainly across your face. Going to string me along and make Tim jealous, were you?'

She reddened until she was roughly the same colour as the prosciutto. He leaned over and patted her arm. 'It's a fine plan,' he conceded, 'and usually I'd be up for it. But I'm afraid I'm helpless where Elizabeth's concerned. You see, I promised myself a long time ago that I'd never interfere in her love life. You may think me incapable of understanding whatever it is you feel for Tim, but let me tell you: I love Elizabeth. She's my closest friend.'

'Are you going to tell her?' she asked, sulkily.

'Tell her what?'

'What I said. To Tim, last night.'

'Ah, I see. Tell her that you're after her man? No. Like I said, I don't interfere. Tim should be the one to tell her, if anyone.

Besides, at the moment, you don't seem like a credible enough threat.' He grinned, amused.

Bernadette scowled deeply. 'If you dislike me so much, why do you want me to interview you?'

'Because I like to have the best,' he said, throwing his hands open apologetically. 'And you're the best.'

Bernadette was only twenty-two when she accompanied Carl Adams to interview President Wibawa at his tropical island home. A delegation of journalists had been chosen by the President himself, to be hosted with his blessing.

Carl was Bloomberg's foreign correspondent out of London, and he, along with seven equally distinguished colleagues, was to fly out and have the chance to interview the President in depth about his views on everything from human rights to nuclear disarmament.

President Wibawa, the self-appointed political, religious and royal leader of a little-known archipelago, had found himself at the centre of a global controversy when he wrested control of the islands from the peace-loving incumbent (his uncle), proceeded to commit atrocities against his people and dictated an extreme foreign policy. This ungentlemanly behaviour, combined with a penchant for flamboyant dress and a habit of violent hyperbole targeted against the West, meant the eyes of the world were fixed firmly upon him.

It was the opportunity of a lifetime, and Carl was nearly hysterical with excitement when he told Bernadette that he had managed to secure her a place on the trip too.

Bernadette had been working with Carl for six months, and had already come to the conclusion that journalism was not the career for her. She had pursued the internship as a way of distracting herself from grown-up heartache. Because Bernadette had just had her heart broken thoroughly, by an incredibly charismatic scoundrel, a notorious bachelor and much-admired Conservative MP, who had made love to her for a number of months and then abandoned her with little ceremony. Instead of the romantic hero she had been expecting, her first real encounter had been with a man very like her father. A man she had, in fact, been warned to stay away from by numerous parties. This was when she made the decision to swear off men for ever, the sins of this particular gentleman casting a long shadow.

Carl was a safe haven. He looked and acted like Tintin come to life, and was as sexually non-threatening as a sweet, single Englishman in his thirties could possibly be. Had enough time passed, Bernadette might have been able to convince herself that she was in love with him, with his gentle amiability and complete lack of resemblance to her father and the MP. But the wounds were still too fresh, and as it was, his constant boyish enthusiasm and desire for adventure only grated on her nerves.

His reaction to the Wibawa invitation had been typical. He was so thrilled, he could barely form coherent sentences, and he was flushed pink round the face, but his most pressing concern had been to make sure that Bernadette felt included. 'Of course,' he had stammered apologetically, 'you won't have the chance to actually *do* much, you know – I've told them you're my invaluable secretary – but just to be there! To see it all! It's going to be awfully exciting!'

Bernadette didn't have the heart to refuse his kind offer there and then, but she planned to tell him tactfully in a day or two that she wouldn't be joining him. It sounded like the stuff nightmares were made of. The political unrest, the bombings of nightclubs frequented by Western tourists, the images of young boys toting machine guns, the diabolical treatment of women. The idea of being thrust into a literal war zone absolutely terrified Bernadette. Her self-preservation instinct was more than unusually strong, and meant she did not share Carl's enthusiasm for this particular adventure.

That evening, over dinner, she mentioned the invitation to her mother. Bernadette planned to boast a little about how invaluable Carl found her, and how hard he had worked to secure her a place on the trip, for she had never outgrown the girlish desire to please and protect her mother.

Rose St John was a tall, slender woman, with a long white neck that rose from perfectly squared shoulders. To Bernadette, her mother's shoulders seemed Atlas-like, never hunched in pain or misery, for Rose faced the world with graceful equanimity and a placid detachment that nothing could excite.

Bernadette had never seen her mother truly discomposed, never heard her utter a curse or a harsh word, and the sound of her laughter was a distant memory. The last time Bernadette remembered hearing Rose laugh was actually the day her father disappeared. It was a beautiful August day, the best kind of English summer, where the sun was warm and seemed everlasting, as though winter had been a made-up hardship. Bernadette had woken late, and when she checked the time on her bedside clock was surprised she had been allowed such a luxury. She had wandered from her bedroom, still in her nightdress, and had found the house remarkably quiet and still. Rose was in the sitting room, a flower on the chintz sofa, clutching a hand-written letter to her chest.

'Mummy?' Bernadette had enquired, cautiously.

Rose looked up and said, 'Your father's gone.'

'Gone where?'

'I don't know.' And then Rose began to laugh. At that moment, understanding flooded Bernadette, and she knew that this laughter marked a new chapter for both of them. This was the giddy thrill of emancipation, the warmth of a new era springing into being. Bernadette laughed too, and clapped her hands, and tried to show her mother how well she understood these adult emotions, but at the sight, Rose stopped laughing, gasped in fact, and her hand went to her mouth, as if something terrible had happened. She drew Bernadette close into a hug and whispered, 'Oh, I'm sorry. I'm so sorry,' and Bernadette had felt her mother's tears in her hair.

Bernadette loved her mother with a devotion that matched nothing else in her life but was testament to her obsessive nature. Rose was Bernadette's heart and soul, her conscience and her lifeline. She showed her very best face to her mother, and tried always to seem sweet and temperate, hard-working and self-possessed.

'Of course, the fact that I'm allowed to go at all, being – you know – a *woman*,' said Bernadette, in a hushed tone, 'is quite an honour. Carl really feels that I could bring something to the piece; he's quite anxious that I . . .' She trailed off as she looked up and saw her mother's face.

Rose's cheeks were flushed and she was almost smiling, with a light in her eyes that was usually absent. 'It's a glorious achievement, my darling,' she said. 'I'm so proud of you! To think you get to be right at the heart of everything; you get to witness history first-hand, perhaps even to help shape history. It's so wonderful.' She reached forward and clasped Bernadette's hand. 'I'm very, very proud of you.'

And so Bernadette's fate was decided. She would have endured a far harsher nemesis than President Wibawa if it meant witnessing that warm glow in Rose's eyes and hearing the pride in her quiet voice.

A few weeks later, Bernadette came face to face with the controversial dictator. It was at his ocean-front palace compound, a myriad of pavilions, lush gardens and intricate temples. The humidity was almost suffocating. Armed guards surrounded the complex, and everywhere she looked, Bernadette could see men in fatigues, nursing Kalashnikovs.

The President greeted the foreign delegation like old friends. Tables had been set out in the shade of a spectacular courtyard garden, surrounded by large palms, and a party atmosphere pervaded the little group, who sipped sweet iced tea.

Several of the journalists had been allowed to bring assistants or secretaries, and Bernadette hung back with these lesser creatures, trying to hide her face under her headscarf. Despite the extensive security detail, she was convinced that at any second there would be gunfire, and she would be riddled with bullets and drop stone dead in an international diplomatic incident, along with the other fools standing around her.

The President was not at all what she had expected. He was young and handsome, and had been educated at Eton. His crisp English accent and horsey laugh bounced off the marble and stone as he shared anecdotes with Carl and the other journalists.

He made a point of greeting everyone individually, shaking hands and learning names.

Bernadette had murderous feelings in her heart as he approached her, but they were tempered somewhat by her old-fashioned English deference to rank, for after all, despite his reputation as a ruthless tyrant, he *was* basically royalty – a living deity. Any man with such immense power must be a source of fascination.

As they shook hands and he sought her eyes with his, for she had lowered her lashes in an exhibitionist show of submission, along with trembling fingers and a theatrical intake of breath, she realised that he was just like any other man, victim to the same insecurities, vulnerable to feminine wiles. He smiled broadly at her and said that her name was very pretty. She gave an awkward little bob-curtsey in response and he roared with laughter at the touching formality. 'Are you frightened of me?' he asked, loud enough for all to hear.

'Yes,' she declared, looking up at him for the first time, and quite taking his breath away with the innocent frankness of her gaze, and the certainty of her answer.

'We can't have that!' he boomed, smiling round. 'See, no one else is afraid.'

The journalists laughed, a couple of them nervously, and the President patted Bernadette on the shoulder. 'I predict you will not be afraid for long.' And with that ominous remark, he moved on to the next waiting guest.

The party of journalists and their assistants were being put up in great style at an American chain hotel in the middle of the nearby town. By the time the armoured vehicles and police convoy had taken them back to the hotel, Bernadette's room had been filled with one thousand long-stemmed red roses. A card on her bed read, *Do not fear what you do not know.*

Her delight was tainted with dread, but the fragrance of the roses aroused a giddying sense of her own power. Had she not been so recently heartbroken, she mightn't have realised that Wibawa had an ulterior motive. But after her dalliance with the MP, she was newly attuned to male bullshit. Wibawa had no real romantic or sexual interest in her; he placed no value on any individual female – which must mean there was a darker reason for the extravagant display. He needed a conduit to the West, and one that he could control. It was a dangerous game to enter into, but in that moment she felt completely equal to the task. She had been born to seduce princes.

She went to find Carl to show him the spectacle. 'Look,' she said, simply, throwing open the door to her room.

Carl's jaw seemed in danger of dislocating, it dropped so fast and so heavily. He did not seem to think the roses were anything other than a grand seductive gesture. Bernadette thrilled at his amazement. Seeing his reaction simply compounded her growing belief in her own invincibility. It was intoxicating.

'Crap,' Carl muttered, under his breath.

Bernadette laughed.

'You've got to be careful, Bernie,' he said. 'The guy's a notorious womaniser. The Demonic Don Juan, they call him. Seriously. This is not good. This is not good. Fuck. I should have foreseen this. I shouldn't have brought you.' He tugged at his hair in a puerile fashion and shook his head back and forth in despair.

It was incredible how Carl could ride through a war-ravaged landscape and not bat an eyelid, and yet come completely undone at the sight of a few flowers. Bernadette, on the other hand, felt safe for the first time since they had landed. Machine guns and roadblocks scared her; roses she understood. 'I think it's sweet,' she said, shrugging.

Bernadette, who was paranoid by nature, half believed her room must be already bugged, and she was careful to say nothing damning of the President. Carl stared at her, dumbstruck, as if seeing her for the first time.

That evening at dinner, she was seated next to the President. Much to the chagrin of the journalists – especially, she noted, the one female journalist in the group – Wibawa had eyes and ears for no one but Bernadette. He questioned her about her family, her education and her dreams.

'My biggest dream is to be a recognised journalist,' she said with a tone of awe. 'But I'm scared I'm not good enough.'

'You're afraid of a lot of things, aren't you?' he said, poking her arm jovially. 'You're a little scaredy-cat.' She simpered the correct amount. 'I think you're a remarkable young woman,' he continued. 'But why do you want to be a journalist, when you could do anything you choose?'

Bernadette looked at him, her eyes dark pools. 'There's so much bad in the world that I can't make sense of. Every day we're bombarded with information, with shocking pictures and descriptions of violence. It's too much. I want to find the good in the world and report it,' she said, with a saintly expression etched firmly on her countenance. Wibawa turned away, hiding his smile of delight, and Bernadette knew then that this was a game she could win.

Two days later, the President sent the other journalists home, cutting their trip and their expectations short. He had given

Bernadette the gift of sole interview rights, a gesture that would secure her self-professed dream of becoming a recognised journalist. Carl was beside himself with worry, still not understanding the reality of the situation, which Bernadette did not dare relate. Before his return to the UK, he begged her to reconsider and fly back with him, offering all kinds of assistance in the case of an emergency, from the personal numbers of people very high up in the UN, to the full weight of Bloomberg as an organisation.

Completely in the grip of the seduction, Bernadette had few qualms about being left alone. And, she comforted herself, if she *had* committed herself to certain death, at least it was all for the love of her mother.

She was moved from her room at the hotel and installed in an exquisite temple-style room in the palace. The individual low hut, with its carved wooden beams and pretty thatched roof, had a large four-poster bed and a view of the turquoise ocean. Mosquito nets and white linen curtains gave a soft romance, as did fragrant pink blooms and bronze statuary.

The plan was that she should stay for a week, and in that time she was to follow the President in his everyday life, in order to best understand the man he really was.

Their unusual relationship had already sparked a flurry of media interest overseas, and people waited anxiously for Bernadette's first reports. But she claimed that she felt too pressured by the attention of the world to write sensibly, and so Wibawa decided that she should compose her article when she got home to England, and spend her time with him taking notes. She followed him around like a faithful puppy. He allowed her to ask anything, and promised to give an honest answer.

She focused less on his political policy and more on his personal ideals, and they had many intimate conversations that lasted for hours at a time, whilst they walked along the golden sands, or dined in splendour.

Bernadette worked a constant game of opposites, flaunting her desire for independence and a successful career, whilst hinting sometimes that she would appreciate the attention of a good-hearted man. She also offered up the idea that her relationship with Carl was more than platonic, and that she felt a certain amount of loyalty to him. The President listened carefully to everything she told him and, in turn, played a subtle hand. He paid her all the attention a woman in such an exotic and romantic situation would expect, but was cautious never to push too far. He was aware of his own reputation, and the last thing he wanted was to scare Bernadette. He often hinted that he needed to find a wife, and he spoke fondly of his education in Britain. Their dynamic was a layered one. More than anything, he seemed determined to spoil her, and offered her lavish gifts, which she refused to accept.

'I can't take anything from you,' she said conscientiously. 'It would be seen as a bribe. I have to remain impartial in order to profile you accurately.'

He would back off immediately, with profuse apologies, and reiterate his belief in her as a writer and his desire to see her succeed in anything that would make her truly happy. But then, a matter of hours later, he would try to give her another extravagant gift, this one even more immoderate than the last.

'What are you trying to do?' she asked huffily at one point. 'Purchase a woman for a herd of cattle and twelve bales of hay? It doesn't work like that. This is the twenty-first century, you know,' for she had learnt that the President liked it when she bossed him a little.

Two days later, a herd of sorry-looking cattle was paraded, in great state, around the palace walls, and a decorated pyramid built using twelve bales of hay was erected outside her bedroom. Bernadette had to laugh when she saw the President's cheeky face, his delight with his own joke, and the way he practically danced up to her begging to be admired. Like all despots, he had a taste for the whimsical.

'Very good,' she had said, laughing too. 'But don't think you own me now.'

'I know I can never own you,' he said, suddenly serious. 'But I hope that perhaps one day you will come to me of your own accord.' She looked away with a troubled expression, biting her lip. 'I won't push you,' he continued. 'I know how gentle you are, and how much you dislike pressure. Just know that I feel this way. But no expectations – I am happy to have you as a friend, if nothing more.'

Bernadette tried not to marvel at her victory too soon. It was an exhausting activity, and she was watched and tested constantly. She had been appointed a personal security detail, and one night her burly close-protection officer, a South African man with bright red hair, spoke to her about the President. 'Be careful,' he whispered one evening, as he escorted her to her room. 'The guy's a killer.'

Bernadette, ready for such a warning, turned cold eyes on him. 'There's a war. He's had to make choices,' she said. 'But he's working for the greater good. He cares passionately about his country. And his people.'

'Just you watch your heart,' the man said, nodding earnestly.

'He likes Western women. He flies planes full of prostitutes over every month.'

Bernadette clicked at him impatiently. 'Have you ever actually seen these planes full of prostitutes?' she demanded. The officer thought for a moment, and shook his head. 'It's all lies,' she continued. 'They make things up about him to fuel Western hatred. I've heard all the stupid stories, but they're completely unsubstantiated. I'm not saying he's perfect, but he's absolutely not the pantomime figure of evil that he's made out to be.'

Bernadette quite enjoyed the theatrics of it all, to the extent that she almost convinced herself of Wibawa's greatness. But at night, alone in bed, she silently prayed for the President's numerous victims, remembering that he was a cold-blooded killer.

When certain periods of life are full of excitement, danger and novel experiences, time takes on a peculiar habit and seems to stretch itself wide, simply in order to accommodate the number of grand events. Careful observation is impossible under such an onslaught, when the rush of spectacle abuses all senses, despite the dilation of the minutes and hours. Detail has to be carefully stored to memory, to be meditated over at leisure. So it was for Bernadette and her week with President Wibawa, which seemed to have lasted a lifetime, so much had been crammed into the days. She had seen impossible fantasies, and worked herself to near exhaustion with the fatigue of constant deception. Yet nothing was clear in her mind, and the specifics of her various encounters evaded order, dancing in a colourful haze of confusion that would not settle and be seen. Some greater force must have been controlling her actions, for when she looked back, she couldn't remember making a conscious decision the whole time, and her behaviour seemed to be that of a stranger. The disembodied feeling lasted for a while and she found peace in it. Bernadette liked to escape the burden of accountability whenever possible.

Her parting from the President was a spectacularly tender one, and she shed a few tears. 'There's part of me,' she whispered, 'that doesn't want to go home.'

His face lit up. 'Would you stay with me?' But then his gaze clouded, and he patted her hand. 'But what about your mother?'

Bernadette moved past him, her heart racing. 'I can't turn away from my life, my real life. But I'll miss you. That's all.' She felt rather like an actress in a cheap daytime soap opera, and wondered at life, and its absurdity.

He gave a small laugh. 'That's all! Will you let me know, Bernadette? If you get back, and you still miss me?'

'You'll be able to know how I'm feeling when I get home. All you have to do is read the article I'm going to write,' she said, staring up at him devotedly. 'My heart will be in my words.'

He moved to kiss her, but she demurred, as she had done every other time he had tried. She knew that withholding physically was part of her power, and it was a part she was loath to give up. Instead, they hugged, gripping one another tightly, as if they would never let go. 'I like that you are a chaste woman, Bernadette,' he murmured into her hair, as over his shoulder she gave her most lascivious smile.

Back in England, in the wondrously safe and quiet environment of Rose's compact house, Bernadette was a changed girl. She locked herself in her bedroom for two weeks and barely came out. She hardly ate, and spent many sleepless nights worrying herself sick. Rose could hear her typing madly away at her laptop at all hours, fingers clicking feverishly at the keys as if she were hammering out a grand sonata.

The resulting article caused a global sensation and made Bernadette a minor celebrity in her own right. It was entitled 'Who's seducing whom?' and her damning account of President Wibawa contributed to a final, successful violent uprising in his country.

The President, she wrote, *is a cunning man, whose Machiavellian mores and morals more than equal those of any of history's greatest tyrants. His mind, shaped by a Western education and poisoned by the inherent ascendancy of his birth, seeks to abuse any weakness. He exploits the current political climate, inciting anti-American hatred among his people, whilst profiting from their poverty. His hypocrisy knows no bounds, and though he may preach the value of a religious life, he enjoys the worst excesses of a liberal society. He is responsible for the deaths of thousands of his citizens. He maintains a brutal oligarchy whilst courting the affection of international allies. He is no great leader. He is, however, a political animal, and this is where I come in.*

I was accompanying Carl Adams in the role of reporter's assistant, as part of the delegation chosen by the President to record a biographical series for dispersal around the world. I do not believe President Wibawa ever intended for this series to be written or published.

Despite his insistence on wanting to present an honest account of himself for public scrutiny, the President must have known that anyone with half a brain couldn't spend any significant time with him and help but see him for what he really is: a ruthless killer and a monster. What he wanted was a sympathetic foreigner, a woman, someone with limited journalistic experience, who would be flattered by any attention he might show her. I was the youngest person in the group. I am a woman. I was an assistant, not a journalist. The President automatically believed me to be a vulnerable and impressionable person, susceptible to his powerful charisma, and the ideal courier for his message to the West.

He sent me mixed signals. He had to flirt with me – he is aware of his own reputation as a ladies' man, and to have avoided any kind of pass at me would have upset my feminine pride. For my part, I played the role of dumb female and allowed him to believe his manipulations were succeeding. It was a gruesome task. He wanted me to think he was under my spell, that I was in control, that he was unthreatening. It was an extravagant and insidious seduction, involving a certain amount of effort, and we must wonder why he is so keen to court our good opinion.

The article went on to detail the intricacies of their mutual inveiglement. Bernadette unabashedly explained her own duplicity; how she had purposefully acted exactly as the President expected her to. Parts of the report were so extreme in denouncing the stupidity of men, as embodied by the President, that a few commentators suggested Bernadette might be as mad and dangerous as her subject.

But these critics were in the minority. Bernadette was almost universally praised for her unique slant on the situation, and people were so caught up with the nationalistic politics, and her impassioned rhetoric, that they completely missed the misandry that worked its way throughout the piece, snaking through the narrative like a wild thing.

Bernadette was offered book deals, guest appearances on

news shows, and could now write for any publication her heart desired. She took it all in her stride, and accepted her new-found success with little fuss or astonishment.

The most significant thing to come out of the President Wibawa escapade was the fact that she met Tim. Hollywood came knocking at Bernadette's door, as it is wont to do when-ever there is a notable story involving a good-looking female activist, and she flew out to LA to talk to potential agents and managers. Tim was the first person she met, and she signed with him immediately, despite having been counselled to take her time and shop around.

With Tim's help, she managed to carve out a credible, respect-able and profitable career. She refused all the grander offers, and instead chose to concentrate on writing articles for quality publications. Tim marketed her as 'The Man Whisperer' and found her gigs interviewing high-profile men, where she would encourage them to share intimate details of their lives, and give away trade secrets. It was a bandwagon that the men seemed thrilled to jump on, and celebrities, tycoons and princes alike lined up to be 'whispered' to by Bernadette. Her articles always had a 'gender agenda', as she called it, and were written from a purely female perspective. But now, tempered by Tim, instead of the strident arrogance of her first piece, she crafted a happy, seductive character that people could relate to. The tone was flirtatious and provocative, titillating without becoming tawdry.

And so she found herself celebrated at a tender age, achieving dizzying heights of career success that most people could only dream of, and yet she was dissatisfied. Despite lacking passion for her work, she was good at it. She had a passion for Tim, and that sufficed. But she was filled with self-loathing, knowing that her empire was built on sand. Her piece on President Wibawa had been driven not by bravery, or the desire to shape the world for the better, or journalistic integrity. It had been inspired by youthful prejudice, and pain, and the fact that the universe had responded by reaffirming that sentiment, by rewarding her for her act of violence and for the darkest part of her character, sat uneasy in her heart.

Her disappointment with the opposite gender only increased. It was true that she was suddenly surrounded by the most successful men on the planet, and spent her days in conversation with exalted characters, but men who have achieved greatness, who take risks and make decisions at a level the majority would baulk at, are not necessarily the first people you would turn to when looking for examples of 'good' men. And she moved to live in Los Angeles, which is not noted for the virtue of its citizens.

For her part, however, Bernadette was ungenerous and judgemental, silently critiquing the people who loved to be interviewed by her. The philanthropists were glory-seekers, the geniuses were nerds, and the wealthy were capitalist pigs.

As for the President, a few days after the article came out, he sent Bernadette one dozen long-stemmed red roses, with a card that read, *It was I who should have been afraid.* Bernadette was not moved by the gesture, but she was relieved.

Bernadette sighed and slowly nodded at Radley Blake. 'All right,' she said. 'I'd like to interview you. I'll do it for *Squire*. We'll make cover. I'll need to shadow you for a couple of days, preferably when you're following a normal routine.'

'Normal?'

'Well, not on vacation, for example, or doing things that you wouldn't normally do. I like to write slice-of-life articles, as close to your everyday experience as possible. Of course, a lot of the people I interview have an incredibly warped perception of what normal is, and I'm sure you're no exception. But normal for you is what I'm trying to achieve. Whatever is normal for you, I want to see it.'

'Okay.'

'And I usually like to interview over the end of the week: Thursday, Friday, Saturday. That way, I see you at work and at play. Fine?'

'Fine.'

'And I'd like to interview people close to you – family, friends, girlfriends, co-workers, employees, et cetera.'

'Oh, good.'

'And you're really not expecting a puff piece? Because you should know, I speak as I find. I'm not going to write exclusively about your genius. If I think you'd make a lousy lover, then I'll put that in my article. If I think you treat your staff like shit, then I'll write about that too. The Man Whisperer is an entity of her own, you know; she has a voice.'

'I've already told you, I don't want a puff piece. *You* may speak as you find, but *I* say what I mean. If I've said I don't want a puff piece, then you can take it as truth.' He leant over and refilled her wine glass.

'Do you not think that *I* say what I mean?' she demanded, downing the wine indignantly. 'The way you said that, it sounded as though you don't.'

Radley laughed. Not in his usual sardonic way, but a proper full-blown laugh. The strength of the hearty peal startled

Bernadette, and made her think that below Radley's acerbic exterior there might lurk an actual human being.

'My dear, I've never known anyone more deceptive than you. You hardly ever say what you mean, and you certainly never say what you think. You're an actress.'

'I'm not an actress, I'm a journalist,' mumbled Bernadette, stunned into stupidity.

'Ah, but you *are* an actress. What is acting? Nuanced mimicry. And you have it down to a fine art. You listen and repeat, like a parrot, trying to sound like the rest of us, but you don't *believe* in what you're saying. Your heart and your mind are elsewhere.'

Bernadette took several more large gulps of wine. 'I don't know what you're talking about,' she said.

3

Rose was going to join Bernadette in Los Angeles for Christmas. It was with some trepidation that Bernadette waited for her mother in the soulless environs of the LAX International Arrivals terminal, two days after her non-date with Radley Blake. She stood nursing her Starbucks cappuccino, shifting from foot to foot like an annoyed llama, worrying that she hadn't brought a welcoming bunch of flowers. It seemed wrong to wait for someone at an airport gate without some sort of offering, and she glanced pettishly at two small children who proudly held up a big home-made banner that read, *Welcome Home Dad!*

With unaccountable tears in her eyes, she fiddled with her sapphire ring, whilst clutching at a small bag containing a pink-sprinkles-covered doughnut, which she had bought at the same time as the coffee and was to serve as a last-minute 'Welcome to America!' gift. The grease was forming dark patches on the brown paper it was wrapped in.

Bernadette hated waiting; it was a habit that went entirely against everything she believed in. She watched incredulously as person after person streamed from the arrivals gate, and none of them was Rose. As if drawn by the spectacle that awaited him, the father of the small children was one of the first passengers to make it out through the gate, and Bernadette watched with a lump in her throat as the children leapt on him, squealing in delight, effusive in their kisses and exclamations of love.

She peeked in the paper bag to check on the sorry little doughnut, which surely had no magic attractive quality, and as the smell of the warm dough hit her, it was all she could do to stop herself from eating it.

When Rose finally emerged, looking immaculate, considering she had just stepped off a long-haul flight, Bernadette actually squeaked in excitement. She was embarrassingly fond of her mother.

Growing up, Bernadette had had a hard time reconciling her father's oxymoronic statements about her mother – such as 'frigid whore' and 'cheap dependant' – with the day-to-day reality of the kind and patient woman who was so good to her. The fact that Rose never fought back was maddening to Bernadette, but reinforced the idea that her mother was a creature who must be protected.

Now she wanted to run to Rose and throw her arms around her, but there was something so delicate about her mother that she worried a fierce hug would crush her. So instead, she approached carefully. 'This is for you,' she said, awkwardly thrusting the paper bag at Rose.

'A doughnut! How beautifully American! Thank you, darling,' Rose murmured, putting her arm around Bernadette's shoulders and grasping the bag as though it contained rare treasure.

The drive to her apartment seemed unusually long, hampered

by rush-hour traffic and the usual shyness that she always experienced when face to face with Rose again after some absence. But they managed to maintain a steady stream of conversation, politely exchanging news, and planning their menu for Christmas lunch.

'Tim got engaged,' Bernadette said lightly, glancing at her mother out of the corner of her eye.

'Tim your manager?'

'Yes.'

'That's nice.'

Bernadette noted afresh how miraculous it was the way Rose's dignity lent everything perspective. There were no catastrophes in Rose's world, no all-consuming passions, no dire misfortunes. The way she had said, 'That's nice,' as though talking about the sunshine, or a non-remarkable pair of shoes, made Bernadette feel that a lukewarm reaction was the pinnacle of human understanding when dealing with affairs of the heart.

Bernadette enjoyed the Christmas preparations with her mother present. Living alone, there was little incentive to partake in the celebration of a season that everyone else seemed unnecessarily bound to, and Bernadette rather prided herself on her lack of consumer support for an antiquated religious festival. But Rose insisted on a Christmas tree. In fact, she seemed somewhat disappointed to arrive at her daughter's bare apartment and find no jolly red-and-green welcome; not reproachful, never reproachful, just a little dispirited at the lack of effort, so much so that Bernadette hasted to assure her that she had been overly busy with work, and had been waiting for Rose's arrival.

The tree, of course, spawned lights, and tinsel, and other bits

of material happiness that littered the otherwise muted bachelorette pad. And then there were the mince pies that Rose set
to baking, which filled the place with the most delicious spiced
scent, and the angelic choral music that she liked to listen to
whilst wrapping enticing book-shaped gifts.

They had turkey on Christmas Day, and opened their presents,
and watched old movies, and Bernadette spent the day in a new
pair of red tartan pyjamas. On Boxing Day, still eating turkey
and still in her tartan pyjamas, her cell phone buzzed with a
message from Radley Blake.

Are you at home?

Yes, she texted back.

Good. Over in ten with a bottle.

His presumptuousness actually excited her, the thought of
an unexpected visitor made her unaccountably happy, and she
jumped up to dress without responding to his text. Rose was
bemused by the suddenness of the arrangement on such a day.

'But is he a *good* friend?' she asked.

'No, not exactly. I wouldn't really call him a friend. I don't
actually like him that much, truth be told.'

'Why are you having him over if you don't like him?'

'He's a sort of . . . a business friend. I'm going to interview
him, have to be polite, you know?' She couldn't resist adding
a boast. 'And he's hardly ever given interviews before. He hates
the press. He'll only speak to me. It's sort of an honour.'

Bernadette absent-mindedly straightened decorations and
poured dry shampoo over her hair. It would be fun to have
someone smart and relatively young to spar with for the afternoon.

Radley rapped loudly on the door when he arrived, and

Bernadette waited a good few moments before heading to open it. Rose gave an enigmatic smile.

'Merry Christmas,' said Radley, stooping to kiss Bernadette's cheek.

'Merry Christmas,' she said cheerfully, stepping aside to let him enter. He stopped when he encountered Rose, who stood waiting to receive him with her usual look of patient beauty.

'I'm sorry,' he said, glancing back at Bernadette. 'I didn't realise you had company. I won't disturb you for long. I just wanted to bring you this.' He handed her a bottle of red wine. 'And these,' he added, depositing a box of English Christmas crackers in her arms. 'To remind you of home.' He moved to Rose with his hand outstretched. 'Radley Blake.'

'I'm Rose St John, Bernadette's mother,' she said. They shook hands solemnly, like a picture from an etiquette textbook, a quiet reflection of one another, and Bernadette knew with unusual foresight that Radley would appeal to Rose, and vice versa. He had a new air of solicitousness, and a tone in his voice that she had only heard him use with Elizabeth. She was relieved; she didn't like to expose Rose to the company of loud, forceful men.

'I was worried you were alone,' he said apologetically to Bernadette.

'Why would you think that?' she demanded.

He shrugged, helplessly. 'It was, I see now, grossly impertinent of me – but people living alone often make plans for Christmas lunch, Christmas Day, but then forget to make plans for the days that follow, and there's an inevitable anticlimax, the Christmas come-down . . . or maybe that's just me?' he said, grinning ruefully.

'I hope you'll stay and have a drink with us,' said Rose, sitting down and gesturing for him to do likewise.

'I don't want to impose,' he offered delicately.

'Too late,' scoffed Bernadette, 'so you might as well have a drink. Sit down . . . *Please*,' she added, after a glance from Rose.

Whilst she uncorked the wine and heated some of Rose's delicious mince pies, she could hear her mother chatting pleasantly to Radley about her visit. Rose's voice had a stronger note than usual and the sound of conversation carried well enough that Bernadette could tell there was a pattern of equal contribution, no awkward pauses, and both parties sounded amused and interested.

She set the snacks in front of them on the low coffee table, and sat back, determined to be entertained rather than entertaining. Radley proceeded to open the box of Christmas crackers. Taking one out, he offered the other end of it to Rose, with a droll look. Bernadette first laughed at them, and then squealed, as the cracker popped and the little gift went flying into her lap. 'Whose is it?' she demanded, holding up the tiny bundle.

'Mine!' claimed Rose almost triumphantly. She was practically smiling as she held up the larger end of the cracker as evidence.

The prize was a small set of silver manicure implements, with the obligatory paper hat and riddle. 'You must wear the hat,' insisted Radley. 'I would take it as a slight if you didn't.'

So Rose obediently wore the purple crown, which dented her decorous image only slightly, and seemed, if anything, to add a regal touch to her greying head. Bernadette was secretly thrilled by her mother's relatively clownish behaviour.

The three of them shared the bottle of wine and polished off the mince pies. They pulled all the crackers, wore a hat apiece and laughed. Even Rose was laughing. Radley looked at Bernadette fondly and said, 'I don't know why I find you so amusing,' and Rose urged earnestly, but with a tipsy lilt, 'Oh, Bernadette is really very, very funny!' and then they all laughed again, and couldn't stop for quite some time.

'One of the main reasons I wanted to see you,' Radley said as he was preparing to leave, 'was because I wanted to personally invite you to my house-warming party. And now you too, Rose, of course.'

'When is it?' asked Bernadette.

'On the twelfth.'

'Oh, I'll be back in England,' said Rose. 'Bernadette, you'll have to tell me all about it.'

Bernadette hesitated. She had enjoyed the past few hours with Radley more than she had anticipated, but attributed most of that to gratitude – she was grateful that Radley had been able to entertain Rose, that he had understood immediately the type of woman that her mother was, and had been able to reach her with chivalry and humour.

'Tim will be there,' said Radley, with forced casualness. 'And Elizabeth.'

'Yes,' said Bernadette, recognising the lure with a roll of her eyes. 'Of course I'd like to come. It sounds lovely. Thank you for inviting me.'

Radley inclined his head in his usual formal manner. 'Feel free to bring a date.'

David Schmidt was a middle-aged, unusually short Democrat who wore an almost permanently startled expression on his soft face, and blinked a lot. He reminded Bernadette of some small woodland creature that had accidentally wandered on to the freeway, blinded by the lights of an oncoming truck. Wiry tufts of dark hair declared war on the circumference of his shiny domed head, and seemed determined to deafen him by growing thickly in his ears. He was the West Coast editor of *Squire* magazine, and had a literary-minded ex-wife whose sole pleasure in life derived from sending him abusive emails interspersed with loving ones.

He had seemed extremely pleased when Bernadette had told him about her exclusive interview with Radley Blake. A beatific smile replaced the startled-rabbit look, and he blinked a furious approval. Bernadette was mildly fond of David, mostly because he was entirely harmless, too absorbed in his own particular affairs (he was a fusspot) to look at her cleavage or make her feel objectified. He beamed a scholarly friendship, and allowed Bernadette to have her own way in everything, which suited them both perfectly.

The idea of asking David as her date to Radley's housewarming had occurred to her almost immediately. There would be something about turning up on the arm of a plain poor innocent that would lend a certain gravitas to her case. No one could accuse her of frivolity, or believe her to be lacking in substance, if she was with someone like David. David was practically a male Elizabeth, so straightforward and decent did he seem – his conversation intelligent and inoffensive, his manner diffident and unobtrusive, and his physical appearance so utterly charmless. Bernadette warmed to the idea so much that she began to think it might not be a bad thing if she and David were to become a semi-permanent item. Dating David, even for a short while, might be enough to force Tim into action. And she really was very keen on David; there was something extremely comforting about him – he would always be kind, never unfaithful, and he wouldn't want much from her other than the obvious.

Once Rose was safely back in the UK, after a non-tearful but extremely fraught goodbye at LAX, Bernadette was free to carry out her plan. She sashayed into the offices of *Squire* magazine like a Japanese schoolgirl, flaunting her sexuality in a blatant and generic way, dressed in an outfit that bordered on being a costume. Her theme was 'naughty secretary', complete with black stockings and wire-rimmed glasses. She had a desk at *Squire* that she rarely used, but today she set up her laptop and worked diligently, tapping away at the keys and ignoring the baleful looks of other staff members. David wandered by her desk, eating a sandwich and reading from a competitor's magazine, dripping mayonnaise down his tie. He was entirely oblivious to her presence.

'David!' she trilled in a sing-song voice, smiling up at him.

He started, and dropped an extra big glob of mayonnaise down himself. 'Bernadette. Hi, hi. Didn't see you there. How are you?'

He seemed unaffected by her dress, and blinked at her in his usual cordial way. She sighed and surreptitiously hiked her skirt up a few inches to reveal lace stocking tops.

'Oh, David! I'm good. I'm really good, thank you!'

'What can we do for you?'

Bernadette blushed prettily. 'I was wondering if I could speak to you? It's . . . it's sort of a silly thing.' She looked at him with an expression of such helplessness that his chest perceptibly puffed with protectiveness.

78

'I'm sure it's not silly. Not from you.'

She leant forward with a confiding air. 'It's just . . . You know Radley Blake?'

He nodded. 'Has he cancelled the interview?'

'Oh no!' she gasped. 'Nothing like that. No, that's all fine. But you see, the thing is, he's having a house-warming party in a couple of days. And I was wondering if . . . if you would come with me?'

David blinked once, and then blinked again. He looked painfully confused.

'As a sort of . . . date,' she clarified.

Clearly David had never entertained the slightest possibility that Bernadette would ever see him as anything other than a colleague. Bernadette didn't make fun of him and laugh behind his back, the way the other women in the office did. Of course, David didn't know that she was not on speaking terms with any of the women in the office, but for this charity alone he should be grateful.

'Would that be wrong?' she asked, innocently, with just a hint of perversion, letting her tongue roll over the final word. 'I mean, would the magazine mind?'

David gulped and found his voice. 'No, no. I think. I don't think. That would be fine!'

'So will you come with me?'

'Yes!' he cried, emboldened. It was a dream moment for David, a once-in-a-lifetime moment.

'Oh, good! It should be fun. I'll email you the details,' and Lady Bountiful bestowed upon him her most generous smile, a tinkling laugh and rosy cheeks.

He stumbled away on his short legs, trying to make sense

of it, looking as though, at last, the fates were rewarding him for a thus far fairly miserable life.

As she watched him move away, Bernadette thought he looked like a wind-up toy whose key had just been turned tight enough to send him off at a rollicking pace, and his jerky, robot-like movements made her want to laugh out loud. David's ardour had rather revolted her, and he had fallen far in her estimation. How easily he had given in to the fantasy, after years of luke-warm friendship. Any sensible man would have questioned her sudden change of heart, and been more prudent in his response.

Radley Blake's new house was an impressive construction of glass and stone and steel. It sat high on a hill with views of the city and the ocean. The grounds were immaculate: terraced lawns, neat desert flowers in regimented beds, and a steamy infinity pool that fell away to nothingness. David had picked Bernadette up in his Prius, and she had been flirtatious and teasing the whole journey, questioning his choice of music and keeping up a steady stream of banter that fortunately allowed him to say very little. David had not been favoured with the gift of easy conversation. Especially when faced with bright, beautiful girls like Bernadette, he was liable to get tongue-tied and say something foolish. But she prattled so constantly that he was saved the labour of having to answer, for which blessing he seemed excessively grateful.

The cooling walk from valet stand to the large front door allowed Bernadette to pause and reflect. She had been mindlessly chattering for the past half-hour, and her cheeks felt numb from all the smiling. But David wasn't really so bad, and she felt with some certainty that Tim would be more annoyed by her showing up with David than if she had been with Radley Blake himself. She and Radley were an altogether too believable pairing, but it would be difficult for Tim to watch her happily wasting herself on the oafish David Schmidt.

The front door was made of rough oak and looked somehow like a living tree trunk. It stood hospitably open, and guests streamed into the open-plan space beyond. There were a number of people already at the party, and to Bernadette's horror, the majority of them were stunning young girls. The house was elegant, warm and modern, and used a lot of natural materials – slate and wood, stone and iron. A fire roared in a huge hearth, a DJ played an eclectic mix, and the beautiful people enjoyed each other and the flowing liquor.

Suddenly Radley had both her hands in his and was kissing her gently on the cheek. He smelt like strong whisky and expensive cologne. 'Hello,' he said.

'Hey,' she said, gulping. 'This is David Schmidt. My editor.'

David preened and held out his hand.

'Welcome!' said Radley. 'I'm looking forward to being whispered to for your publication. I read *Squire*, actually. I like it. Good articles.'

'You'd better watch our Man Whisperer!' said David, his face pink with fearless joviality. 'She's a tricky one. She can make men do anything! Say anything!' He looked quite overcome with the myth and grinned covetously at Bernadette as if she were once an untamed creature, and now his own particular pet in a cage.

Radley raised an eyebrow. 'Do *anything*? Is that so?'

Bernadette felt colour rise to her cheeks. 'That is not possible, for anyone,' she said. 'And nor should it be.'

'But you're a marvel!' cried David, who had decided that Bernadette was his favourite topic of conversation. 'You're a vixen with a pen—'

'David, could I have some wine, please? Red,' asked Bernadette desperately. 'I'm very thirsty.'

David looked aghast at his failure as a date. 'Yes! Yes, of course. Radley, anything?'

The host shook his head to decline, and David scuttled off with all haste. Bernadette met Radley's clear gaze with a defiant look.

'Poor sod,' he said, nodding after David.

'I *like* David,' she began.

'I should hope so. He seems like a nice man.'

'Where's Tim?'

'He and Elizabeth are in the garden. Elizabeth has something very special she wants to talk to you about.'

Bernadette immediately became dizzy, and clutched at Radley's arm in fright. 'She's not pregnant, is she?'

He shook off her grip, annoyed. 'Control yourself, woman. No. She's not pregnant.'

'You have a nice house,' muttered Bernadette, gathering her wits and changing the subject.

'Now I just need the right woman to make it a home,' he laughed, mock-sentimentally, slapping his hand across his heart and smiling widely at her.

'I'll be sure to include that in my article,' she said. 'I'm taking notes, you know.'

'Not tonight you're not.' He placed his heavy hands on her shoulders. 'I'm quite serious, Bernadette. Other than our allotted interview time, I don't want anything on the record, thank you very much. I want there to be room for you and me to develop a friendship, separate from anything else.'

'Oh,' she said, taken aback. She wondered if he meant a genuine, platonic friendship, or if it was clever long-game subterfuge.

'Don't you think we could be friends?' he asked, peering at her oddly.

'We could be friends,' she responded carefully.

'Then let's divide our working relationship, in which you as the Man Whisperer are to give an honest but accurate account of what you find, from our personal relationship . . . where who knows what will happen? I want to be a friend to you.'

Bernadette didn't like the way he looked at her, and was relieved by David's return with the wine. 'I want to find Tim,' she said, and nodding politely, moved away from Radley, with David in tow. David had a jaunty spring in his step, and the alert look of a cocker spaniel on a duck hunt.

Tim and Elizabeth were in a small knot of people lounging beside the infinity pool, protected from the New Year's chill by strategically positioned heat lamps. Bernadette wanted to cry when she spotted her love with his hand in the small of Elizabeth's back, laughing at the centre of a happy group. He caught sight of her looking and she smiled meekly, shrugging her shoulders. As he beckoned her over, everyone in the vicinity turned to watch her approach. Elizabeth was rushing forward calling a cheery greeting, and Bernadette found herself grabbing David's hand for support. He clutched back at her with his clammy fingers and gave her hand an exultant squeeze.

'Bernie!' said Elizabeth, enveloping her in a hug and standing on tiptoes to give her a quick peck on the cheek. 'You're here!'

'This is my date, David,' Bernadette said, and felt David jerk beside her, no doubt vivified by her choice of words.

Elizabeth was all politeness, and Bernadette sensed rather than heard them exchanging the relevant details. Her eyes were on Tim, who was still involved in conversation with the others. She went to him and took both his hands in hers, vaguely noting that this was the method Radley Blake had used to greet her merely minutes before. She kissed him on the cheek and said, 'Hello.'

'Bernie! Hi!' He didn't linger over the greeting, as he usually would, but turned swiftly to indicate the people he was standing with. 'These are our friends Stephanie and Mason, and Gina and Chris, and the lovely Miss Lauren Paul.' Bernadette nodded and acquiesced as Tim put his arm around her shoulder and said, 'This is the infamous Man Whisperer! Bernadette St John.'

She didn't like the look of the lovely Lauren, who was eyeballing her with obvious distaste and had raised an eyebrow at Tim's introduction. Lauren had extremely blonde hair, piled on her head in an overly complicated style that looked like it had been inexpertly copied from Pinterest. Her jaw was too square, and her eyes too close together, and her lips were thin and mean-looking. Despite these deficiencies, she was, Bernadette conceded, a fairly attractive girl. Her figure was good, her skin looked smooth and tanned, and she had a sharpness of feature that implied a quick mind.

Elizabeth and David had followed her over, and David was rocking up and down on his heels in a manner that demanded attention.

'And this is David, my date,' Bernadette said to them all in a dull voice.

Tim looked at her, dismayed, and she trembled with guilt. David stepped forward on cue and pumped Tim's hand, not noticing the other man's distraction. The only person who seemed aware of the exchange was Lauren, who squinted at Bernadette and Tim with speculative furrows creasing her forehead.

The two men knew each other through work, and they began swapping news. Bernadette desperately wanted to listen in, especially when she heard Tim probing David for details of their 'date', but Elizabeth was tugging at her sleeve and pulling her away. 'I have a favour I wanted to ask you,' she whispered, and Bernadette's attention was caught; she wasn't used to being on the receiving end of such a statement. 'I know how close you and Tim are,' Elizabeth continued, and Bernadette held her breath, waiting for the next accusation. 'I *love* how close you are, and I'm dying to know you better. I kind of feel like I know you already. I've heard so many stories from Tim, and I've read all your columns. And I wanted – I'd love it if you could be one of my bridesmaids.'

Bernadette gave no answer, and made no movement, and Elizabeth hurried on. 'I don't want it to be too much of an imposition. I've got three other bridesmaids and we all know how busy you are. You wouldn't have to be that involved, only as involved as you'd like to be. I'd just love to include you in the ceremony. Radley is my best friend in the whole world, and Tim is having him as one of the groomsmen. It would mean a lot to me. A real lot.'

Bernadette stared down at the older woman, wondering how deep the layers of denial must run. Elizabeth couldn't possibly believe, in her heart of hearts, that her fiancé had a purely disinterested female friend.

'I'll be your bridesmaid,' said Bernadette, thinking of all the inevitable extra time she would get to spend with Tim. 'I've never been a bridesmaid before.'

Elizabeth hugged her again, and for the first time Bernadette deigned to return the hug with feeling. It was brave of Elizabeth to open the field, and there was something quite pathetic about having to have one of Tim's friends as a bridesmaid. The combination of foolhardiness and loneliness was finally something Bernadette could relate to.

'David is cool,' said Elizabeth. 'Did I push too hard with you and Radley? Tim said I was being overbearing at our Christmas party! But you know when you get the feeling that two people would really get on? I had that with you and Rad. But . . . but David is great.'

'The thing with David is kind of new. But he's more my *type* than Radley,' Bernadette fibbed gleefully.

Most women would find it difficult to swallow that David Schmidt could be more of *any* woman's type than Radley Blake, but not Elizabeth. Elizabeth nodded and smiled with sincere acknowledgement.

At that moment, David interrupted, boldly grabbing Bernadette's hand and clasping it like a baby with a pacifier. 'Tim has come up with the most incredible idea for you!' he squeaked. 'It's extremely interesting. The magazine will definitely support it!'

Bernadette turned her almond-shaped eyes on Tim, who was quick to dampen the announcement. 'We'll talk about it, Bernie,' he said softly, as if he was asking her to dance. 'But not now.'

She didn't care to talk of work anyway, but turned and kissed David showily, purring, 'I can't wait to hear what you boys have come up with.'

David flushed pink, and beads of sweat, already in existence from the torture of the heat lamps, quivered on his forehead and threatened to roll down into his eyes. He looked like a lobster about to be dropped into a pot of boiling water, with no idea of the fate awaiting him. Tim glanced at him with understanding, and with pity.

'Come meet your fellow bridesmaids!' Elizabeth said to Bernadette.

'Hi again,' said Bernadette, as she was duly re-paraded in front of Lauren and the others. She waved her hand once through the air in greeting, which she meant as a friendly thing but which came across as a gesture of jaded indifference.

'Welcome on board,' smiled Lauren icily.

Bernadette absolutely didn't care about the women, or their relationship to Elizabeth, or what they did for a living. But she tried to look as though she did. She tried to behave as a friendly and interested person might. She asked questions, she laughed when they laughed, she kept her eyes focused on whoever was speaking, and she didn't look round to Tim once.

The husbands had melted away at the start of the bridesmaid talk, and were now in loud and animated debate with Tim and David. Bernadette wished she could join them. Her misandry did not extend to segregation, and in fact she preferred the company of men. Better to be the judge than the judged. Women were too smart.

She bore the farce as long as humanly possible, but ducked away with a mumbled excuse just as Gina began a lengthy exposition on the pros and cons of colonic irrigation.

Relieved that David was occupied, Bernadette slunk quietly off by herself, the vague thrill of emancipation fighting feebly against her generally depressed spirits. She wondered how many of the people at the party were sad, hiding lovelorn sighs behind affected smiles, disguising a yearning touch as a handshake, experiencing the present as a form of purgatory.

It was in this maudlin fashion that she entered the house, collected another glass of wine and propped herself against an interior wall to philosophise in peace. She spotted Radley at the centre of a group of admiring women, who were hunched and stretched and practically exploding with the effort of keeping his attention. Primped and plucked and waxed and stuffed, they laughed in chorus while trying to distinguish themselves one from another. It was to squeals and protests that he extracted himself, and made his way over to Bernadette.

'Where's the very likeable David?' he asked.

'Talking to Tim.'

'Awkward.'

'Oh, shut up.'

'This is precisely why I asked you to bring a date. It doesn't suit you, this woebegone solitary loitering. Stop chilling my house-warming with your sulky face.'

'Your house seems well warmed already,' she said, staring darkly at his group of female admirers. 'What are you, the Girl Whisperer?'

'Oh-ho! Those beautiful eyes of yours are green for a reason!' he laughed.

'You'll never find a wife if you carry on like that,' she sniffed, tossing her head in the direction of the other women.

'A wife? Who on earth said I wanted a wife?'

'You did. You said you were looking for a woman to make this house a home.'

'I said that for comic effect. And a woman is not a wife, you know. There is a difference.'

She rolled her eyes at him before he added, 'I'm not a one-woman kind of man. I'm certainly not the marrying type.'

The puritanical old-school romantic in Bernadette died a small death as she spat back, 'Well I'm certainly not the give-a-fuck type.'

She was disappointed in Radley Blake. He had been beginning to map himself on her consciousness as an interesting and almost decent male human, but now – alas! – he had proved to be as dull and wrong-headed as all the others.

Bernadette was a girl who believed in defined gender roles and Regency literature. In her mind, a real man did not flirt indiscriminately, and declare himself anti-marriage and anti-monogamy, whilst purporting to be the perfect bachelor. A real man chose a sensible, good wife and married her, and loved her with every ounce of his being until the day he died. Unwittingly, she glanced outside to the infinity pool, but the friends gathered there seemed to have dispersed.

'I'm not going to be put off by your prickly exterior,' Radley declared. 'I know there's a warm and fuzzy girl in there some-where.'

'You're wrong,' she said, matter-of-fact. 'Deep in my heart there is nothing but ice. It's a cold and barren interior, just glaciers, and icebergs, and a polar bear named Borghild. Borghild likes to eat men for fun.'

'*Borg*-hild?'

'Borghild,' she nodded.

'I think Borghild is a social animal. She just needs to find the right society.'

'Well *this* isn't it,' said Bernadette. He took the insult with temperance and merely smirked his omniscient smirk. 'You're a bad man,' she continued, with a slug of wine. 'I'm on to you. You're a bad, caddish man who pretends to be a knight in shining armour. All those poor girls over there truly think they have a chance of becoming Mrs Blake. And you bring them here, and show off your giant house-made-for-a-wife, and act all obliging and sexy and available. You have no integrity.'

'Oh yes, please do lecture me on integrity . . . Where's David again?' She didn't answer him, but instead busied herself with drinking the remaining wine from her glass in several connected gulps, as he continued, 'I told you, Bernadette, I told you the night we first met: we are the same, you and I.'

'No, we're really not.'

'No? I'm able to flirt with pleasant women I have no intention of marrying, and I present to them the best possible version of myself. Sound familiar? You make yourself irresistible to any man that crosses your path, while actively despising them, it seems. Which of us is worse? Which of us contributes most heavily to a greater evil?'

'There is a difference,' Bernadette insisted, stepping close to him, half because she didn't want to be overheard, and half because he was so handsome. 'You are laying a false foundation that *might* hurt others but will *certainly* damage you. Play the part for long enough, and trust me, you'll wish you could be the man you've pretended to be. But you'll know you can't be that man, because that man was created – and no man can inhabit his creation without first cutting out the part of himself that did the creating. And that part is the hardest to cut away.'

He took a moment to process her words, and smiled patiently, 'Well, aren't we bitter and world-weary?'

She shook her head in frustration. 'This isn't about me. By closing yourself off to the idea of one woman, and behaving as you do, you're writing a story that can have no satisfying end, you're playing a game you've declared you'll never win, you've asked a rhetorical question . . . and how sad to be doomed to the same behaviours for ever. To never progress beyond what you currently are.'

Radley had stopped smiling and was instead studying her face intently, his dark eyes seeming to cover every part of her. With one hand he pulled her to him, his arm encircling her waist; with his other, he pushed her hair back from her forehead. She could feel his fingers tracing over her scalp and tugging through the strands from root to end as he systematically pulled it all back over her shoulders. She found it almost unbearably erotic, but he was doing it in a methodical, contemplative fashion, and being no more seductive than usual. While he worked, he spoke to her softly, slowly, almost whispering. 'So you're worried that I'll end up a lonely old bachelor, bored and boring, regretting past transgressions for the rest of my days, longing for one companion in the winter of my life? I thank you for your compassion, I do . . . but you still haven't answered my question: how are we different? We who seduce the masses.'

'I do flirt,' said Bernadette, equally quietly, 'and I do try to be appealing. And I do it unfairly sometimes, and badly at other times, and I've practically made a career out of it – but I do it because I believe so strongly in the end result. I do it because I'm a person who wants love and wants to give love. I'm in *love* with Tim and I'm trying to find my way to him. I'm blundering towards him, taking no prisoners. And I might seem stupid to you – I *know* I seem stupid to you – but my love for Tim is the best part of me. The truest part. So that's the glaring difference between you and me. We're both skilled in the art of love, and both impressed with our own prowess, but I'm the one that truly wants it. I'm *in love* with Tim, I'm cut-my-own-arm-off-and-eat-it in love with him, but you . . . you're in love with no one except yourself.'

There was a painful pause. He looked hurt almost, his black eyes round with surprise. She wanted to kiss him as an expression of friendship, but managed to avert the tragedy by biting the inside of her lip. She hadn't meant to sound so harsh. This time, surely, he would be irrevocably angry with her. But after an intense silence, he simply said, still whispering, 'What about Borghild? Borghild who eats men for fun?'

'I said that for comic effect,' she returned, and removing herself from his arms, she walked away.

She hadn't moved far before Tim was beside her, falling into an easy stride next to her as she weaved her way through the party.

'What are you doing, Bernie?' he asked, gravely.

'What do you mean?'

'With Radley? What was that? What was he doing to your hair? He looked like he was going to kiss you right there and then.'

'Would you care?'

They had ended up outside, and Bernadette headed towards a quiet part of the garden so that he had to follow.

'You know I care about you. And what about David? I mean . . . David! Come on! What are you doing to yourself?'

He looked so exasperated, in a polite, intellectual way, that Bernadette smiled at him lovingly.

'Are you jealous?'

He turned his head, a red flush on his cheeks and neck. 'You can't ask me that.'

'Why not? Why can you question me, but not the other way round?' He looked at her helplessly, as she stood proud and poised and challenging. 'Here, darling,' she said, removing his glasses and cleaning them on her dress. 'You're getting all hot and bothered. Let's not steam these up.'

He took his glasses back and settled them on the bridge of his nose. 'Bernie!' he sighed. 'You're torturing me.'

'Actually, Tim, I think you're torturing both of us.' They stood a foot apart, neither one moving, both filled with regret. 'I just want you to know that you are my motivation . . . for everything. I'm not interested in Radley, or David, or anyone but you. You're it. Do you know that? The rest is just silliness on my part, because I'm so demented and distracted by you, I forget how to behave properly. And I'm filled with constant pain, and loneliness, that needs an outlet. But if we were together, I would be the very model of propriety and sobriety. You wouldn't fault me.'

'You're fine as you are,' said Tim, his voice cracking. 'I like you the way you are.'

Her eyes threatened to fill with tears as they gazed at each other, but then they both noticed David puffing his way towards them, waving cheerily at Bernadette. 'Hello, hello!' he said. 'I thought I'd lost you.'

'Apparently not,' she smiled. 'I was just asking Tim where the bathroom was. I'm going to go and freshen up for a minute.'

David looked disappointed as Tim said, 'If you head upstairs, you should find Lizzie and the other girls. They wanted to escape the party for a bit. There's a powder room up there that won't be as crowded as the ones down here.'

Bernadette nodded and set off, ignoring David's obsequious little bow as she passed.

She felt strange walking up the staircase of Radley's house, as though she were violating something unwritten. She hoped none of the guests noticed her sneaking up the stairs, and she particularly hoped Radley Blake himself wasn't watching. At least she had the legitimate excuse of going to find Elizabeth, and could say so if questioned.

The house was so large that the upstairs landing had three corridors leading in different directions. Bernadette hesitated, as though at the labyrinth of Crete, but took the corridor to the right, after hearing women's laughter emanating from that area.

Her footfalls were silenced by the thick silk carpet, and she walked slowly, looking at the black-and-white art photographs on the walls. As she neared an open door, she heard laughter, louder now, and a clear voice saying, 'The Man Whisperer! That is so passé. And she's not even that good-looking.'

Bernadette stopped and listened.

'Lauren, that's not kind,' she heard Elizabeth's soft voice respond. 'And I think Bernadette is one of the most beautiful girls I've ever seen.'

'She's not all that,' said Lauren. 'And the guy she's brought with her – what a joke! He's got to have some serious cash.'

'No!' Elizabeth exclaimed, distressed. 'She's not like that. Honestly, Radley was absolutely crazy about her from the moment he saw her, and she didn't want him because he's not her type.'

'Not her type?' exclaimed one of the other women. 'Now that I don't believe!' There were mumbles of assent, Lauren's loudest of all.

Bernadette had pressed herself against the wall by the open door as she listened in distress to Elizabeth defending her honour. She heard a noise at the end of the corridor and, looking up, to her absolute horror saw Radley emerging from a doorway further down. He spotted her immediately and grinned widely at the sight of her in such a stealthy and compromising position. Keeping his eyes locked on hers, he crept forward like a jungle cat, until he too could listen on the other side of the doorway undetected. Bernadette made a frantic gesture for him to go away, but instead he just made an exaggerated silent show of putting his hand behind his ear, like a creepy French mime.

'Radley Blake is every straight girl's type!' Lauren exclaimed, loudly. Radley waggled his eyebrows triumphantly at Bernadette and gave her a thumbs-up. 'If she didn't make a play for him when she had a chance, then there's a reason . . . and I think I know what it is.'

Bernadette was paralysed with dread. Radley had stopped his clowning and was instead listening carefully, his eyes fixed on her.

'Don't hate me, Lizzie,' Lauren continued, 'but I think your friend the Man Whisperer is after Tim. She's totally into him, in a big way. It's obvious.'

'No!' Elizabeth exclaimed. 'They're just friends. She loves him like I love Rad!'

In that moment, Bernadette hated Lauren with all her ice-white heart. She hated Elizabeth too, and Radley Blake, and humanity in general. She could hear Elizabeth's clear laugh. 'Bernie is not "into" Tim!'

'I'm telling you,' said the indefatigable Lauren. 'You watch her. She's got "whore" written all over her.'

It was at this moment that Radley decided to step through the doorway and startle the women on the other side of it. He startled Bernadette too, who realised too late what he was doing and didn't have a chance to pull him back. She pressed herself against the wall, wondering what he was up to, and hoping that he wasn't going to give her away.

She heard the temporary silence, and then Radley's smooth, commanding tone. 'Sorry, ladies, I don't mean to interrupt, but I couldn't help overhearing you. I got in trouble recently for eavesdropping, so thought I'd better make my presence known.'

In the corridor, Bernadette held her breath. She didn't trust Radley Blake in the slightest, and believed him perfectly capable of compounding the horror with his sorcerer's ways.

'I just wanted to confirm that Bernadette eluded me. I tried every trick in the book – and I know quite a few tricks.' Bernadette heard the girls laugh, and a couple of them mumbled something that sounded vaguely conciliatory and apologetic. 'Personally, I'm not sure she's "into" me, or Tim, or any man, in that kind of a way. Must be a hazard of her job: extreme boredom with the male gender . . .'

Bernadette didn't stop to hear any more. Taking the opportunity to escape, she retreated back the way she'd come and down the staircase. She headed straight for the bar, determined to drown in vodka and choke on slices of lime.

*   *   *

It was half an hour later that she swooped down on David like an intoxicated eagle, her talons sinking into his fleshy sides as she grabbed him round the middle and squeezed. 'David! I've been looking for you.'

'I've been looking for you!' he gasped. 'We must have been walking round in circles just missing each other!'

'Must have!' she cried, matching his excitement in pitch, tone and timbre.

She rested her chin on the top of his head. 'You're really a very convenient height, David,' she sighed. David, who was squashed against her chest, couldn't help but offer a muffled agreement. 'You're just convenient in general. All-round convenient, you.' She cuddled him harder.

'Oh no you don't.' Radley had appeared like the Wizard of Wor in front of her, and took her boldly by the shoulders, squashing David between them. 'Excuse me, David,' he said, looking down at him, 'but I need to borrow Bernadette.' He took her by the hand and led her towards the kitchen. 'You're impossible,' he said.

'Well you're improbable,' she returned. 'Look at you. Who's seen the like of you, you sexy genius billionaire? You're ridiculous. Every woman's type!'

'How are you getting home?'

'David!' she smirked coquettishly.

'Not on my watch.'

'He brought me.'

'Well, Mick's taking you home,' he said, poking his head through an archway to a large kitchen, where bar staff and caterers rushed around. In a corner sat Mick, eating a large sandwich and reading *Motor Trend* on his iPad. Radley signalled to him, and he hastily left his sandwich and followed them.

'No,' said Bernadette, literally digging her heels in and throwing her weight in the opposite direction, like a disgruntled Yorkshire terrier on a leash.

Radley gave her a grim look, and picked her up bodily, putting her over his shoulder in a fireman's lift. 'Come on, Mick,' he said.

'Put me down!' screeched Bernadette. 'Seriously, Radley, put me down! This is dangerous!'

He carried her through the house, people laughing and cheering as they passed, and out through the large front door.

'You bastard. This is utterly humiliating.'

'Surely you're used to humiliation? I thought you actively sought it.'

'I hate you! Put me down!'

'Fine,' he conceded, plonking her somewhat unceremoniously on the tarmac at the top of his steep driveway. 'Mick is going to see you home. No more arguments. And one more thing: I don't mislead women. I'm always entirely upfront about my intentions. I've told you before, I say what I mean. I don't play a part as you do. I am myself. And women seem to like it. At least, I've had no complaints so far.' Here he grinned. 'I always make it known I'm not in the market for anything long-term.' He turned and walked into the house.

'Not soon enough!' Bernadette called stroppily after his retreating back. 'You don't make it known soon enough!'

He was gone. Sighing, she turned doleful eyes to Mick, who discreetly held out his arm to steady her. He steered her towards the large detached garage.

'You must have a very bad impression of me,' she said. 'I'm not always this drunk, I promise.'

'Uh-huh,' was Mick's only response.

4

Bernadette opened her eyes. David was lying in her bed, staring at her breathlessly, not moving a muscle lest he disturbed her. 'You were dreaming!' he said. 'I could see your eyeballs moving backwards and forwards under your eyelids!'

Bernadette closed her eyes, courageously counted to ten, opened one eye and then opened both. David was still there.

They had been sleeping together for about a week now, and she still couldn't get used to the naked sight of him. Especially in the morning, when the soft light of a new day seemed so far removed in time and space from the transgressions of the night before. Allowing him to stay the night was pure self-flagellation; she might as well tear all the hair from his incredibly furry chest and wear it as a cilice.

She tried to smile at him; after all, he was a human being, and deserving of civility, at least. 'Would you like breakfast?' she asked, dutifully. She fancied that she could don a fetching apron and cook him an omelette. She would open the windows, turn on the radio and serve him coffee. She could be the woman of his dreams this morning.

He nodded, already accustomed to the privilege, and rolled over on to his back, stretching in a self-satisfied way, and with a master-of-the-universe smile that made Bernadette shudder.

A naturally energetic person, she did not often experience the sensation of genuine fatigue, but this morning her whole body felt heavy with exhaustion. In the kitchen, she opened cupboards and banged a skillet down on the stove, yanked at the refrigerator door and sighed a heavy sigh. For a moment, it seemed as though she might start crying, right there over the eggs. But she managed to gulp down whatever true emotion was threatening to surface, and focus instead on a general sense of victimisation.

She was already sick of the making-breakfast routine. It was an unpleasant mix of boredom and self-loathing. Playing the part of a sweet-tempered housewife was somewhat limiting. She didn't know how long she could continue this charade with David.

She wanted to lie in her bed alone, stretch out, check her emails and then head to a café for brunch. Instead, she was arranging an omelette carefully over a piece of toast, fussing about how much milk to add to the coffee, and feeling very lonely.

'Here you are!' she said, forced-cheerfully, re-entering the bedroom and placing the artfully styled plate and a mug of medium-brown coffee on the bedside table. David was on his stomach in her bed, scrolling through his emails. 'You're welcome,' she added, as he didn't look up.

'Hmm?' He reached absent-mindedly for the coffee, and dripped a couple of medium-brown drips on her white cotton sheets. 'Tim wants to meet us, to discuss his idea,' he said.

'Great,' said Bernadette unenthusiastically, perching on the edge of the bed and drawing both knees up to her chin.

'He's a genius!'

'No,' said Bernadette quietly, 'Radley Blake is the genius.'

It was interesting, Bernadette thought distractedly, to be sitting in a room with the man she loved, while the man she was sleeping with looked on benignly.

Bernadette, David and Tim were in the latter's office. He was behind his desk, just as he had been the first time she'd met him. She wished they had met in a garden, or in a wooded dell by a stream, or some other equally romantic location, but they had met here, in this rectangular white-and-glass place.

The office had two walls of windows, which looked down on Beverly Hills and allowed the light to play prettily over Tim's flaxen head. White shelves were lined with books, awards, and pictures of Tim's travels: there he was riding a camel in Rajasthan, petting a stray dog in Burma, swimming with turtles in Hawaii – and there he was kissing Elizabeth.

Bernadette scowled at David, who rustled and creaked in the seat next to her in a most irritating manner, trying to find a comfortable position for his pursy form. He was struggling with excitement at what Tim was suggesting. Bernadette was wriggling too, but for entirely different reasons.

'A tour?' she repeated, looking at Tim sceptically.

'I think it's the next logical step,' he said, holding her gaze steadily. 'We need to get you out there, connecting with real women.'

'Oh yes, real women. I love those,' she said drily. 'But I'm afraid I don't understand. Why would I do a tour when I haven't written a book?'

'Tour is the wrong word. Think of it as a lecture series.'

'That sounds very grown-up. What would I lecture on?'

'On being you! On being the Man Whisperer!'

'Hmm. Not so grown-up then.'

'You'd be allowing real women – normal women – in on your secrets.'

'Do you not think I'm a real woman, Tim?' she asked, her eyes suddenly alight with playful fire.

He looked down at his hands, suppressing a smile. David was doing the classic tennis-match-spectator head-swing, looking first to her and then to Tim, with his mouth hanging slightly open, his mind always a thought behind and never truly catching up.

'Your readership demographic is overwhelmingly male,' Tim continued. 'Not surprising, but I think we're missing something. I've noticed how enamoured Elizabeth is with you. She thinks you're an admirable role model—'

'No need to sound so dubious,' interjected Bernadette. 'I could be a role model.'

'Elizabeth feels that you are this modern, together, go-get-'em, kick-ass woman. A rarity.'

'How sweet,' said Bernadette with a glint in her eye that made Tim blush. He removed his spectacles and cleaned the lenses with his shirtsleeve.

'David,' he said, turning large, unfocused eyes in the other man's direction, 'would you mind leaving us for a moment? As Bernadette's manager, I feel she needs to be *managed*.'

'Oooh!' Bernadette purred. 'How thrilling. I love it when you're so obviously dominant.'

David laughed delightedly, as though he were included in the joke. 'Of course, Tim, I'll leave you to it!' he said, pleased to answer a direct appeal, having found no other way to insert himself into the conversation. 'And you know, Bernie,' he simpered, heaving himself from the chair, '*Squire* would follow this with great interest. We could even have *you* on the cover! Maybe. It'd be a nice change for you, wouldn't it? In lingerie? We could do something exquisite. Black lace, I think.'

Tim ushered David out the door, and Bernadette immediately kicked off her heels and put her feet up on the desk, her long legs glinting, revolver-like, in the sunlight. Tim wandered over slowly, thoughtful, and leaned on the edge of his desk, delightfully close to her bare feet.

'How are you doing, Bernie?' he asked, with a complete change of tone.

'How am I doing? I'm doing fine. Thank you for asking.'

'Come on, Bern. Seriously.' He stroked the top of her foot. 'Are you okay?'

'I don't know what you're asking,' she said, jerking her foot away from him. 'I'm still in love with you, if that's what you mean?'

Tim groaned and straightened up. He paced the room while Bernadette watched. It gave her a comfortable sense of déjà vu. She wished she could explain things to him properly, wished she could drop the seductive mantle she wore and explain that she was scared. That she had been hurt too deeply by men in the past. That she had almost given up on the old idea of love. That Tim, and his goodness, was her last hope. But instead, she drawled provocatively, 'What's with this lecture tour? Are you trying to get rid of me?'

He stopped and turned to her with a doleful look in his cornflower-blue eyes, and she realised with a metallic sickness in her throat that she had hit upon the truth. 'Oh. You *are* trying to get rid of me.'

'It's not that. Of course it's not that. I'm just trying to think of something that will challenge you, something to take you to the next level professionally. You're too smart a person to waste yourself on . . . on . . .'

'On *you*? You're trying to distract me from the pain of a fruitless love? That's very kind of you, but I don't need charity.'

Tim knelt down in front of her so that their faces were level. 'I'm not trying to get rid of you. I need you in my life, Bernadette.'

'You look like you're asking me to marry you,' she said, resting a hand on his shoulder like a queen with a knight errant.

'I'm not,' he said, simply. 'That's the one thing I can't do. I love you, Bernie. I think you're an incredible woman. I need you in my life. I'm selfish . . . I *want* you in my life. But I can't marry you. I've made a promise to someone else.'

Bernadette smiled sadly at him. The innocence and pure feeling of his declaration, the almost childlike vein of need and the beauty of his eyes overwhelmed her. 'All right,' she gulped. 'I'll do your stupid lecture tour.'

In the end, it turned out that the lecture tour was to be a bi-coastal speaking event, consisting of only two evenings. Bernadette was to speak for one night in Los Angeles, and a second in New York. Despite the lack of dates on her tour, the prospect was still a daunting one.

Although she had a successful career as a journalist, communication was not Bernadette's strong point. She preferred to simmer philosophically in a world of inner torment, relishing thoughts too scary for public consumption. The idea of standing on a platform in front of hundreds of women, trying to sell them some kind of world view, was anathema. And there was a big difference, she realised, between putting words on a page – words that could be laboured over and edited at will, even by a third party – and the nakedness that would be a consummate part of standing unchecked on stage, non-concrete vocalisations pouring forth from her untrained lips. Oh, the horror of immediacy.

She lay, fitfully discontent, in bed, contemplating the oddness of having to present a complete version of herself to strangers. It was nice to be on her own, for once, without the short, dark presence of the Dwarf of Doom.

Her home was a vision of tranquillity and unity, at odds with her inner life. The wide, soft bed was furnished with high-thread-count cotton, pure white. Hand-crafted oak side tables displayed mother-of pearl-trinket boxes, a glass carafe of infused water, an artistically stacked pile of sensible literature – and nothing else. There was a faint, not overpowering, floral scent, and the lighting was low and discreet. The true ornament of the room was Bernadette herself, exactly as she had intended. It was a room ready, at any unexpected moment, to receive Tim.

Her phone vibrated from the depths of the voluminous duvet, interrupting her reverie. It was a text from Elizabeth: *Hey! Can I call you? I suck at texting.*

Bernadette rolled her eyes. She texted back: *Now's not good to talk. Ever so busy. What do you need?*

The cell beeped back: *Are you free tomorrow to do bridesmaid stuff?*

Bernadette plunged her face into her pillow and choked out a small scream. *Yes*, she texted back.

It was an extremely disgruntled Bernadette who dragged her feet along Wilshire Boulevard the following afternoon, en route to 'bridesmaid stuff'. She perked up enough to notice a stunning sapphire-blue cocktail dress in the Neiman Marcus window, but mostly her eyes were downcast and distraught. She couldn't help but wonder why it was that *she* was not the bride. Bernadette had been born to be a bride. Elizabeth had been born to be an NGO worker, or a pioneer in the field of urology.

Reaching the corner of Wilshire and Rodeo, she stopped as instructed and looked around for Elizabeth's unremarkable form. Instead, she saw Radley Blake striding towards her.

'Oh no. What are you doing here?' she asked.

'Lovely to see you too,' he said, stooping to kiss her cheek. 'I'm here in the same capacity as you.'

'As a bridesmaid?'

'Naturally.'

'I have no words,' she said.

'I have plenty.' He smiled, his body too close to hers. 'Do you want to hear them?'

'No,' she said, stepping away just as Elizabeth arrived.

It was hugs all round, with Elizabeth apologising profusely for being all of three minutes late.

'Should we wait for the others?' asked Bernadette.

'I didn't ask the others.' Elizabeth smiled impishly. 'This is a very special bridesmaid outing.'

'I feel honoured,' said Radley, as Bernadette gave a tight smile.

The three of them trooped up Wilshire in the balmy sunshine, Elizabeth brimming with some happy secret, Radley striding along contentedly and Bernadette dragging behind like a sulky teenager.

'Here we are!' cried Elizabeth, stopping outside a large shop that sold nothing but wedding dresses.

Bernadette's mood plummeted further. 'Oh gosh,' she said. 'Dresses? I didn't realise this was what we were doing. When you said "bridesmaid stuff", I thought we'd be sampling cake or something. I'm not sure I'm right for this.'

Elizabeth laughed. 'You have more style than any real-life person I've ever met. I totally need you here. I trust your judgement one hundred per cent!'

'Really?' said Bernadette hopefully, with brief visions of steering her nemesis towards a hideous pistachio meringue, but Radley was staring at her in a steely fashion that rendered that idea impractical.

The wedding dress store was an impressive ivory-hued, rose-scented, over-the-top emporium of girlish delight. Several highly manicured saleswomen descended upon them the moment their feet crossed the threshold, and Bernadette shrank back behind Radley, in abject disgust at their overpowering eagerness.

Elizabeth welcomed the exuberance of the shop girls, matching their plastered smiles with a genuine beam of her own, informing them that yes, she had an appointment, and yes, she was Elizabeth Wentworth. The shrill cacophony that accompanied this information had Bernadette starting for the door, but Radley pre-empted her movement and caught her by the arm. 'Be nice,' he hissed.

He pushed her towards the other women, and she found

herself saying, yes, she was the bridesmaid, and yes, she was very excited to help pick the dress. Then, at once, they all seemed to notice Radley.

'Is this the groom?' asked the senior assistant, name-tagged Rita.

'Oh no,' laughed Elizabeth. 'Radley is my maid of honour!'

The girls all laughed uproariously, like it was an original joke. They fussed round Radley, cooing over him as though they'd never seen a man before. 'All my best friends are men,' Rita was saying. 'There's just something so incredible about the male perspective.'

'Isn't there?' agreed Radley, slyly eyeing Bernadette.

She wandered further into the fluffy lair, running her hands over the silk and lace offerings crowding the room. It was a maze of white illusion, and she wanted to get lost in it. The dresses were beautiful, fairy-tale creations made for once-in-a-lifetime wearing. Dresses designed for virgin princesses. She stood humbled at the altar of material goodness, savouring the pleasure of pretty things well made and bounteously presented. Bernadette was a true capitalist. There was something quite magical about the luxury of this place, the pomp and spangle and modern convenience, and all in aid of validating an ancient ritual of rights and obligations.

'Would you like some champagne?' asked one of Rita's under-lings, offering a glass of gorgeous bubbliness.

'Yes,' said Bernadette, not making eye contact, but taking the glass and slinking back to find the others.

Radley had enthroned himself in some kind of atrium seating area. He sat on a cream couch, which rested on a platform over an open koi pond. Potted vegetation surrounded it, creating a

Midsummer Night's Dream fantasy forest effect, and Radley himself contributed a complementary Puckish vibe.

'This is the viewing area!' he called. 'Won't you join me?'

Bernadette carefully made her way over the koi pond bridge, and gingerly placed herself on the sofa, every part of her body quivering with suppressed emotion.

Rita guided Elizabeth into a changing room on the other side of the pond, both women disappearing behind a silvery curtain. The other assistants had melted away, and Bernadette felt suddenly as though she had been transported to Fairyland on a couch. It was a surreal moment, hearing the gurgling of the pond, seeing nothing but white silk and forest greenery, the most corporeal sensation the weight of Radley next to her. These out-of-body moments had been occurring more frequently since Tim had announced his engagement. Any semblance of control over her life had evaporated, and she felt like a puppet of the fates, an empty wooden doll.

'Well, isn't this jolly?' said Radley, bringing her crashing to earth with a bump. There was nothing quite like his mordant harassment to ground a person. She didn't answer, but gulped down more of the champagne. 'I'd go easy on that if I was you,' he continued. 'I don't have Mick with me to take you home today.'

She refused to rise to his teasing and continued to stare doggedly at the curtain whence Elizabeth would emerge. It seemed to be taking her an inordinate amount of time to get into a dress. Bernadette counted to twenty in her head, tried to check her breathing, and decided to completely ignore Radley.

Radley, for his part, after muttering, 'Antisocial . . .' began to check emails on his phone. They sat in silence. After five minutes, unable to bear it any longer, Bernadette stood and called out, 'How are you doing?'

There was a rustle, a pause, and then a blushing Elizabeth appeared, in a spectacularly elegant dress, looking as attractive as Bernadette had ever seen her.

Bernadette sat back down on the sofa abruptly. Elizabeth smiled shyly up at them and hopped on to a small dais, to best admire herself in the three-way mirror. 'Well, what do you think?' she asked.

Bernadette was having trouble with words. A little croak escaped her, but luckily the ever-ready Radley was there for honest praise. 'You look beautiful,' he said softly. 'Lizzie, I really think this is the dress for you.'

Elizabeth laughed. 'But everyone always picks the first dress, right? It's like a trap. Maybe it's just because you don't usually see me dressed up, and this is such a big contrast?'

'What do you think, Bernadette?' asked Radley.

Bernadette found it surprisingly easy to squash the sabotage attempt rising through her, and was able to stammer, 'It's stunning – extremely flattering. I can't imagine anything more beautiful on you.'

To Bernadette's utter discomfort, tears welled in Elizabeth's eyes and she began to cry with joy. 'Oh God, don't cry!' Bernadette gasped, annoyed.

Elizabeth was laughing and crying at the same time, and again Bernadette was struck by the unrealness of the whole situation. It was as though her life was some carefully constructed stage play, and these bit players knew their lines too well. Elizabeth was too appealing.

The shop environment was clearly playing tricks on her brain, and she tried to snap herself back to some clarity. 'You should still try on others, though,' she finished. 'Just in case there's something you like better. Besides, how often does one actually get to do this?'

When Elizabeth returned behind the curtain, elated by Bernadette's words and the excitement of dress shopping, Radley took Bernadette's hand and gave it a squeeze. 'You're doing very well,' he said, gently.

'Thanks,' she muttered back, and didn't pull her hand away. They sat in amicable silence, enjoying the simple sensation of hand-holding as though it was an undiscovered art.

'I'm looking forward to shadowing you for our interview,' she said.

'Me too. That's in a few weeks, isn't it?'

'Mm-hmm,' she breathed, quite dreamily.

He brushed his thumb rhythmically over the back of her hand. It seemed like a thoroughly acceptable and quite pleasant form of timekeeping, much better than the ticking of a clock. 'I hear you're branching out? With a lecture tour?'

Bernadette shrugged modestly. 'Apparently there are a lot of women who're interested in what I have to say. I'm supposedly some kind of twenty-first-century role model, you know? A sort of female guru—'

'That's the most ridiculous thing I've ever heard,' cut in Radley, laughing. 'You're the least spiritual person I've met in my life.'

Bernadette sharply withdrew her hand from his thumb's caresses. 'Well, that was nice while it lasted,' she spat. 'All of two minutes. Why can't you be a decent human being for a respectable amount of time?'

'You know, I've been thinking about what you said.'

Bernadette was momentarily thrown. 'What I said when?'

'The other night, at my house. You said that by shutting myself off to the idea of finding a mate, and yet continuing to pursue women, I'm basically playing a game I've declared I will never win. Interesting. I haven't thought of it like that before.'

'You're welcome.'

'I can see why you're a writer. Because that idea, it really hit home. I don't like losing. I never choose to play anything unless there's a chance I can win.'

'Big talk.'

'Not just talk. I've decided: I'm going to get married.'

'*What?* Who to?'

'I don't know. I haven't decided that part yet.' He looked thrilled with the idea, and she couldn't help but feel a momentary pang of jealousy directed at whoever was to become Mrs Radley Blake. She wondered why jealousy seemed to cloud her reaction when hearing about the successes of other women. Why should she care that Radley was going to make some girl ridiculously happy, turn her into a fairy-tale bride? It wasn't a biological imperative, driven by resource scarcity – there were plenty of other men in the world. There were boundless opportunities for countless women to thrive, so why did she feel the need to stand on the head of any girl who threatened to be happy?

'Well that didn't take long,' she said. 'For you to change your mind. So much for your conviction.'

'I never said I was a man of conviction. I am a man of action, of pure, unguided effervescence.'

'Oh, get over your bad self. I've had enough of you.'

Elizabeth appeared in another creation, not as spectacular as the first. They both gave her the *comme ci, comme ça* hand gesture, and she retired once more behind the curtain in a fit of giggles.

'She seems to be having a good time,' Bernadette said, only a little wistfully.

'I'm having a good time too,' Radley smiled. 'I don't think you understand how much I enjoy your company. We joke with one another . . .'

'I wouldn't call it joking so much as insulting.'

'. . . and the levity does me good. I look forward to spending time with you.'

Bernadette withdrew into herself slightly, as she was wont to do when faced with genuine emotion. 'Thanks,' she mumbled. 'I'm quite shallow. It's easy to be flippant when you don't give a fuck.'

'You're only shallow on the surface,' he grinned. 'Thanks to my skilful eavesdropping, I know just how deeply you feel things.'

'Only certain things.'

'Depth only has one direction.'

They were staring at each other, so that neither noticed when Elizabeth popped out in a third ensemble.

'Hey! You two! What do you think?' she called.

All in all, and given the tragedy of the basic circumstances, it was quite a pleasant afternoon. Helping the fiancée of the man you love pick her wedding dress could have been a more painful experience.

Radley had proved to be a helpful distraction, at turns annoying, charming and controversial. He had even suggested that Bernadette try on a gown, for the fun of it. Rita hadn't looked best pleased, but he had managed to persuade her with his most irresistible smile. There were few women, Bernadette realised, who could say no to him.

She picked out a floor-length, off-white, sleek and modern creation. Elizabeth was eager to join in the fun, and admired her prodigiously when she emerged from the changing room, but Radley had turned his back and refused to look at her.

'It's bad luck,' he called over his shoulder. 'I'm still holding out hopes that I might be the groom. You never know. Best that I don't peek.'

Bernadette was secretly pleased at his theatrics. And the dress fitted her beautifully, hugging her curves and elongating her already lanky frame. It gave her a funny stirring in her breast when she looked in the mirror. The woman who stared back at her seemed serene and full of grace. Bernadette wanted to earn that reflection. She wished she were worthy of the dress, and all its imbued meaning. For the thousandth time in her life, she promised sincerely to be good.

'Can I take you ladies to tea?' Radley asked, once they had chosen the dress and were safely deposited on the sidewalk, seemingly at a loss to know how to give each other up.

'Okay,' immediately agreed Bernadette, who was hungry as usual.

'I can't,' Elizabeth smiled. 'I have to go home and get dinner ready for Tim.'

Bernadette's face contorted with the effort of suppressing her *idée fixe,* and she could feel Radley watching her. Tim should be hers; she should be the one rushing home (hopelessly devoted, with a ribbon in her hair) to cook him dinner and warm his slippers by the fire. 'Do you make him breakfast too?' she asked suspiciously.

'Yes,' said Elizabeth, and then laughed, mistaking Bernadette's look of horror. 'I'm sorry! I'm totally old-school, a disgrace to my gender and our modern times. Does that mean we can't be friends?' she teased, gently.

Bernadette laughed back, wordlessly. Radley gave Elizabeth a big hug.

'Don't worry,' said Elizabeth, turning to Bernadette and hugging her hard. 'It all evens out. I make breakfast, Tim gives great foot rubs.'

Bernadette laughed harder, somewhat hysterically, her mind a confusion of blonde-haired men, wedding dresses, and omelettes. Elizabeth waved to them both and walked away.

'Do you like it?' Bernadette called helplessly after her. 'Do you like making him breakfast?'

Elizabeth turned and smiled. 'Best part of my day! Don't worry, Bernie, no man could ever make me do anything I didn't enjoy.' And with that gut-punch, she left.

'Well there you have it,' said Radley. 'That's why she's getting married and you're single. She doesn't live a lie.'

'You are so *mean*,' cried Bernadette, giving him a shove.

'No, I'm not. I'm actually remarkably nice. I just happen to be socially observant. Perceptive, one might say. And I'm outspoken, which seems to jar with you.'

'It does jar with me. And I hate being observed. Stop it.'

'I can't. You've fast become my favourite thing to look at.'

'Are you taking me to tea or not?'

'Certainly, this way.' He proffered his arm and squired her back up Wilshire. They walked in silence for a while.

'Personally, I am firmly of the opinion that meal-making should be outsourced,' he said.

'Outsourced to whom?'

'To a French pastry chef.'

'You are grossly wealthy and out of touch. It's disgusting.'

They were passing the Neiman's window, and Radley stopped suddenly. 'That dress would look fantastic on you,' he said, pointing to the sapphire-blue cocktail dress Bernadette had earlier admired.

She rolled her eyes. 'You *are* perceptive. But just take me to the food, please.'

He took her to the Beverly Wilshire, where they sat in the window and ordered tea, sandwiches and cake. 'This hotel has always disappointed me,' she said, looking round glumly at the extreme luxury.

'Is there anything in life that hasn't disappointed you?'

'This is the Beverly Wilshire! It's the *Pretty Woman* hotel! It's basically the locale where the whole movie plays out. But you know what's a travesty? This *isn't* the hotel they used for filming. The interior shots were somewhere else entirely. When I first came to LA and someone took me to this impostor of a Beverly Wilshire, I nearly cried.'

'Yes, that's a very sad story.'

She kicked him under the table. 'It *was* quite sad. I hate it when things aren't as advertised. You know what else was disappointing? The Hollywood sign! I was expecting it to be huge, perched on the side of a mountain, glowering down over the whole city. But instead it's just a tiny thing in the middle of nowhere, inaccessible from all but three vantage points.'

'Didn't you find *Pretty Woman* to be a tad depressing? She's a prostitute, and he's a nightmare businessman who treats her badly . . . and then all is forgiven when he brings her a bunch of flowers at the end.'

'It doesn't matter who they are, or what their original intentions were. What matters is that there *is* a happy ending. That's all that matters.'

Radley pushed his chair back from the table, his head tilted to one side as he chewed thoughtfully on a final mouthful of cake, swallowing deliberately before pronouncing, 'You are a study in contradictions.'

'Why?'

'The other evening you told me that all that matters is someone's intention. Not how they act, or who they hurt, or what ultimately happens – none of that matters as long as their intention is good, as long as they have an honest heart.'

'I don't remember saying that.'

'You certainly said something like it. You were reasoning hard, trying to defend your manic pursuit of Tim.'

'I suggest you stop listening so carefully to what I have to say. Most stuff I just make up in the moment. I'm not wedded to any particular philosophy. I'm as changeable as the wind. Don't believe a word that comes out of me.' She said it blithely, in her usual insouciant manner, but looking up and catching his eye, she suddenly felt guilty of some delinquent breach. She waited, nervous as a schoolgirl, for his response.

'I don't know when apathy became fashionable,' he said sadly, slowly, 'but it certainly doesn't suit *you*. For a woman as smart as you to suggest you have no opinion – it's a crime, Bernadette. To ask me not to believe a word you say!'

'You're the one who called me a liar. You're always saying I'm a liar or an actress or whatever . . .'

'I would hope you're clever enough to know the difference between teasing and genuine feeling.'

'I really don't know what I think,' she said, in a small voice.

'Then I suggest you ruminate and reach a conclusion. Don't let a brain like yours go to rot. Pretty-girl brain atrophy is far too common an occurrence. Have a well-thought-out opinion and defend it to the death. The woman I overheard that night declaring her love for Tim – she knows how to have an opinion.'

She sulkily popped a large piece of poppy-seed cake into her mouth, not wanting to meet his eyes. He had such a dark, fascinating gaze, liable to render her silly. 'Okay,' she said, after quite a pause, 'I've thought about it. Bad actions can be excused if a person's intention is good, but only if that person's intentions extend to suppose a happy conclusion. Random, unjustifiable acts are wrong. So a person should work backwards, decide their happy ending and be unrelenting in their whole-hearted pursuit of that goal.'

Radley laughed loudly, his whole body rocking with movement, his face alight with mirth. 'Thank you,' he said. 'You are precious. That was extraordinary reasoning, you peculiarly prim little hedonist. I'm very happy.'

'Well more fool you,' she said, ungenerously, although secretly she was pleased. His laugh seemed like a reward, an honour bestowed, a medal received. 'And on a separate note,' she said, 'you shouldn't tell me to have an opinion or teach me how to express myself as a woman. That goes against the whole feminist bullshit you're espousing. The whole you-are-smart-and-a-woman-therefore-own-it-because-a-smart-woman-is-such-a-rarity thing. Ugh.'

'I'm not espousing anything feminist,' he said. 'Quite the

contrary. If you want to know what I'm doing, you need only ask me. I always tell the absolute truth.'

'What are you doing?'

'I'm simply trying to make of you a woman I would find even more attractive than I already do. I am trying to mould you, in a most *Pygmalion* fashion. So you see, no feminist espousing here. It is up to you, rightfully, to be the feminist at this table. I am just a man.'

'Oh!' cried Bernadette, laughing despite herself. 'That's awful. This had better be one of those times that you're teasing?'

'You're smart enough to know the difference. You'll get no help from me.'

'You're as schizophrenic as I am,' she said, shaking her long mane. 'One minute all kind and caring and moral, the next a complete and utter pervert.'

'I told you,' he smiled. 'We are the same, you and I.'

When they said goodbye in the lobby of the hotel, Bernadette felt inclined to linger and smile a lot at him. The afternoon had been thoroughly pleasant, despite every circumstance being stacked against such a possibility.

Radley was actually excellent company, she decided, for a despicable man. Bad men often were good company. 'I guess this hotel isn't so disappointing after all,' she said, meaning it as a big compliment. It was rare that Bernadette paid compliments, and she felt quite pleased with herself for doing so.

'And so it begins.'

'What begins?'

'You're falling for me.'

'I am *not* falling for you, you arrogant, conceited peacock. I was just trying to be *nice* to you. To throw you a bone – you, the undeserving!'

'If you're naturally this hot-headed, I can't wait to see you on stage lecturing women on the art of . . . What is it exactly you're lecturing on?'

'Never you mind. And there is no way you're coming to see me lecture.'

'Oh, depend upon it,' he said, grinning devilishly, 'I'll be there.'

The problem was, Bernadette herself wasn't exactly sure what it was she was supposed to be lecturing on, and the LA tour date was looming fast. What *was* the Man Whisperer? What was at the heart of the concept? She had never truly understood why Tim had chosen this particular alias for her – the first time she had heard it from his lips, she was completely bedazzled, thinking he understood the darker aspect of her nature and had given it a fun, self-referential label, a cutesy derivation that masked the deviation and made her a socially acceptable creature. It was only later that she suspected the name had less to do with her own psychological failings, and more to do with a concept that could be sold: a woman in control, a woman who could beguile men into confessing secrets. Funny really, given how out-of-control Bernadette herself felt compared to all the together people that populated her existence. Funny too that she had no desire to hear the secrets of men. The less learnt about men the better, she had found.

The interesting part was that the creation, Tim's creation, apparently held some appeal. Her articles were well received and widely quoted, and now a couple of hundred women (and some men too) had signed up to come and hear her speak at the Beverly Hilton. Tim had allowed her utter creative freedom over the content of the speech, which was to be half an hour long, followed by a question-and-answer session. She couldn't help but acknowledge that Radley's caution about putting her on a stage was more deserved than Tim's rampant confidence.

She felt more of a fraud than ever; the guilt that had dogged her ever since her first article, ever since the shaming of President Wibawa, was bubbling to the fore and threatening to consume her overly introspective, neurotic self. Undeserving, untalented and bitter, wordless and poorly motivated, she fretted and fussed and panicked in the days before her speaking debut. But in quieter moments, when her troubled mind stilled, it wasn't difficult to imagine a scenario in which she shone. At heart a self-important little person, she could very easily visualise stunning an audience of women with her right-minded rhetoric. And Tim would be in the front row, admiring, adoring and feeling legitimately responsible for the marvellous spectacle. Overcome by her sophisticated phrasing and well-thought-out argument, he would hand her from the stage, take her in his arms and confess undying love.

Bernadette believed herself absolutely entitled to such an outcome. It was right that she should be honoured and respected by the masses, and that Tim should love her. It was her birthright, a beginning and an ending entwined, a preordained and complete affair that required no impetus from her. To be loved without labour, to be enough without effort, to be praised without process: this was what she wanted. Her superiority should be endlessly evident without supporting proof. Her distinguished inner world, surely, must break free with no showy introduction.

Annoyingly, she recalled Radley's urgings that she be a woman with an opinion. It would not be enough to stand on a stage and expect to be loved; she needed to get up there and actually say something.

The eve of her big speech had arrived, and Bernadette sat in a suite at the Beverly Hilton, feeling decidedly queasy. The suite had been kitted out as a green room, complete with coffee-making equipment, snacks, and a large TV monitor, which displayed the waiting stage and would provide a live feed of her performance to those on her team who cared. Bernadette's eyes were glued to the screen, staring at the empty podium, the chair and the jug of water that awaited her. Her team consisted of Tim, with various assistants and up-and-comers from the management company; and David, there in both a personal and professional capacity, and failing utterly to be helpful in any way. A tattooed and muscled man with a ginormous bag arrived to do hair and make-up, and Bernadette soon found herself being cleansed and polished and breathed-upon by the guy, who was chewing gum and smelt overly minty.

David hovered like an overweight fly, zipping from person to person in a surprisingly nimble fashion, asking pointless questions about the AV set-up that no one in the room was able to answer. By contrast, the only visage of peace, the voice of calm and reason, the person whose eyes Bernadette sought with her own, was Tim. He stood tall and proud among the rabble, his blonde head luminous and lovely, his smile serene, his blue eyes piercing and direct. He was a prince, a knight, a prophet, and theirs might have been the only two bodies in the room. It was as if a light connected them, an unseen affinity that no other person could pierce. Bidden by her thoughts alone, Tim walked over and took her hand. He squeezed it.

'How's she doing?' he asked the minty make-up artist.

'She's great,' the guy drawled, his breath engulfing her as he leant in to colour her eyes with kohl. 'She's looking good to go. Fierce.'

It wasn't long after that that she was taken from the sanctity of the green room and led down some stairs, through a maze of carpeted corridors, Tim beside her, guiding her, and David hopping along behind.

'You're going to be fine,' Tim said.

'More than fine!' chipped in David. 'This is a turning point! This is going to be huge. You should see how many people are out there – and they're all waiting to hear you! I can see something big coming from this. I see—'

'I've never wanted anything big,' Bernadette said to Tim, not waiting to hear what it was that David saw.

'I know,' Tim assured her. 'This isn't that.'

'What is it then?' she asked, stopping so suddenly that David crashed into her. Tim turned to face her in the dark hotel corridor, their bodies aligned. 'What is this, Tim?' she pressed.

'It's what you make it,' he said. 'It's whatever you want it to be.'

Waiting behind the screens that formed the backstage area, she could hear the rumblings of many women talking together. The noise was thunderous to Bernadette; it was an alien dialect, a hostile growl of anticipation that beat louder than her heart. The screens were covered in adverts for *Squire* magazine, and Bernadette couldn't help but imagine David as a true Shylock, his palms sweaty, his greedy eyes alight with desire for *her*, his golden hoard.

There are moments in life, acute, taxing moments, when our true selves are brought to the fore, when we revert to type and rely on instilled behaviours to guide us through certain unpleasantness. Unfortunately for Bernadette, she had spent if not a lifetime, then certainly many years mulling a toxic brew of antipathy, exemption and paranoia that would cause a scalded throat when swallowed, undiluted, to the last acerbic drop. The time had come to taste her own medicine, and she was borne to the stage not on a happy cloud of optimistic modesty, prepared to stand humbly at the altar, but on a thorny bed of doubt and defensiveness, every atom of her kicking and screaming and fighting for approval.

She vaguely heard David's introduction; she only knew that the mass of female voices had hushed, that they were listening to him speak, and that he said her name. She walked out to tumultuous applause and was heartened by it; it allowed her to reach the podium, take a gulp of water and clear her throat. The vast function room was cold, and she felt the hairs prickle on her bare arms. The prickling sensation continued down her whole body, and she tensed, like an animal preparing for flight. There must have been hundreds of people in the room, rows and rows of them stretching back into darkness. The lights focused on her were too bright, too blinding, the stark nakedness of the beams stripping her psyche and bleaching her dress.

She cleared her throat again and looked down. Elizabeth and Radley were right in the front row, Elizabeth staring up with all the fervour of a teenage girl at her first concert. Radley's face was blank and oddly comforting, the plain look of it easy to project upon, his coal eyes fixed on hers in challenge.

She looked up and began to speak. 'Thank you for coming this afternoon. I'm Bernadette St John, otherwise known as the Man Whisperer, and I'm here to impart some fairly scandalous secrets. I want to tell you about some of the things I've learnt from interviewing the most illustrious men on the planet.'

A random woman in the audience cheered, there was an impromptu round of applause, and Bernadette sighed, feeling like a Kardashian. It was clearly easy to work an audience if you told them what they wanted to hear, but less obvious how they would react to a non-sexy message.

'Firstly I want to go into a little detail about my background, so you understand the particular colour I bring to my articles. Obviously, I'm young' – this got a big laugh, and Bernadette ascertained that the average age of her audience was probably well above forty – 'I'm female, and I have a particular world view. It's well thought out and it's my own, and I'm fond of it.' Here she glanced at Radley, who was beginning to smile. 'So you should know that everything I write is tainted by who I am. I often decide what I'm going to write about a person before I interview them. It's called having an "angle". The Man Whisperer's angle is as sneaky and nefarious as it sounds: I'm a lipsticked Eve, a friendly face with a filthy purpose, and I am out to lambaste any guy that signs up for it.'

The audience was silent, bewildered by the hostility in her voice. She could feel their uncertainty shimmering like a breaking wave. Her crisp English accent and harsh tones were not the norm. She hadn't lost them yet; they were just confused. She hastened to reassure them, to guide them to understanding.

She spoke eloquently of her dissatisfaction with telling stories about real-life men; she confessed that her infamous piece on President Wibawa was more about her than it was about him; she focused on gender politics and dissatisfaction. 'I am sick of the inequalities that still exist. I am ashamed to be defined by terms that men dictate – the very word "feminism" was originated by a man!'

It was here that the booing began. 'You're forty years too late!' called one disgruntled woman.

Bernadette tried to ignore her and the crushing hostility, but the noise entrenched her further in her own position, her excitable nature flaming with each taunt. 'You're fools if you don't recognise it!' she said, her voice ringing loud across the auditorium, a note of panic rising sharply. 'We have been emancipated to the lauded rank of up-for-it bimbo sex toys—'

'Speak for yourself!' someone yelled.

'I usually do speak for myself,' Bernadette shouted back. 'But you've paid money to come and listen to me speak, so listen!'

Several members of the audience got up out their chairs and began to leave. Bernadette felt hot tears stinging her eyes and willed herself not to cry, not to even snuffle. Her views were extreme and she was a defensive fundamentalist. She was a woman with an opinion, and she was on her own.

She looked round desperately, trying to find Tim's face in the crowd. David was standing offstage, all colour drained from his flabby face, his worried jowls slack and weak. Elizabeth was for some reason still gazing rapturously up at her, undeterred. Radley was staring venomously at departing audience members, looking like he would hit them if he could.

'I can't be the only woman fed up with being called a "good

sport" if I accommodate a man's fantasy-girl persona, and considered lesser if I don't live up to his raunchy ideal,' she tried again, reasonably. 'I say it's time we stop whispering and start shouting!'

She stopped as she noticed David ascending the stage, pushed up the steps by Tim, who had miraculously appeared. David almost snatched the microphone from her trembling hand. 'Thank you, thank you, Bernadette,' he said shrilly, facing the audience. 'We're unfortunately running slightly short on time, so now would be a good moment to open discussion up to a question-and-answer format. I'm sure we'll have lots of good questions.' He thrust the microphone back at Bernadette and shaded his eyes with his hand, straining on tiptoes to find a raised hand in the audience. 'Ah, yes! Yes, young lady with the blue sweater, what is your question?'

There was a pause and a shuffle as a runner delivered a microphone to the waiting blue-sweatered woman. 'What about journalistic integrity?' she asked upon receipt. 'You've just said you make everything up. Why should we believe anything you say about anything?' Her tone was a pompous *gotcha*, and Bernadette bristled, her heart still pounding rapidly.

'I didn't say I make everything up! What I said was, what I write is corrupted by who I am, and that often I work in my own assumptions. I ask leading questions, I tease and flirt, and often I intentionally mould answers to fit my view. That's not the same as making everything up. I never misquote a man – if he's stupid enough to say it, I print it, that's all!'

David laughed nervously. 'I think Bernadette is joking with us a bit; it's that dry British sense of humour. We, of course, have a great editing team at *Squire*; no one has assumptions there—'

'But *her* assumption is that all men are raunchy pigs?' asked blue sweater, clinging on to the microphone longer than her turn.

'No, no!' laughed David.

'Not *all* of them,' Bernadette answered glumly into her own mic.

'Next question!' called David desperately, pointing to a hand in the sea of faces.

A middle-aged woman with soft curling hair stood up and said, 'I kind of hear what you're saying. But in all honesty, I didn't know this was a political thing. I just came here to see if you could get me laid. Do you have any tips on that . . . please?'

'Probably not ones you'd care to hear,' said Bernadette, softening at the woman's tone. She pointed to David, and shrugged. '*I'm* sleeping with *him*.'

There was a gasp from the audience, a noise of general squeamish disgust, and a call of 'You're sleeping with your *editor*? Whore!'

'Next question!' yelled David, practically crying.

The runner dutifully delivered the microphone to a painfully thin girl with a pinched face. 'Yeah, I just want to know if you think you're all that,' she said, gawking aggressively at Bernadette.

'If I think I'm all what?'

'Hotter than the rest of us. Do you think you're fucking Beyoncé or something?'

Bernadette stared in quiet loathing at the woman, while the room waited with bated breath for her answer. She couldn't believe that this was what she had been reduced to. 'Sometimes I feel attractive and sometimes I don't,' she answered evenly, her voice lifeless now. 'Do I think I'm hotter than everyone in the audience? No, statistically that's unlikely. Do I think I'm hotter than you, as an individual? Yes.' The audience gasped and she heard David squeak with despair beside her.

'Oh no you did not!' cried the thin woman, enraged.

'My question to you is: does it matter?' asked Bernadette, as the poor runner tried to wrestle the microphone away from the angry guest.

'Next question! Next question, *please*!' David implored. Bernadette heard his voice lighten considerably as he said, 'Yes! Yes! Man in the front row. If I'm not mistaken, it's Radley Blake!' He was obviously relieved to land on a friendly face, although his cheer was short-lived as he noticed the dark intensity of Radley's eyes. 'Er . . . er, Radley Blake, ladies and gentlemen!' he choked out, as the runner puffed over to Radley.

The audience was aflutter, enlivened by the appearance of such eligibility in their midst. Those who recognised his name seemed to telepathically communicate his net worth and physical attractiveness to the unenlightened. Scores of women jostled to get a good look, and any camera phones not yet in operation were whipped out and readied. Bernadette was humiliated on their behalf, cursing the dopes of her gender.

She forced her eyes to meet Radley's. He was waiting patiently for her attention, quite still and serious, and scowling slightly. 'Bernadette,' he said into the microphone, his voice low and deliberate, 'will you marry me?'

5

Bernadette sat alone on the bed of the green room suite, head in her hands. Her long dark hair fell forward around her face, loose and tumbling. She focused on the sound of her breath and the sensation of moving this life energy through her body.

She was not one to be easily overcome. Even in the depths of despair she was happy to be alive; she could appreciate the beauty of her skin and the comfort of her environment. The hotel was luxurious and handsome, and she was lucky to be sitting in that room at that moment. She was lucky to have a brain and a body. The past meant nothing and the future didn't exist. Right now, she was clean, sane and calm; she was unhurt, educated and young. She warmed her body with her breath, inhaling slowly and exhaling through her mouth, making a small puffing sound with each count.

There was a knock at the door, and she heard the whirring sound of a key card allowing access. She looked up as Tim entered, her eyes still raw from crying.

'You did this to me,' she said unfairly, falling backwards. He said nothing, but came to lie next to her on the bed. He wrapped his body protectively around her, and she felt their legs instinctively entwine. He buried his face in her hair, and they lay still, and quiet, and so close. His heart was beating under a layer of thin pinstripe, and she basked in his soft-cotton, soapy scent. They lay like gorged lions on warm stone.

'Aren't you going to speak?' she asked, after a long silence. The moment was bliss, and yet nothing could lift the dull indifference, the dead weight, the grey cloud.

He moved slowly, pulling his body back so they could see each other clearly. She knew she could have him then if she moved at that moment; he would be hers if she kissed or touched or sighed the right way. But her body refused to be roused from its current lethargy. She was alive, yes, but not as alive as before. Something hurt.

'What made you do that?' he asked.

'I'm still not entirely sure what it is I've done. I said some words, that's all. I stood in front of some people and said some words. And I could feel their judgement like a bullet. Their hatred pierced me, and now I know it's the end, even though I don't know why.'

Tim shook his head as if he were trying to rewrite history. 'I really think you must be a bit crazy,' he said, not unkindly.

'I'm not crazy,' she responded hastily. 'I'm just lyrical.'

He laughed, the kind of laugh that precedes tears, and pulled her close again, hiding his face once more in the crook of her neck, under the cover of her soft hair. She felt his lips brush against her skin, near her sensitive nape, as he spoke.

'What was that?' he asked.

'I've told you I don't know! I don't know what capital crime I'm supposed to have committed—'

'Not that. What was that with Radley? What *was* that?'

'Oh,' she gasped softly.

When Radley had asked her to marry him, for one crazy moment she had wanted to say yes. She'd wanted to scream the word into the microphone and deafen the hateful crowd with her affirmative. His eyes were locked desperately on hers, but instead of his usual mesmeric mastery, he seemed . . . vulnerable. Radley Blake looking uncertain was nothing she cared to see, and so to block out the image, she moved. What followed was a blur, as she moved quite rapidly.

She shoved the microphone at David and strode off the stage. She pushed past people and fell through a doorway. She ran down a passageway and leapt up some stairs. She careered down corridors and stumbled on her heels. Finally she found the deserted green room, where the monitor still displayed the empty stage. She had rested on the bed, and remembered to breathe.

'I don't know what that was,' she replied.

'Well, that's a bad sign.' He pulled back again so he could look at her. His face was agitated behind his spectacles.

'Why?'

'That means it's real. If it was nothing, you'd do your dismissive thing – you'd say he's madly in love with you and can't help himself, or you'd say he's a crazy attention-seeking lunatic and make fun of him. But to not know!'

The numb feeling began to ease, to be replaced with a gruesome air of wrongdoing. 'That means it's real,' she heard him say again. 'That means it's real.'

'Why is everyone so keen for me to have a definite opinion?' she asked.

'Because you *are* opinion! You are opinion itself!'

'Well, I sound *great*,' she sighed, sarcastically.

'You *are* great,' he said, too low. She knew that now was the time to lean in and claim him. He was ripe and unprotected and spiralling in free fall. It made her think that what she had done on the stage must have been very bad indeed. Tim was unflappable. He'd climbed mountains and trekked through rainforests. But now, clearly, he was unnerved.

'Is this the end of my career?'

He looked surprised that she had asked; not quite offended, but certainly caught off guard.

'No, no, don't think like that. There'll be damage limitation, of course, but that's what *I'm* here for. Nothing is ever final. Asking you to speak was a mistake, I see that, and you were right to say it's my fault. It was a bad suggestion on my part and I'm sorry.'

As he spoke, they had instinctively uncoiled their bodies, separating and standing apart. He was blushing.

Suddenly the whirring sound of an access key card rumbled through the door, and David entered without knocking. He was beside himself, frazzled and sweat-drenched, and wringing his hands in misery.

'Bernadette!' he cried. 'What *was* that? Why did you say those awful things about yourself and the magazine? I just don't understand the sabotage, the self-sabotage! *Why?* When you had them eating out of the palm of your hand, when you can make people do anything you want! Why would you throw it all away?'

'Let's calm down,' said Tim, coldly. 'These kind of things are never as bad as they seem. It's entirely containable.'

'It is?' said David, a drowning man grasping at a life raft. 'Containable? You think so? I don't know how the magazine is going to feel about this. It's most unfortunate, but it was really was quite libellous—'

'David,' said Tim, 'you *are* the magazine. Come on, now.'

'I'm not! I'm not! I'm just the West Coast editor, I have to answer to—'

'Are you saying you don't want the world exclusive? Radley Blake has never given an in-depth before. And there's no such thing as bad publicity, you know. The magazine isn't going to want to abandon their Man Whisperer at this point. That's just bad business, David.'

David struggled, floundering like a line-caught tuna, his pasty face a tragicomic mask of agony. 'But will Blake even want to do the interview?' he gasped. 'He was there! He heard everything – he heard her say how she likes to make a fool out of the men she interviews, for God's sake!'

'He asked her to marry him,' said Tim pointedly, as though he were talking to a simpleton.

'That doesn't mean he'll do the interview!'

'He'll do it,' said Bernadette quietly, an authority on the subject. 'David, I'm guessing *Squire* will still want the Radley Blake interview. I'm hoping Tim will be able to work some magic and salvage my career. But I totally understand if you want to stop dating me. I wasn't very kind to you up there. It was unintentional, a reflex, but that's no excuse. Sorry.'

David looked like a weasel in a trap, his eyes searching anxiously for escape, his brain working through possibilities.

After an anxious few seconds, he gulped peevishly. 'Well, it was quite hurtful. I just don't understand it. It isn't like you . . .'

'David, I—' she began, but he held up a silencing hand.

'But,' he said, smiling a martyred smile, 'I'm willing to stand by you. I don't think I'll ever understand what made you go crazy up there, but you're my girl, and the rest of the world can go to hell!' He looked like he expected applause and a parade for his chivalry, and Bernadette could sense Tim stiffening with distaste.

'Okay,' said Bernadette, who would have resigned herself to far greater punishment. Clearly, as shocked as David was at her behaviour, it would take something pretty significant to make him give up the frequent sex and omelettes.

'Do you want to have dinner with me and Elizabeth tonight?' Tim asked, turning to her. The idea of leaving her to David's overbearing forgiveness was clearly too much for him. She nodded and smiled her thanks. 'We'll just leave you to . . . freshen up a bit,' he added, gesturing vaguely to her face, which reminded her that she had been wearing stage make-up and crying hard. 'Come on, David.'

She was grateful when they left. Strangely, the only person she wanted to see was Elizabeth. Elizabeth reminded her of childhood Easters in England. Elizabeth was newborn lambs frolicking by hedgerows, daffodils, and hessian, and marbled ink-blown eggs. Elizabeth was a woman who had decent thoughts, and spoke sense.

One Easter, when Bernadette was about seven or eight years old, she had spent a long time decorating an Easter bonnet; it was a school project, and there was to be a parade. She painstakingly sewed a pretty yellow flower trim around her hat, and added a wide blue silk ribbon as fastener.

Young Bernadette presented her effort somewhat timidly to her father, who placed the bonnet on her head and tied the blue ribbon beneath her chin, peering at her under the brim as he did so. 'You know, I can tell how proud you are of this bonnet,' he said, smiling. 'Women place great stock in silly things like this. Who can sew the best piddly flowers. Who can bake the most ridiculous fondant fancies. You're starting young, aren't you? You're making of yourself the perfect little doll – an accomplished plaything with artful prevarications, your plumes and feathers designed to attract the men around you. But wait till you see what it is men really want from you! Wait until you see the arena you'll actually have to compete in. You're in for a shock. It's nothing to do with daisies and cupcakes, believe me!' He laughed. 'Now, go and find your mother. She'll no doubt marvel at your tarted-up cuteness, and tell you everything you want to hear. She'll feed the delusion for you. But remember, you'll get nothing but the truth from me. Run on, little doll.'

The morning of the school Easter parade, Bernadette looked around her at the other girls, girls in their best party dresses, with decorated bonnets demonstrating various levels of skill, girls who were smiling and actively trying to look pretty, waving and smiling at the mothers and fathers who watched them adoringly. She felt as if she was in a carnival of fools. She tore her bonnet from her head in the middle of the parade and actually stomped on it in rage, causing several of her classmates to cry, and her teacher to condemn her forever as an actual heathen.

* * *

Bernadette washed her face, carefully reapplied make-up, practised her breathing, and then made her way back down to the conference room. She walked stealthily, half afraid that audience members would be lying in wait and ready to attack, but no one was around, and it wasn't until she pushed open the double doors that led to the backstage area that she heard voices. She moved as quietly as a cat, keeping behind the *Squire*-covered screens, peeking through a partition into the largely empty auditorium. Radley and Tim were standing on the other side of the screen chatting with the runner and a couple of sound guys.

'She's just got to be tamed,' Radley was saying. All the men laughed, except Tim.

'Dude, she is a piece of work!' laughed the runner.

'I like a challenge.'

'But she was, like, seriously lesbian up there. She's loco.'

'She is.' Radley grinned. 'She's bat-shit crazy and confused, and—'

'And your future wife, man!' They all laughed again, but Tim looked intensely uncomfortable.

'I said that for comic effect,' Radley smirked, waving his hand through the air in a dismissive and lordly gesture. 'She may not be my future wife, but let me tell you, I am going to have her if it's the last thing I do.'

'*Have* her?' the runner guffawed. 'I hope you mean you're going to bang her? She looked like she could do with a good—'

Radley opened his mouth to say something, but Tim cut him off. 'Bernadette is my friend and my client. For the record, she's not crazy. And I think, given the point she was trying to make up there, we should stop objectifying and demeaning her.'

137

The other men laughed at him. Radley shrugged. 'Just being honest.'

Bernadette was shaking behind the screen, her teeth chattering with rage. Tim's defence was so wonderful and so like him, and she loved him even more than before – but the betrayal she felt from Radley was a pain she couldn't take. A blinding migraine of hatred and shame engulfed her.

'I'm just joking around, man,' the runner was saying, appeasing. 'And I never said she wasn't hot.'

At that moment Bernadette emerged from behind the screen like an avenging fury, bearing down upon the small group of men, evoking the image of a living Medusa.

'Holy shit!' said the runner. He scarpered, the sound guys hot on his heels.

'Well if it isn't Charlie Sheen,' grinned Radley pleasantly. 'Seminal speech, my dear, but entirely the wrong crowd. You need to know your audience.'

'I hate you,' she said.

'I'm guessing it's a resounding no to my proposal then?'

'How could you talk about me like that?'

'Eavesdroppers really should be careful what they listen to.'

'Don't talk as if we're friends. I just heard everything you said.'

'So?'

'So? It was disgusting.'

Tim looked intensely uncomfortable; he had his head down and his hands thrust deep in his pockets.

'What about it was disgusting?' smiled Radley. 'I didn't say anything I wouldn't say to your face. What part offended you?'

'You said I was crazy!'

'You *are* crazy. You are a manipulative, perturbed little madam. You are a minx and a menace and a madwoman . . . I could go on. *Shall* I go on?'

'*Me* mad? You just proposed to a crazy woman!'

'I'm good at making quick decisions.'

Tim cleared his throat and stepped towards Bernadette. 'Bernie, we should go,' he said.

But Bernadette was too busy looking daggers at Radley to heed Tim properly. 'What you said about "having" me. That was . . . that was *wrong*. So gross and backward and—'

Radley covered the space between them before she realised he had moved at all. He enveloped her in his arms and shifted so his mouth was pressed up against her ear. 'I will have you,' he hissed, so low that Tim couldn't hear. 'And I want you to know it. I want it to be the only thing you think about.'

His lips tickled her as he spoke, and an awful thrill ran through her body, the same kind of spooky anticipation that she felt when she had heard ghost stories as a child. She looked up at him and thought about kissing him right there, but Tim had had enough of their display. He took Bernadette gently by the arm and frowned at Radley. 'Given her speech, Rad, I doubt she likes being grabbed like that.'

'I wasn't going for a grab so much as a tender embrace,' said Radley, backing off with both hands in the air. 'And given her speech, I *doubt* she likes you intervening on her behalf, and I *doubt* she likes being spoken of in the third person when she's right here.'

'I think you need a drink, Bern,' Tim said, ignoring Radley and moving her towards the exit. He was acting the part of

139

reasonable mediator, wearing his sanity like a scarlet sash of honour, but Bernadette could tell he was annoyed. He didn't like the tempestuous vortex that existed between her and Radley. He didn't like being the odd one out, the obtruding stranger.

Bernadette turned to look back at Radley as Tim led her, like she was an invalid, away from the stage. 'The next time I see you,' she called back to him, 'it will be in a professional capacity.'

He nodded and bowed in agreement and waved a jaunty wave. She couldn't help but smile at him a little, even though she was still angry. He returned her smile wholeheartedly, flashing his brilliant teeth in a quick spark of goodwill. 'Bernadette, you may not have accepted my proposal, you may have found it confusing and possibly insulting – but I think you will come to appreciate it sooner or later. In one way or another.'

The way he said it, like a magician with one final, peerless trick, made her wonder about his motive. It seemed like he was trying to include her in some wider secret.

It wasn't until the next day that she realised what he meant, and what exactly he had sacrificed by proposing in such a public way. For a man who shunned publicity, there was suddenly a whole lot of press about Radley Blake. Anything that might have been written about her cringeworthy speaking appearance was totally overshadowed by the fact that one of the most influential men in the country had made such a 'romantic' gesture. Gossip columns and business pages alike reported that Radley Blake, the elusive entrepreneur, had blatantly declared his love for Bernadette St John, the Man Whisperer. The Twitterverse was buzzing; Bernadette had been approached by every morning talk show to comment; pictures of her and Radley graced countless blogs, and video footage stormed Snapchat and YouTube.

Bernadette had mixed feelings, but the fact was, Radley's gesture had saved her from a lot of bad press. The numerous articles barely mentioned her talk, and if they did, it was simply to say that Radley had interrupted a 'heated girl-on-girl debate' or a 'spirited rant on the unresolved sex wars'. The fact that a man – a young, intelligent, good-looking, enormously wealthy man – had proposed during a talk entitled 'The Man Whisperer Speaks!' led most people to assume that Bernadette had been divulging siren secrets. Advance ticket sales for the New York event increased so dramatically they had to switch to a bigger venue. David was obnoxiously overjoyed, Tim was saved from a PR nightmare, and Bernadette found herself once again lauded for no reason. As grateful as she was for the miraculous turn of events, she couldn't help but feel a nagging disappointment in the pit of her stomach. Radley's proposal had been nothing but a trick, a very kind trick. He had obviously been fully aware of the outcome of his gesture when he stood up to ask the crazy question. He had pre-empted and prevented her career catastrophe, and had sacrificed himself to do so. As lovely as that was, it was not a genuine marriage proposal.

She approached the Radley Blake interview a fortnight later humbled and a little shy. It was discomfiting to be in a man's debt, especially a predatory scoundrel of a man like Blake.

It was a Friday morning, and she had dressed in her very best journalistic attire: a black pencil skirt, nude suede pumps with a sensible two-inch heel, and a caramel collared silk shirt that was provocative in all the right ways. It was a classic look that made her feel braver and appear deadly efficient.

She arrived at Radley's glass-and-metal mansion at exactly 7 a.m., as appointed, her Dictaphone fully charged and loaded. She gave her name at the gate, which swung silently open to allow her to drive up to the main house.

It was interesting to see the place in daylight. The grounds were meticulously maintained, and she noticed a large vegetable garden, and a gleaming array of solar panels, which she had not been able to see at night. The solar panels were placed in regimented rows, like sowed plants, and looked more like a modern art installation than a utility. There were panels on the roof of the house too.

She stopped at the top of the driveway and Mick materialised to open her door. She leapt out, grabbing her bag of equipment and smiling widely at her old friend. 'Good morning! Thank you, Mick!'

'Uh-huh,' was all she got for her efforts, as usual.

Radley stepped from the house, dressed in nothing but a pair of navy pyjama bottoms. His chest and stomach were as well defined as an athlete's, and Bernadette quivered at the sight of him. He really was spectacular. She had forgotten what a toned man looked like, let alone a muscular man, having been presented so often recently with David's pudgy nakedness.

She pulled out her Dictaphone and spoke into it as she approached. 'He appears in nothing but dark blue pyjama bottoms. Poser.'

Radley heard her and laughed, holding up his iPhone and speaking into it. 'She appears dressed like Catherine Deneuve. Tease.'

'Well, Mr Blake,' she said, holding out her hand for him to shake. 'Here we are: a day in the life of . . .'

'And right on time.'

'Perfect. What are we doing first?'

'First up, breakfast,' he said, turning and loping back into the house.

'Breakfast?'

'Yes. It's the most important meal of the day, you know.'

She followed him into the large open-plan living area, which looked quite spectacular in daylight. Morning sun streamed through the glass walls, displaying a hazy cityscape and a shining ocean view. A large table, a single piece of rough oak, was laid with two place settings and a simple arrangement of white tea roses.

'This is very civilised,' she said.

He held out a chair for her to sit on, and she approached it as one might a crumbling cliff edge. 'Okay,' she said, dropping into the chair, 'I see what this is going to be. You're going to pretend to be Mr Perfect for two days. But I'm still angry with you, you know.'

He laughed and seated himself. 'I wondered how long your professional demeanour was going to last. And I was so enjoying it. I can see why it works, this sexy, dominating persona of yours – I was very willing to confess my innermost secrets, darkest childhood memories, and then beg for forgiveness with my cheek resting against that soft silk blouse of yours. You look like the perfect mix of schoolteacher, mother and—'

'You are endlessly provoking. Please stop sexualising me.'

'Can *you* please stop sexualising you?

She almost growled at him, and he laughed again before

continuing. 'Well, you needn't worry that you're not getting a genuine slice of life. I am prepared to bare my soul and share my daily routine. Unlike some, I do not dissemble.'

She raised an eyebrow. 'So you always have breakfast like this? At a table set with silverware and cloth napkins and cream roses?'

'But of course. The only difference is, there's usually only one place setting – I eat breakfast alone – and I eat at seven a.m. on the dot. I am a creature of habit.'

'Okay then,' she said sceptically, arranging her napkin over her knee, as a tall, thin man in a white chef's coat placed plates in front of them.

'I thought you could eat what I eat. But Alexi can make you something else if you'd prefer?' Radley offered.

Bernadette looked down at the perfectly shaped half-moon omelette on her plate, garnished with a sprig of coriander and halved cherry tomatoes. It was somewhat different from her own amateur attempts. Fresh orange juice was being poured into her glass. 'This looks fine,' she said.

'So how does this work? This two-day interview thing?' asked Radley.

'Well, most of the time I want you to pretend I'm not here. I'm going to observe you, make notes, record you, if that's okay?' she said, waving the Dictaphone. He nodded his assent. 'And I might have to ask you questions about what you're doing.'

'What if I'm in the middle of doing something really important and don't want to be disturbed?'

'I'm not stupid. I won't interrupt you if you're doing something important.'

'Okay.'

'Then we'll need a good couple of hours – tomorrow, maybe – where we can sit down and I can ask you about what I've observed. I'm trying to give readers an insight into what makes a man like you tick.'

'A man like me?'

'A successful man.'

'Successful? Ugh. How diminishing.'

'And then at a later date, I want to interview some of your friends, employees, relatives. You don't have to be there for that – in fact, I'd rather you weren't – but I'll need you to provide me with some names.'

'As you wish.'

'Great. Okay. So just . . . go about your business.' She placed the Dictaphone prominently on the table, angled towards him. He shrugged and set to work on his omelette, eating one-handed with a fork while checking emails on his iPhone.

'What are you reading?' she asked, after a short pause.

He held up one long, silencing finger. 'You said you wouldn't disturb me when I was doing anything important. This is extremely important.'

She rolled her eyes and drank some juice. His face was a study in concentration, his attention thoroughly absorbed by the tiny screen in front of him. His expression would change quite dramatically as he worked his way through his emails, and Bernadette tried to guess from the appreciative chuckles, or horrified stares, what he could possibly be reading that moved him so much.

She pulled out two extra Dictaphones, and her iPhone with its special microphone attachment, and arranged them on the table with the first device, angling them carefully so that they might pick up any sound from Radley. He looked up in surprise, staring at the array of equipment with some astonishment.

'That's my back-up arsenal,' she explained, helpfully.

'How many back-ups do you need?'

'Well, sometimes they break, or I haven't timed them properly, or I've forgotten to put the tape in . . .'

'That sounds like an awful lot of human error. Can't you just learn to use one of the damn things properly?'

'You'd be surprised at how often they go wrong. And there's varying sound quality. I like to be prepared.'

'But I'm not even saying anything right now,' he muttered, returning to his screen.

Bernadette realised it was the first time in their acquaintance that she had not had Radley's full and undivided attention. His iPhone was a goddess more divine, and he worshipped with no half-hearted posturing but with the complete adoration of the devout. His fingers tapped and jabbed and stroked the screen with such skill that the phone almost seemed to be an extension of his body.

Eventually he looked up. 'I was answering email.'

'Do you enjoy it?'

'Enjoy it?' he asked, knitting his brows to suggest she was mad. 'No, it's necessary. It's how I run my company. At this point, I'm basically an email processing machine.'

'Do you find that makes you very antisocial? At . . . meals and so forth?'

He looked at her, exasperated. 'You just told me to pretend that you're not here and go about my business. I usually answer emails at breakfast.'

'I'm not offended. I was just asking generally.'

'You *are* offended. You can't bear the fact that I'm not mooning all over you.'

'What would you have done,' she said, unable to help herself suddenly, 'when you asked me to marry you. What would you have done if I'd said yes?'

'I'd have married you,' he said casually, rising and tossing his napkin on the table in a debonair fashion. 'Have you had enough to eat?' She nodded, dumbfounded, and stood up too. 'Excellent. Now I'm going to get dressed . . . Coming?' he asked, a cheeky glint in his eye.

'I'll wait here.'

'Are you sure? What if I say something really profound in my closet? Don't you need to keep an army of recording devices on me at all times?'

'I'll wait here,' she said, firmly.

'Okay. Next on the schedule is yoga. Do you want to join the class? You won't be able to do it in that' – he pointed at her skirt – 'but I could probably fashion something to fit you.'

'I'll just watch, thanks.'

'Suit yourself.'

He wandered off upstairs, and Bernadette rather regretted not following him. It would be interesting to see his bedroom. She worked her way towards the large sitting area, a square of squishy couches around a low bronze-and-glass coffee table. There was a beautiful orchid arrangement on the table, a small glass bowl of mints and a selection of magazines. Bernadette picked up the copy of *Squire* and was pleased to find it well thumbed. It fell open to her pages.

Radley came back downstairs looking like a fitness model,

dressed in a grey T-shirt and simple black sweatpants. He beckoned to her with one hand while checking email with the other. Bernadette, having diligently collected her Dictaphones, followed him obediently outside, past the lovely swimming pool, across a stretch of lawn and into an airy studio. It was as bright and light-filled as the rest of his home; a sprung wooden floor stretched from two mirrored walls to two walls of glass. One section was full of high-tech gym equipment and Pilates reformers; the other half of the room was left clear, like a dance studio.

A bubbly blonde girl with fantastically long legs emerged from a bathroom at the back. 'Hi!' she called, bouncing towards them.

'Janie, you remember I told you I'd have a journalist with me today? This is Bernadette St John. Bernadette, Janie is my yoga instructor. She's originally from England, like you.' The two girls sized each other up as Radley added, 'I do like English people.'

Janie giggled and shook Bernadette's hand. She had quite a strong grip, for such a delicate-looking girl. 'Where are you from?' she asked.

'London,' said Bernadette, non-committally. 'I hope you don't mind me observing your session?'

'Not at all! Do you want to join us?'

'No. Thank you,' said Bernadette primly, gingerly seating herself on a recliner and taking out her beloved Dictaphones. 'Is it all right if I record you?'

Janie looked at the array in interest. 'Am I going to be in your article?'

'Probably not.'

'What magazine do you write for?'

'*Squire.*'

Radley had pulled two yoga mats to the centre of the room and settled himself on one in a relaxed cross-legged position. Janie gave Bernadette a sweet acknowledging smile before moving to the wall and pressing a button. Calming music flooded the room.

Janie and Radley worked side by side on the yoga mats, beginning with an obviously familiar routine of stretches. Bernadette didn't like it. Radley hadn't struck her as a yoga fanatic, and she certainly didn't appreciate the intimate way Janie kept touching him to adjust his position. He seemed to be quite an advanced practitioner, and she watched as the poses and stretches got more and more elaborate. She couldn't help but notice his arm muscles, braced and bulging, as he balanced his whole body inches off the ground, just his palms touching the floor and his legs folded up over his supporting arms.

He then held a very stable headstand, Janie timing him for a minute exactly before telling him to come down. Bernadette admired the way his T-shirt succumbed to the effects of gravity, and slowly slid down his body to reveal his incredibly honed stomach muscles. She whispered into her Dictaphone, 'Skilled at yoga. Body built and bendy. V. serious about practice. Implies extreme vanity.' Both Janie and Radley looked up at her sharply, their faces red from the inverted pose, but Bernadette stared innocently back.

As their session began to wind down, Janie pressed another button and electronic blinds silently glided down the glass walls, submerging them in near darkness. Radley came out of Child's Pose and turned to lie on his stomach. Janie massaged him for a couple of minutes, working the knots out of his shoulders and lower back. Bernadette thought it entirely unnecessary that she chose to straddle him in order to perform this service.

After the blinds had gone up and the music was turned off, Janie turned to Bernadette, smiling in an annoying way. 'Did you record us all that time?' she asked, pointing at the range of Dictaphones. 'We didn't say anything! You've just recorded an hour of meditation music!'

Bernadette crossly gathered up her little machines and shoved them in her bag. 'Yes, well, it was doubtful you were going to talk during yoga, but you never know. I once interviewed a very famous director who muttered details of his childhood abuse during pauses in the Mass at his local church, so you see, I always like to be ready.'

Janie looked at her in wide-eyed silence. Radley headed for the sliding door. 'Come on, Bernadette,' he said with a grin. 'Shower time. Bring your Dictaphones.'

Bernadette smiled a sweet farewell at the horrified Janie and headed out after him.

'Thanks, Janie,' he called back.

'Thanks, Rad!' she squeaked, finding her voice. 'See you on Monday.'

Bernadette took two strides for every one of Radley's, which caused her heart rate to rise a little as she tagged behind him on a weaving path through the garden and into the kitchen, where Mick was eating a muffin. They went on through the main living area, where no trace remained of their earlier repast, and Radley headed upstairs without saying a word. Bernadette followed, also silent.

She remembered the soft carpet, and the choice of three

corridors at the top of the stairs. Radley took the corridor to the right, and she followed him past the bathroom where they had listened in to the other bridesmaids, down to the doorway she had seen him emerge from that particular evening.

His bedroom looked out over the pool and garden, and the valley beyond. It had a very masculine energy, as she had expected. The bed was low, with a dark wood frame, crisp white sheets and the minimal number of pillows. It was quite a stark room, the only decoration a selection of old family prints arranged neatly on an antique sideboard.

She realised that he was watching her scope out his most intimate possessions. He smiled at her kindly. 'Do you approve?'

'Your home is fantastic. Obviously.'

'It's not to everybody's taste. I sometimes worry that it's too stark. Not homey enough.'

'Only stupid people could dislike it here.'

He smiled wider. 'Well, I'm glad I fall on the right side of your black-and-white judgement.' He stripped off his T-shirt and Bernadette gulped. 'Make yourself at home,' he said, indicating that she should sit on the bed. She plopped herself down where he pointed. 'I'm going through here to shower and change.' He strolled into a large walk-in closet that led to a modern bathroom, but reappeared moments later, poking his head round the door frame. 'Just think, that could have been our marital bed.' With that he left her properly, and she heard the sound of a shower running.

Bernadette felt somewhat unbalanced. Radley Blake had an unsettling effect on her, because despite the fact that he looked and sounded exactly like the type of man she most despised – arrogant, powerful and assertive – she actually found him worryingly attractive. She tried to remind herself of the pain that could be the only outcome of indulging in this attraction, the despair of being badly treated and abandoned. But Radley was managing to break through her misandrous mantle, and he had one very strong advocate: Elizabeth.

Bernadette's subconscious mind allowed that Elizabeth was a good person, in the same way that Tim was a good person; they were both better than she would ever be. And Elizabeth valued Radley as a true friend.

She stood to look at the framed pictures. There was a large one of Elizabeth and Radley, both looking significantly younger, both grinning to camera. Bernadette was pleased to note that Elizabeth was not particularly attractive even with youth on her side. She picked it up for a closer examination. It was odd to see a youthful Radley; he was so completely at ease as an adult man that it seemed almost as though he had come to life fully formed, in need of no growth or incubation period. Yet here he was, younger and leaner. The rest were family photos, including several of an elderly couple Bernadette assumed to be Radley's parents. They looked sophisticated and a little intimidating. There was also a photo of Radley holding a puppy, a black-and-white bundle of fluff, nestled happily in his powerful arms. She snorted at the ridiculous appeal of the picture. The shower water cut off, and she hastily went to sit back down on the bed, careful to replace the frame in the exact position she had found it.

When Radley re-emerged, he was wearing jeans and a T-shirt, and the damp, fragrant scent of shampoo clung to him. He crossed to the other side of the bed and lay down, plumping a pillow behind his head.

'What now?' asked Bernadette, wanting to lie down too, but worrying about the inevitable consequence.

'Now, we head into the office.'

'I'm looking forward to seeing you at work. I suspect that will be the real meat of my article, unless you have something spectacular planned for tomorrow?'

'Tomorrow? No. You just want to see me in my normal routine, right? On Saturday I usually just hang out, maybe do some work, watch some television . . .'

'Really?' she asked, incredulous.

'Er, yes. Is there something wrong with that?'

'It's just that usually . . . usually if a person knows I'm profiling them, they tend to do something impressive when I'm around, like skydiving, or reading to blind orphans or something. I've never shadowed anyone where they just sit around and watch TV.'

'But you said normal routine.'

'I know – but nobody actually *does* their normal routine! They have an agenda. The actor who wants to look intelligent goes to a reading of contemporary philosophy at MOMA. The politician who wants to come across as sincere takes me along on his visit downtown to the women's shelter.' She had turned her body to face his so that she was practically lying next to him, propped up on her elbows.

'I don't have any agenda,' he said. 'But if you'd like to add a little colour to your article, other than my charming self, I'm happy to do anything you suggest.'

'I'll think about it.'

'You're already going to frame any answers I might happen to give you into the body of a pre-written article. You've decided who I am, so go ahead and match up a weekend activity with your chosen angle and I'll oblige. What is your angle, incidentally?'

'I was going for pig-headed narcissist.'

'And what does a pig-headed narcissist do on a Saturday?'

'I wouldn't know. But I was imagining some kind of extreme gesture. Something that would highlight an expertise of yours, allowing you to shine. A situation that you could dominate.'

'Well, I should let you know that I am an *excellent* watcher of television. I own that shit.'

The mattress was the perfect tension, not too soft and not too hard. The sheets were so smooth and inviting, Bernadette would have been happy to settle down there for the day and conduct the interview from Radley's bed. She wondered if that would add an interesting 'between the sheets' slant to her piece. Her readers would already be speculating, given the famed marriage proposal. Perhaps the ultimate gimmick here would be to ham up the sexual chemistry and go for broke.

'I have to ask . . .' she said, turning on her back and lying down flat next to him, staring up into his dark eyes. She licked her lips, and batted her lashes, allowing her gaze to linger and the faintest smile to play at the corners of her mouth. 'People will want to know, given the fact that I'm writing about you . . . why did you propose marriage on my lecture tour?'

'I'd hardly call it a tour. It's only two speaking engagements.'

'Oh, just tell me why!' she demanded, nasally persistent, her seductive mask slipping like the strap of a cheap satin negligee.

'I don't want to talk about my personal life.'

'*What?*' she said, sitting up so quickly she almost cracked him under the chin, 'What do you mean, you don't want to talk about your personal life?'

'Just that. I'm happy to bare my soul to you in many ways. I'll open up my home and work to you – and you should know that the company I've created is a big part of my soul. But I'm not going to talk about my family, nor girlfriends past or present. Nothing that involves a third party; it's not my place.'

'But I *am* the third party in this case!'

'And you have the right to say whatever you like publicly. I'm sure you'll find some special, clever way to work it into your writing. But I won't comment.'

'So it was personal?' Bernadette asked, in a small voice.

A frown darted across his face, knitting his brows like thunderclouds. 'Are you quite mad?' he said. 'I asked you to marry me. That's as personal as it gets.'

'I thought it was a joke . . . a trick – a sort of jokey trick,' she finished lamely.

He stood up, still scowling, took both her hands in his and pulled her up to a standing position. 'Don't get too comfortable in my bed,' he growled.

She followed him back downstairs as meek as a kitten, into an office at the back of the house. It was a high-ceilinged room with tall bookcases on every wall save one, crammed full and overflowing. The remaining wall was a sheet of clear glass that allowed yet another spectacular city view. Books seemed to cover every available surface and there was no order to it. It was similar to the rest of the house in its design, but quite different in feel. This room was warm and well used, and seemed the perfect place to settle with a novel, curled up on one of the ample couches.

'Is this where you work?' Bernadette asked, uncomfortable despite the serenity offered by the surroundings. It was the type of room she had dreamed of as a child, a luxurious literary escape, a gentleman's study, the perfect book nook.

'I work everywhere. But this is not where I spend the working day. I came to pick up my bag.'

Radley collected a laptop from a large mahogany desk that was a jumble of papers, cables and books. He carefully placed it in a soft leather satchel, and slung the bag over his broad shoulder like a cowboy catching a calf by its hind legs, then, still glowering, and without a word to her, strode from the room. She followed him through the house and out to the drive, where Mick and the gleaming sedan were already waiting.

The three of them travelled in silence. Bernadette was a vexed mess. No matter how hard she tried, she couldn't fathom Radley's motivation. He was attracted to her, of course – but the attraction was of the superficial kind, based purely on her youth and good looks. She preferred it when men were drawn by a combination of her physicality and the unthreatening persona she preferred to project. But Radley had never been fooled. He could read her mind and predict her every move in a Gandalf-like fashion. He knew and he ridiculed, hiding his disgust behind a thin veil of flirtatious raillery.

When they turned down a road running parallel to large aircraft hangars and a private runway, Bernadette remembered that Radley's company was based up in Silicon Valley. 'How often do you fly to work?' she asked him.

'Twice a week,' he replied, somewhat gruffly.

The car stopped at a large metal gate, which slid silently aside to let them pass, before heading towards a brilliant-white Falcon 7X that rested birdlike on the black tarmac, its three engines stirring the hot air, creating an aura of energetic expectation. As they exited the car, the noise and the heat made the breath catch in Bernadette's chest, and filled her with a powerful desire to match the kinetic force of the plane – she wanted to scream and run and cartwheel and jump. Instead she followed Radley up the extended staircase, calling out to him, 'How do you justify flying private?'

'I don't,' he said, rolling his eyes. 'If you don't understand the math, that's your problem.'

Mick followed them on to the plane but stopped short of the main cabin, seating himself in the jump seat by the pilots. Radley led Bernadette into a cream suite and pointed to the chair she should take.

She desperately wanted to engage him in conversation, but he was still in a foul mood with her, no doubt insulted that she hadn't realised his proposal was a serious one. But just because it had been genuine didn't give him the moral high ground. She knew that his motivation was corrupt, and his heart was not truly in it. Just like a man. She scowled slightly as she sat opposite him, watching as he fiddled with his precious cell phone. He looked up, saw her expression and promptly laughed.

'What?' she asked, surprised at his sudden mirth.

'Are you feeling hard done by?' he asked.

'A little.'

'You are funny,' he said appreciatively. 'You might be the most selfish creature I've ever met.'

She opened her mouth indignantly. 'I'm not selfish.'

'You are a passionate soul, impulse-driven and pleasure-seeking and thoroughly self-serving. The only true hedonist I've ever met.'

'I don't know where you get all this codswallop from,' she said, her throat dry. He thought her selfish, and it stung. But in a world rife with self-interest, one *had* to be selfish so as not to be made a fool of.

The plane was taxiing down the runway, jolting slightly over bumps, the lithe machine tripping and shimmying like an excitable colt. Bernadette fastened her seat belt. 'Why did you move to LA if your company is based in Silicon Valley?' she asked.

'For a change in scene and society.'

She looked at him doubtfully. 'You came to LA for the society?'

The plane rose from the ground in a simple joyful leap, and Bernadette turned involuntarily to look out of the oval window by her chair, watching the ground recede with giddying pace. The network of roads and houses and the LA grid system below looked so peaceful and complete, a well-ordered testament to human triumph.

'Do you really think I'm selfish?' she asked softly.

'Yes.'

'You're probably right.'

They both gazed out of their respective windows, Bernadette careful to blink away the salty tears that were forming at the corners of her eyes.

The seat-belt sign darkened and Mick appeared from the front of the plane to stand deferentially by Radley.

'I'll have a ginger ale, please,' Radley said.

Mick turned to Bernadette. 'Water, please,' she said, in response to his carefully raised eyebrow.

Once they had been furnished with beverages and Mick had disappeared to the front again, closing the pocket door carefully behind him, Bernadette felt the need to come clean. 'I used to be kind, you know,' she faltered, somewhat desperate. 'I used to be very kind. Truly I did. I mean, I think I was kind, when I was a child.'

Radley glanced up at her, his eyes as soft as she had ever seen them. He hastened to reassure her, speaking quietly. 'Yes,' he said. 'I know it. I can tell.'

'I think I was hurt. And it was the kind of hurt that deadens one.'

'Yes?' He looked at her with compassion as she stumbled over her words, making little sense, fiddling with her sapphire ring all the while.

'When someone you love – someone you're supposed to be able to trust! – tells you things about yourself and about the world that seem wrong, it's a strange feeling,' she began.

'Someone . . . like your father?'

She nodded. 'I was a millstone around his neck. A helpless dependant. I just expected him to love me! Without having done anything to earn it.'

'That's not an outrageous expectation. Parents do usually love their children.'

Bernadette nodded absently, her mind alive with the past. 'I was so eager for his love, so open and hopeful and . . . I just expected it. I thought I was beautiful, you see, and lovable, and that the world was that simple.'

'You are beautiful. And lovable. Very,' Radley said, quietly.

Bernadette shook her head this time, with a small, tight laugh. 'He showed me how wrong I was, and how the world would judge me.'

'Judge you?'

'For being a woman, for being so weak and open. The simple sin of circumstance, the stain of inferiority.'

'No,' said Radley, quiet but firm. He looked to be almost in pain. 'You can't really think this?'

'It's not so much how I think as how I feel. Sometimes I feel so weak and helpless, because of everything I was told. Feelings can overpower thoughts, no matter how hard you try to rationalise them.'

'This weakness you talk of: it is *not* weak to expect and express love. It's an incredible strength. It's one of the most admirable things about you.'

Bernadette looked at him, lifted suddenly. 'Yes, I knew that love was real, even as a child. I had such a joy inside me – and ultimately, it was that hopeful expectation that he couldn't crush.'

'The very quality he was so keen to undermine.'

She smiled at him. 'I felt love myself, love for him, love for my mother, so I knew it was a real thing – and I read about it! I read how other people experienced love. I learnt it was something that could exist, and that it could be simple, and uncomplicated, and not greedy, or grasping, or some strange form of trickery.'

Radley watched her silently, witnessing something that few people had a chance to see: the tender side of Bernadette's nature.

'But then the awful thing,' she continued, 'was that reality seemed to confirm his view of things, and not mine.'

'What do you mean?'

'Well, everything he had warned me of came true. All around me men just seemed to care about the way I looked, and the way I made them feel about themselves, and what I could do for them. They degraded me, and compared me, and discarded me like an object.'

'Has it really been as bad as all that?' Radley asked, looking quite sorrowful.

She nodded. 'Men are bastards. All of them.'

Radley shifted in his seat. 'Now hang on, I know lots of wonderful men. Do you not think that these things happened to you because of the hurt your father inflicted? If you didn't deal with his influence, it could go on affecting you in . . . strange ways.'

She looked at him, her eyes like pieces of warm copper, tears brimming but not falling. 'Possibly. There was a man . . . he was a bit like you, actually, except older than you, and not as good-looking . . . and I loved him. He was my first love. He – he wasn't very nice. But he was smart and funny, and I didn't care that he wasn't good to me. I was just consumed with wanting to be with him. I suppose, with hindsight, he was similar to my father. They both had a reputation for being immoral and dangerous. But I couldn't help myself.'

'What happened?'

'I thought that as long as I was with him, as long as I could keep him, earn him, be worthy of him – trick him into feeling something for me! – nothing else mattered. I compromised myself and my ideals in order to be with him. Over and over again I tried to be someone I wasn't, just to keep up with him. And then he left me. And it seemed so wrong, because I had given everything, and he . . . It meant nothing to him. My soul was worthless to him, but important to me, and yet I had given it away so easily, and ultimately all for nothing . . .'

Radley reached over and took her hands. 'You were born with a great belief in romantic justice. And you were too soon disabused of your credo. I'm sorry you experienced such pain.'

She gazed at him with something approaching surprise. She hadn't realised he could be so nice. It was a relief to confess her weakness to someone. 'I wish I could go back to being the person I was before. I wish I could get my soul back. But I can't.'

'You can!' Radley urged, his voice quickening. 'You never lost your soul, as you call it. You are still a kind person underneath it all. You are still full of love, and passion. You just need to channel that passion in a productive way, and not at Tim!'

Bernadette recoiled, suddenly aware that Radley was too close to her. He had said the last as a half-joke, but something in his manner was off: he was holding her hands tightly and looking far too sincere. His emotion frightened her. And he had used the information she had given him to attack Tim; just like a man! His concern had been an elaborate show, when all he wanted was to make his own point.

Suddenly Mick popped open the pocket door. He hesitated in the doorway, sensing that he might be unwelcome.

'Would you like something to eat?' Radley asked Bernadette, his eyes never leaving hers. 'A snack? Some fruit? Bagels? A cookie?' She shook her head. 'We're fine, thank you,' he finished, still not looking in Mick's direction. The door was shut with all possible haste.

'You don't understand,' said Bernadette.

'Of course. I'm sorry.' He let go of her hands and shifted back in his seat. 'Too soon, Radley, too soon,' he muttered.

'You don't want to know details? Of the man? He's quite a famous British MP, you know.'

'I don't need to know details. I know he was a shit. There are any number of ways a girl like you could have been hurt by a man. They are all tragic enough. But I've garnered the material point: your father was the man who hurt you first. You made a bad choice in life because of that hurt, and I know this much – neither the MP nor your father is anything like Tim Bazier. And because you have decided never to be hurt by a man again, that is why you're now so deeply "in love" with someone who's no good for you.'

'Oh, you are awful!' she exclaimed, relieved at the rush of red-hot feeling returning, bringing much-needed vim to her weakened body.

'I might be awful, but I am also right. And I suppose, by some horrible irony, there are things about me that remind you of . . . ugh, I hate to say it – I was already conscious of the age gap between us: I'm nearly a decade older than you – but there are things about me that must remind you of your father!' Radley dropped his head in his hands in a gesture that would have seemed almost comical had he not been so genuinely distressed.

Bernadette felt like herself again, no longer caught in Radley's spell, but hard and self-contained, with a sudden rush of power. 'You are quite old,' she agreed, callously.

He gave her a wry smile and her heart seemed to thump harder in her chest. She smiled back prettily and turned her head away. 'Yes, well, I'm supposed to be interviewing you, not the other way around. I didn't mean to impose with my sob story. It could be a lot worse.'

'Oh, I'm not crying for you,' he said in his usual playful manner.

'I mean, here I sit with the genius Radley Blake. Things could be *a lot* worse.'

'You know, I think that's the first real compliment you've paid me.'

'It's not; you just haven't been paying close enough attention.'

'I've been paying very close attention,' he said, simply. The cabin suddenly seemed very warm, and Bernadette rested her head against the oval window, cooling her forehead.

'How long are we staying up north?' she asked.

He didn't answer, and she turned to look at him with a questioning eyebrow that rivalled Mick's in its propriety and self-assured dignity.

'Well,' he said, hesitating, 'that depends.'

'On what?'

'On whether or not you want to get a room.'

It took her a moment to register what he was asking. 'A hotel room?' she clarified.

'Yes.'

Her mind was spinning. 'You're suggesting that you and I get a hotel room in the Bay Area, and go back to Los Angeles tomorrow? After spending the night together? In a hotel room?'

'Yes.'

She couldn't understand why he wouldn't offer two rooms. They could get two rooms. It was such a bold and brazen move.

'On the record or off the record?' she asked.

'Whichever you like.'

'On the record.'

'Okay.'

Bernadette hesitated, giddy with the pleasure of a lust finally acknowledged. 'Okay. On the record, Radley Blake, I accept your offer to spend the night with you.'

'Well then,' said Radley, grinning. 'On the record, I succumb to you.'

6

A fresh sedan was waiting for them at the bottom of the aircraft steps. Bernadette alighted carefully, thanking the pilots as she passed, and smiling girlishly at Mick, who handed her down the stairs and into the car.

She slid across the cold leather back seat, with Radley following close behind. As soon as the door was shut, he took her hand in his. Her breath quickened with anticipation. She had not been expecting to be propositioned so boldly. And she had accepted him – refused an offer of marriage, but jumped at the idea of sharing his bed.

He leant across her suddenly. 'Here, let me,' he said, a gentleman, pulling her seat belt around her body and fastening it in place with a click, the sound like a wink of acknowledgement.

'I can fasten my own seat belt,' she said automatically, shifting uncomfortably.

'I know you can.' He gazed sympathetically at his wriggling companion. 'We could go back to Los Angeles this afternoon if you'd prefer. You seem a bit discomposed. I didn't mean to shock you.'

'No,' she heard herself answer, too quick. 'I don't take fright easily.'

He smiled, and turned his attention to his ever-present iPhone. 'Well, it's never too late to change your mind.'

How wrong he was. She was no fickle woman; she had made her bed and now she must lie in it. The space between them was unnecessary given their understanding, and she moved her legs closer to his, in silent confirmation of her choice. A small sound of mirth puffed from his lips, and he gently patted her knee, not taking his eyes from the screen.

Bernadette's was a confusing, fast-paced life, and she could focus only on one compelling idea at a time. Everything was currently lost behind brazen desire. She had forgotten love and revenge, integrity and pain. She had been reduced to a lust-addled fool. As long as Radley was being honest about what he wanted from her, she was happy. Better that they sleep together and get it over with, rather than keep getting entangled in unnecessary semantic tussles. He had patted her knee, but kept the gesture fast and brief, as though he could tell she would be too easily stirred. He was waiting. Waiting until they were alone in a hotel room.

An impatient and transparent person, she turned in the seat with a longing groan, but all he did was laugh. There was more to her than this, she knew it – her brain was filled with facts. She knew all the kings of England, and the Latin dative; she knew the story of Voltaire's mistress, and how to turn a horse chestnut into a winning conker. And her mind could take the facts she knew and find linking patterns; she could assimilate and create. But since Radley had suggested they spend the night together, nothing had ever seemed so interesting. The facts were void and her selfdom ceased to be.

She was intrigued by the idea of being intimate with him, and her perversion was more than sexual. It was arousing to know she would be sharing personal space. She would be a witness to his nightly ablutions, see what snacks he chose from the hotel minibar, know what time he set his alarm for in the morning. Radley Blake was the kind of person who exuded such a mannered superiority, it was difficult to imagine him performing tasks essential to mere mortals. But now she would see him tie his shoelaces. It was vulnerability that she desired. It would be satisfying to see him weak and duly at her mercy. She hoped that he snored.

'Do you need anything?' Radley asked. 'We'll have dinner with some friends of mine. Should I send for a dress for you?'

'I'll go like this,' Bernadette assured him. 'Unless this isn't formal enough?'

Radley laughed. 'This is Silicon Valley. A T-shirt is formal enough.'

'Good. Then I'll go as I am.'

'Would you like anything at all?' he persisted solicitously. 'Toiletries? Hosiery? Anything?'

'Hosiery is a word that went out with haberdashery. And no, I'm fine, thank you. All I need is toothpaste, and the hotel can provide that. I'm pretty low-maintenance.'

'I hope not,' he said grimly. 'I don't like it when women describe themselves like that. It always makes me feel like I'm being sold a pup.'

'Okay, I'm hideously difficult to please and like to have my own way. Better?'

'Much,' he said, grinning delightedly. 'Although I still hate that phrase. For the record.'

Northern California reminded her of England. Verdant hills undulated in a most unassertive manner, large-eyed, shiny-nosed cows grazed happily behind post-and-rail fences, and there was a distinct lack of dust and palm trees. The large office building that housed Clarion Molecular sat back from the freeway in a sympathetically designed industrial block, its clean white walls and angular structure making it look like a Mormon temple, or an edifice to high-designed futures technology. The large blue-and-green Clarion sign read like a challenge to lassitude, and a call to arms for capitalist endeavour. Bernadette approved. It was bright, modern and appealed to her sense of scale.

They walked towards the large glass entrance, past box hedges and a herb garden that looked like it had sprung from the pages of a horticulture magazine. 'What's with the garden?' asked Bernadette, noting the neat rows, and the almost spooky spotless pathways between pristine beds.

Radley shrugged. 'We're biologists. A lot of us here like plants. I come out and snip herbs for my sandwiches at lunch sometimes. It's all organic.'

'I'm sorry . . . You snip herbs for your sandwiches?' she repeated, a note of unmistakable ridicule in her voice. He didn't flinch, just swerved into a side path and stooped to pick a few leaves of mint. 'Here,' he said, thrusting them in front of her nose. 'Eat it.'

'I don't want to eat it.'

'Eat it,' he encouraged, tickling the leaves against her lips. She chomped down, narrowly avoiding the tips of his fingers.

169

'What other interesting features does the building have?' she asked, with full mouth and fresh breath.

'You can't see it from here, but we have a jogging track, and a Japanese tea garden on the roof. We're completely energy-self-sufficient with our solar-panel field out back. We have a crèche, a gym, state-of-the-art wave pool, Pilates studio— '

'Are you kidding? I want to come and work here. It's like a spa!'

Radley shrugged with genuine modesty. 'It's nothing original.'

'Er, a Japanese tea garden on the roof sounds pretty original to me.'

He smiled at her. 'I don't know that I've seen you animated like this about anything other than Tim.'

Bernadette grew grave for a moment, but was distracted quickly enough by the advanced biometric entry to the building, where a compact machine scanned Radley's retina, and a computerised female voice said, 'Good morning, Radley.' Bernadette shrieked with delight.

'I have a guest with me,' he informed the surrounding air.

'Welcome, visitor. Please check in at reception,' replied the computer, and the large glass doors swept silently open.

'That is extreme!' Bernadette whispered, as they entered an immaculate lobby. 'That is some serious James Bond shit.'

'Nothing tacky,' Radley assured her, smugly. 'It's the most up-to-date system that actually works. There are others considered more advanced, but they're not quite there yet. They crash frequently, need a lot of babysitting, that sort of thing. Doris, as we call our access control, actually works. She's a one-machine facilities management superstar.'

'Who makes the decisions round here?' Bernadette asked.

'Well, it's not Doris,' he said, grinning. 'Are you worried about a HAL-type situation?'

'No, of course not. I meant, how did you end up with Doris? Who made that decision?'

Radley looked immensely affronted. 'Who on earth do you think?'

'But decisions about security, facilities management, human resources . . . the tea garden on the roof? Is that you too? Do you micromanage?'

Radley sighed as they reached the reception desk, behind which sat a very pretty girl. 'Hi, Rachel,' he said. 'Do you have Bernadette's access card?'

Rachel, who wore a snug, low-cut cardigan and bejewelled nails, smiled pertly at Radley and pulled a card from a recess in the desk. 'Good morning, Mr Blake,' she said, in an excellently modulated telephone voice. Turning to Bernadette, she held out the card and glanced at her curiously. 'Good morning, Ms St John, welcome to Clarion Molecular.'

'Do you think that's what Doris would look like, if she was embodied?' Bernadette asked, sneaking a look back at Rachel as they walked away. Radley's loud answering laugh echoed round the high-ceilinged lobby.

They headed towards a bank of elevators, past a comfortable seating area and a living wall decked out with ferns and green leafy plants. It gave a fresh scent to the air, and a bright splash of colour to the otherwise stark white gleam.

'More herbs?' asked Bernadette, pointing.

Radley shook his head. 'For decoration only.'

He pushed a button to call a chrome and glass elevator. 'To get back to your ridiculous question about micromanaging –

another term that I hate, by the way – I'm intimately involved in every aspect of this company. My background is biological engineering, and that is what I am at heart: a biologist. But I am also the CEO and founder of a large organisation, and I take that role very seriously. I'm perhaps not as good at managing as I am at engineering, but luckily I am a superlative engineer, so even if my management skills fall far short of my engineering skills, I must still be pretty good.'

'Now we're getting down to it,' said Bernadette, as they entered the elevator. 'There's the pig-headed narcissist I've come to know and love.'

'You may know me, but you don't love me. Not yet, anyway,' said Radley, as the doors slid shut behind them.

'How can I love you?' asked Bernadette, quietly.

'Charming. I'm not so thoroughly bad, you know.'

'No, no, I wasn't being hostile. I meant it as a genuine question.' She turned her green eyes up to gaze at his face, wanting very much to kiss him. 'How can I love you? Help me to love you.'

She jumped as Radley banged his fist against the emergency stop button and the elevator came to an abrupt halt. It was an electrifying moment, and after staring at him for a split second to judge the crackling lust, Bernadette threw herself into his arms, nuzzling her head under his chin and pressing her cheek against his chest. His strong arms encircled her, and she was overcome with the sensation of rightness. It felt so comfortable and pleasant, and her body fitted exactly into his. She wanted to drown herself in the physical reality and forget everything: forget her own name, forget the existence of Tim, and of every man who had hurt her, forget that Radley was as dangerous as every other bastard out there. She wanted him to wipe every thought from her mind, and to leave her numb and oblivious.

'Do you mean it?' he asked, pulling her back to look at him. 'Do you really mean it?' His lips were so close to hers, and her body tingled.

'Yes,' she said, in a small, sad voice, 'I suppose I do. It would be ever so convenient to love you.'

He let go of her sharply, and she felt the immediate lack of him, the emptiness of not being surrounded by his warmth and overpowering energy. 'Damn!' he said, stepping back and shaking his head fiercely. 'You're unbelievable.'

Suddenly Doris's voice rang out, the clear electronic sound cutting through their absorption. 'Radley,' the voice asked, 'is there a problem?'

'No,' said Radley, loudly and firmly.

'Shall we resume service?' asked Doris.

'Yes.'

'Resuming service,' and the elevator whirred to life, moving upwards once more.

'Can they hear everything?' asked Bernadette, glancing nervously at a camera installed in the corner.

'No, thank heaven,' said Radley, refusing to look at her.

At the fifth floor, the doors drew back to reveal a vast open-plan space, with rows of desks in low-partitioned cubicles. People buzzed efficiently, typing at their desks, or moving through the office labyrinth with important gait and shining eyes. Radley changed as he entered: he too walked faster and with more purpose, and he appeared to forget the incident in the elevator. Bernadette kept pace, weaving with him through the rows until they reached a desk somewhere in the middle.

'This is me,' said Radley, seating himself at a nondescript workspace.

'Don't you have an office?' she asked, surprised. 'Shouldn't the CEO of the company have an office, or at least a desk that can be distinguished from the others? Where do you take meetings?'

'I take meetings in one of the conference rooms, like everyone else. This is Silicon Valley. We're very egalitarian here. You wouldn't like it.'

'Just because I'm English doesn't mean I'm some hard-nosed elitist.'

'No, being English doesn't, but being *you* does. Now, I need to answer emails for a bit. Would you like to sit with me? If not, you can take a tour of the building with my assistant. I can join you in an hour.'

'I'll wait,' said Bernadette. 'I'm here to shadow you.'

'You're here to torment me,' muttered Radley, turning to wake his computer. As soon as the screen came to life, he ignored her presence, so utterly taken up was he with his bright, shiny machine. Bernadette stood somewhat stupidly by his desk, glancing around at the hive of activity.

A pleasant-faced man about her own age popped his head over the partition of a neighbouring cubicle. 'Ms St John?' he stammered nervously. Bernadette knew she had seen him before, but she couldn't quite place him. His features were vaguely familiar.

'Have we met?' she asked politely, with a winning smile.

'Actually . . . yes,' said the forlorn boy. 'At Tim Bazier's surprise engagement party. I was in town with Radley. You . . . um . . .' and he blushed a pretty crimson.

Her stomach lurched with embarrassment. Of course! This was the random young man she had rebuffed and then pretended to know. Why must all past transgressions haunt her? 'Call me Bernadette,' she said wanly.

'Nice to officially meet you, Bernadette. I'm Sam, Radley's assistant.'

'Oh. We emailed. Good to put a face to the name.'

In their email exchanges Sam had seemed scarily efficient and middle-aged, helping Bernadette schedule her time with Radley and answering various logistical questions with prompt ease. But in reality he appeared easy-going and casual – and he was young and good-looking too. Why had she been so quick to repel him at the party? He must think her very odd.

'Are you sure you don't want to stretch your legs and look around? A trip to the cafeteria might be more fun than staring at Radley's back for an hour,' he said persuasively.

'Well, perhaps the cafeteria would be nice. And could I ask you a few questions for my article?'

'Of course,' he said. 'Come with me.'

Bernadette moved to follow him, but was stopped short by Radley, who, quick as a snake, grabbed her by the wrist and pulled her towards him.

'Sam's a nice boy,' he hissed, so that no one could overhear. 'Lay one finger on him and so help me . . .'

'Don't threaten me,' Bernadette huffed testily, shaking off his grip.

'Well don't make cow eyes at my assistant.'

'I do not make cow eyes!'

'Try to have at least one non-flirtatious encounter with another human being.'

175

'I don't know *how* to interact with someone without resorting to flirtation,' she hissed back. 'I do it when I'm nervous. It's a sort of insecurity thing.'

Radley snorted. 'You, nervous? Chance would be a fine thing.'

She stared at him challengingly, and then quite deliberately strutted over to Sam, who was waiting patiently.

'So, Sam,' she said in a friendly fashion as they walked to the elevator, passing workers who gave cursory glances in her direction, but not the rapacious looks she was used to – the employees of Clarion Molecular seemed to have a higher purpose, a subtle superiority that elevated them above the scandalous or the mundane. The room buzzed with honest work, like a hive or a colony. 'What's it like to work for Radley?'

The boy's eyes lit up at the question, and he spoke with an almost religious fervour as he rushed to expound on his favourite topic. Radley had no need to fear her seductive charms; there was clearly no room in Sam's life for romance, so completely absorbed was he with his work. 'It's an honour, obviously,' he stammered. 'I still don't know how I landed the job. I wasn't the most qualified applicant, but Radley is a man who likes to nurture potential.'

'So he chose you, the less qualified candidate, and in so doing has won your unfailing gratitude?' she asked, smiling sweetly, showing her journalist's half-smile, half-sneer.

Sam looked askance. 'I wouldn't phrase it exactly like that,' he said carefully, some of the boyish ardour dissipating. 'Not unfailing gratitude. But I trust Mr Blake and his vision.' He had obviously fallen for Radley like a giddy schoolgirl. He began to seem less attractive.

On the ground floor, they walked out to a pleasant courtyard, where white benches were positioned around an array of exotic plants and flowers, and subtle jasmine provided the base note in a tropical medley.

The cafeteria was housed in a low building. On entering, it seemed they had stepped into a corporate banquet rather than a simple lunch hall. It was an epicure's delight. Every type of cuisine was available at serving stations scattered around the large room. Stalls were piled high with bright fruits, pizza ovens emitted a warm glow, delicious soups simmered in large cauldrons. There was a dedicated vegan bar, and a 'pick-your-own' orchard of potted indoor trees and fruit-bearing plants.

'This is quite something,' Bernadette said. 'You must dine well.'

'I tend to eat all my meals here at work,' Sam-the-Eager laughed. 'In fact,' he said, warming to his theme, 'going home at all just isn't necessary. I could shower here, eat here, exercise here . . . sleep in the meditation room. It would be awesome! I'd live here twenty-four seven if they'd let me.'

'Wouldn't you feel the lack of something?' Bernadette asked. 'Real life, for example?'

'But this *is* real life!' he exclaimed, his body twisting for emphasis, his face adamant. 'There is nothing more real than what we're doing here, nothing more interesting, nothing as beautiful or as challenging! There is nowhere I'd rather be.'

'Gosh,' said Bernadette drily. 'Lucky you.'

He stared at her with clear blue eyes that reminded her suddenly of Elizabeth, his face registering pity and confusion. 'I'm sorry if I sound extreme to you,' he said frankly. 'But there are a lot of people here like me. We all think we're doing something good and worthwhile. That's not an easy thing to find in this world. Believe me, I've chased that feeling down in all the wrong places.'

'I've never felt that way. I can't really imagine what it's like,' she admitted, feeling suddenly very useless.

'Then I'll hazard you've never really been in love,' he smiled. Her eyes widened so startlingly that he faltered. 'That was rude. Sorry.'

'I *am* in love,' she said. 'For your information.'

He stared at her as though trying to read her soul, and Bernadette felt uncomfortable, a sinner being looked on by a blameless innocent. She wished she hadn't judged him so harshly; that her mind could open to the generous possibility of his naïve world view being the right one, that he wasn't just an impressionable worker, a propaganda-fed, put-upon soldier on the front line.

'We were all kind of shocked,' Sam said, 'when we read that he'd proposed to someone. You must be pretty special.'

She wondered why his statement sounded more like a reassurance than a compliment. It was annoying that he seemed to assume she must be in love with Radley, and it was difficult to squash the overwhelming desire to correct him. She waited for him to say more, to divulge secrets or question her further, but he simply indicated with his arm that she should move on and help herself to whatever food she fancied.

She chose a latte and a delicious-smelling cinnamon roll covered in sticky white icing. They sat out in the courtyard at a picnic table, the sun warming their backs. Sam had a green tea and thin slices of mango, which he chewed thoughtfully, mindful of every mouthful. He looked like a character from a video game, and Bernadette wondered whose avatar he was, wondered who was controlling the words that came out of his mouth, words that led her mind in such funny directions. He seemed to intuit what would most stimulate her thoughts; he was a divine messenger from the gods, not just a puppet of Radley's making, but a mouthpiece for the universe, if she was willing to listen.

He reminded her of a young Tim. He was one of the good guys, a thoroughly nice human being so caught up with his own small part to play that he could offer nothing but pleasant sincerity. A man of faith.

'But isn't Radley a megalomaniac? A tyrant? A slave-driver?' she pushed.

Sam shook his head, but without hostility, used to her probing now. 'No! Don't you know him at all?'

'It's not my own opinion I'm bothered with right now, it's yours.'

'He's so off the back foot all the time – he's so . . . cool! I can't do it! I wish I could be that cool, but I get worked up about small stuff, and I get really crazy about the big stuff. You may have noticed,' he said, ruefully.

'I've noticed you take all this personally,' Bernadette said, waving her arm around to encompass their surroundings.

'Radley's only ever forceful when he needs to be. He doesn't have to rule this place with an iron fist because we're all desperate to be here. The number of applications for internships is twenty times what we can accept. If you have a love for bioengineering, this is the only place to be. Seriously. It's the Superbowl of biotech. There are dozens of companies globally trying to do this stuff, but we're the only one actually doing it. We're the only one with a marketable product.'

'Why?' asked Bernadette, interested in spite of herself.

'Well, because of Radley. Because he's a genius!'

'How convenient. Everyone does seem fond of saying that.'

'That's because it's true. He created the technology. That was all him. It's not some kind of trick.'

'Pride in good regulation, then?'

'I'm telling you, he's cool. Totally reserved, and laid-back. He doesn't really speak much at company meetings; he just sits there listening, and lets everyone else talk. Then he'll come in at the end – boom! – with just a sentence or two, and it's like all the other stuff was unnecessary. He's solved whatever was being argued over, and he's done it without upsetting anyone. I couldn't do that.'

'Nor could I,' said Bernadette, wondering why she was finding it hard to marry her own impression of Radley Blake with this glowing account. 'Can I ask you, is he not often . . . confrontational? Combative? Scathing?'

Sam popped a piece of mango in his mouth and shook his head slowly. 'No. Those aren't the kind of words I'd use to describe him. He's majorly supportive. The only thing would be . . .' He paused.

'Yes?'

'Well, he hates to see unused potential. It's something that drives him nuts. As long as I do my job and put in maximum effort, I'm not afraid of him. And that works for me, because I'm that type of person anyway. But a lazy bum who felt entitled – he'd see that as a wasted resource. He'd go to war on it. So I guess he'd be combative and confrontational with someone like that. But I've never seen it. Why would I? There isn't anybody like that around here,' he said, looking about him innocently. Bernadette narrowed her eyes.

Suddenly Radley's towering form appeared at their table. 'Hello,' he said cheerfully. 'My ears are burning.'

'So they should be,' said Bernadette.

Sam stood, stretching his back and rolling his shoulders. 'I'm going to head upstairs, if that's okay?'

Bernadette nodded. 'Thank you for keeping me company. It's been illuminating.'

'Has she been trying to ferret out skeletons?' Radley asked.

Sam grinned, his freckles crinkling. 'She's nice. I like her,' and with a nod to them both, he ambled away.

Bernadette was touched. The way he had expressed his approval had been so natural and unmannered, she could almost believe he meant it. Radley was watching her shrewdly. 'It's not often you get called nice, I imagine?' he asked.

Bernadette frowned indignantly. 'You imagine incorrectly. I get called nice, and beautiful, and special, and all those kinds of things all the time. That's why I know to ignore it.'

'Then it's a shame if overindulgence has meant you can't recognise the truth when you see it. Sam was clearly taken in by you, and is thoroughly convinced of your niceness. He wouldn't say it if he didn't mean it.'

'Sam's been taken in by *you*, that's for sure.'

'What do you mean by that?'

'He's so grateful that you hired him, when getting in here is apparently harder than getting Centre Court seats at Wimbledon. And he wasn't the most qualified for the job – so he's indebted to you for ever. Smart.'

'He wasn't the most experienced, but he was certainly the most qualified in terms of what I needed from an assistant. He's a great worker.'

'He's a young evangelist. It was quite cultish, in fact. To hear him speak, Clarion Molecular is a house of worship, and *you* can walk on water.'

Radley reddened. 'I don't encourage cult-like behaviour. In fact, I actively discourage it.'

'So that's a problem then?' she pushed, reaching into her bag for the army of Dictaphones. 'You worry about being worshipped?'

'Oh no you don't!' said Radley, offering her his hand and pulling her up from the bench. 'I'm not giving you any fodder to make me sound like some kind of crazed egomaniac.'

'You do know there is no point in trying to protect yourself by being cautious with your speech? I'm spending two days with you. You're going to say enough in the line of normal conversation that I could piece together quotes to make you sound any way I wanted. Like the monkeys typing *Hamlet*.'

'Well, I'm trusting your journalistic integrity. Now, let's tour this place. We'll start on the roof.'

They walked side by side back to the now familiar elevator bank. Bernadette couldn't help but notice the way people greeted Radley as they passed, smiling widely, nodding hello. She had never seen such raw admiration directed at one human being: people were genuinely delighted to see him, and thrilled when he offered them a brief acknowledgement. It must be enough to turn a man's head, she thought.

When they were alone in the elevator, Radley said, 'I don't think we should spend the night up here. We'll head back to LA after dinner, if that's okay with you?'

The manner in which he said it, staring attentively at the ground rather than at her face, made her react more wildly than she would have done had she stopped a moment to consider her actions. But she was so perturbed suddenly by the idea of not spending the night with him, by the rejection, that, copying Radley's earlier action, she slammed her fist violently against the emergency stop button. The elevator abruptly halted.

He was regarding her with only mild surprise as she glowered tempestuously from under thick dark lashes.

'I can't wait to see what happens next,' he said, folding his arms across his chest and leaning insouciantly against the shiny wall.

She paused momentarily, wondering whether to hit him or kiss him, but then realised she was currently capable of neither – he looked too intimidating to kiss, and hitting was the last resort of an infant or an inebriated adult.

'I want to stay the night here,' she said. 'With you.'

'Why?'

'I don't know. Because I want to have sex with you? You want to make me say it explicitly? Why did you suggest it in the first place?'

'Because we were getting on so well. And because—'

Doris cut him off. 'Radley, is there a problem?' she asked in her electronic tones.

'No,' he replied, loudly.

'That thing is really starting to freak me out,' Bernadette mumbled.

'Shall we resume service?' asked Doris.

'No,' said Radley.

Bernadette smiled at the minor victory. 'Because what?' she murmured.

'In all seriousness, no pretence now,' he said. 'Because I

thought that bringing you up here, removing you from your normal environment and showing you all this' – he swept his arm in a large circle – 'might help you to understand me. And change your mind about me. It was foolish, I see that now. I was wrong.'

'What do you want from me?'

He smiled and shrugged his shoulders. 'What do you want from Tim?'

'Everything,' she said, breathlessly.

He let a moment pass before speaking, the air still heavy with her admission. 'I told you,' he said finally. 'We are similar creatures, you and I. I want everything, just like you. I thought, incorrectly, that if I could pull you into my world – which, I might add, most people find quite overwhelming and impressive – you would be overcome with the romance of it.'

There was nothing apologetic about his declaration; it was delivered in the same careful drawl he reserved for most things. She looked for a sign of weakness and found none.

'I'm not going to be overtaken by romance,' she said truthfully. 'But I have been overtaken by something else.'

'You're lusting after me, by your own admission,' he stated, somewhat humorously. 'If you don't like me very much, and aren't succumbing to the empire, then I suppose that is the only reason you would be so keen we stay tonight.'

'I *am* lusting. I don't trust you. I don't particularly like you. I think you could be dangerous to me and my ultimate goal. But you intrigue me, and I want to rid myself of that feeling.'

He laughed. 'I am an itch that must be scratched, a boil that must be lanced, before you can dance off into the sunset with your beloved Tim. What a suggestion!'

'Oh please,' she cried, growing impatient. 'Are you saying you've never spent the night with someone without loving them first?'

'I try to *like* them at least.'

'Really? You've never gone to bed with someone you find just a teensy bit annoying, or stupid? Someone you can't wait to be rid of in the morning? Someone whose welfare you don't care two hoots about?'

He shifted uncomfortably. 'Maybe only half a hoot.'

'And does that make you a bad person?'

'No.' His chest swelled imperceptibly. 'Because at the time, I never pretended otherwise.'

'Well then,' said Bernadette. 'I come to you free of artifice and ask this simple favour. You offered it once; don't back down now.'

'Fine. I'll lower my expectations, my scruples and my pants. Is that what you want?'

'Exactly.' She smiled like the cat that got the cream. 'Somehow I didn't think you'd refuse me, not when it came down to it.'

Radley tapped a number into a keypad on the wall, and the elevator resumed its upward motion. 'Well aren't you insightful?' he said, with a sideways smile.

They took tea on the roof in a surreal Japanese pagoda surrounded by rocks and moss. The small garden was in the very middle of the roof, the view of the freeway artfully screened by large ferns. A running track circled the perimeter, where a few dedicated joggers were doggedly ignoring the midday sun. Bernadette sipped clean-tasting green tea from a handle-less cup and tried to enjoy the serenity. It was not often she was

185

able to stay still and quiet. She was a fidget, impulsive and restless as much in her physical person as she was in manner and thought. Radley was quiet and contemplative, and Bernadette was beginning to suspect him of serious Buddhist tendencies when he suddenly looked up from his small cup and said, 'What shall we do about the stag party and such?'

'What?'

'Well, I need to arrange some kind of party for Tim, a final fling before a life of dull matrimony, and you should do the same for Elizabeth. A bridal shower or a girls' weekend.'

'Me? I don't think so. One of the other bridesmaids can do it.'

'I was thinking, why don't we do a joint party? Men and women together, at least for part of the evening – or we could all go away for the weekend.'

'Why is there so much fuss?' Bernadette complained. 'A whole series of parties and shopping trips. It's too much.'

'You're just jealous that it isn't you. Won't you want all these things when you get married?'

'Yes,' Bernadette admitted. 'Yes. I'll have it all.'

'So, what do you say? Let's plan something fun.'

The thought of arranging a nice surprise for Elizabeth did not appeal, but if they all went away for a weekend together, she would at least get to spend additional time with Tim. She foresaw the possibility to cause trouble. 'All right. Vegas.'

'Vegas?' he said doubtfully. 'I was thinking of a wine-tasting weekend or something. Elizabeth isn't really a Vegas kind of person. And neither is Tim, from what I can tell.'

'Every man is a Vegas man, at least for a weekend. And Elizabeth is an adventurer, isn't she?'

'What would we do in Vegas?'

'Oh, you know, the usual,' Bernadette said airily. 'Clubs, shows, restaurants, bars . . . the Grand Canyon, if you like?'

'I'm not sure this is such a good idea after all,' said Radley.

'It'll be fun. I'm sure between us we can come up with something fabulous.'

'That I don't doubt. But I want to make sure it will be something Lizzie will enjoy.'

Bernadette smiled graciously and nodded with syrupy sweetness. 'Of course. Now, I'm sure you don't spend the whole day at work drinking tea. What now? Get to it.'

Radley stood up, carefully replacing his cup on the small enamelled tray. 'Now, I'll take you to the lab.'

It was on the laboratory floor that Bernadette first began to understand the importance of Clarion Molecular. It was spotlessly clean, scientists working diligently in white coats. Radley walked among it all like landed gentry showing off the bounty of an ancient estate, pointing out particular features, and highlighting the most impressive undertakings. His physical size and scale suddenly seemed perfectly fitted to the environment. He was a big man doing big things. A perfectly formed, highly honed mass of health and energy contributing to a greater good. He knew exactly what he was talking about, and spoke with such easy urgency about rapid sequencing of the human genome that Bernadette begged to have her own biology analysed.

Radley was pleased with her enthusiasm. 'To be clear,' he said. 'What sets us apart here is that we're ultra-fast. Rapid sequencing is essential, including determining what genes are turned on and off. We're able to match accurately the symptoms of a genetically influenced disease with the specific DNA.'

'Designer drugs?' Bernadette asked.

'We're a mechanism for accuracy. Think of it in terms of software. If there's something wrong with the software, you create a software patch. That's what we do here.'

'How involved are you in this?' she asked, looking around at the white-and-glass machines.

'The company keeps growing. Originally it was just me in the lab every day. But now we've perfected the technique and everything has become so big – there's management issues, and marketing, and dealing with clients, and all that torment. I'm not so good at that. I do it because I'm in love with the company, it's like my child. But ultimately I'm looking to step back completely, once everything is as it should be and can go on without me. I miss the start-up days.'

'What will you do then?' she asked.

'Live happily ever after with you?'

'Not an option.'

'Why isn't it an option? Humour me, seeing as I so politely signed away my virtue to you this afternoon.'

'Because we're not proper together. We might be alike, perhaps you're right about that,' she conceded. 'But we don't speak nicely to one another! People who are truly in love are good and gentle with each other; they don't tease or bully or try and catch each other out. I want a gentle love, a true love of the highest order. Nothing less will do, you know.'

Radley looked thoughtful, and patted her on the back in a soothing fashion. 'Poor little girl,' he said. 'I'm afraid you're hankering after something you can't have.'

'Why not?' she demanded.

'Because you yourself are not a gentle person. You are a bull in a china shop. You're touchy and quick-tempered and incredibly passionate. I think you need to know yourself better before you decide the avenue of your fate.'

'Ugh, you do wear me down,' she said, moving to inspect a row of Petri dishes. 'Just when you're at your most attractive – smart and sexy – you have to go and get all preachy and perverse.'

'You don't like hearing things that you don't agree with, even if you're absolutely in the wrong . . . especially when you're absolutely in the wrong.'

'See?' she said. 'This back-and-forth is maddening. We can't agree even when we're trying to get along.'

'The shadow of the evening ahead looms large,' he said, making for the exit doors.

'Exactly! You'd think we'd be able to get it together in order to get together! But we can't be civil for a minute, even knowing that we're going to . . . to . . . you know.'

They left the lab and walked down a long, wide corridor. 'Out of interest,' said Radley, 'how's the interview going?'

If Bernadette were the type of girl to blush, she would have coloured prettily, but her skin remained its usual peaches-and-cream as she answered, 'Fine, thank you. Sam was very helpful. And I've been ever so impressed with the work you do here. I'd like you to know, this is the first time I haven't come with a pre-planned article written in my head. I'm taking things as I find them.'

The truth was, Bernadette had thought very little about what she was going to write. She knew that since her onstage outburst, she was out of favour at *Squire*, and that the Radley piece was to be a fabulous peace offering. She needed to come up with the goods. But, like always, she found herself so caught up with personal matters, her commitment to the job had fallen far behind. She was thoroughly involved in the scandal and the promise of spending the night in a hotel room with Radley Blake, her moral compass unhindered by thoughts of the devoted David, who was technically her boyfriend. And when she thought of Tim, it was only with a desperate bitterness, a tainted longing and a desire for some kind of feeble retribution. She would make herself miserable with Radley; she would abuse the purity of her love for Tim and damage herself in as many ways as possible.

The working day passed, and Bernadette gathered sound bites from lab technicians and administrative assistants, from the women who served in the café and the primary investor in the company. Radley came in for universal praise, although the words used most often to describe him – 'reserved', 'quiet', 'responsible' – clashed harshly with her knowledge of him. 'You are none of these things!' she said, perplexed, as they travelled to dinner that evening, Mick driving as usual.

'I've told you before,' said Radley. 'You bring out something unusual in me.'

'Really?' she asked, doubtfully. 'Your character as a determined flirt seems fairly well established, as far as I'm concerned.'

'You make me laugh,' he said, lowering his voice. He reached out and let his hand rest non-threateningly on her knee. 'And you appeal to a part of me I mostly keep hidden. I've never met anyone who so clearly speaks to that desire.'

'What desire? You know, with this flattery, you're making me feel almost worthy of my ridiculous pen name.'

'The desire to understand someone fully. I have a great thirst for knowledge. And I feel like I *know* you. I've felt it from the first moment I saw you, as haughty and disdainful as you were that night at Tim's. I understand who you are, and the way you think – and it's intoxicating. You are not a mystery to me.'

'Gosh, you're conceited! And laughably wrong, by the way. I don't think you know me at all. Surely, if you did, you wouldn't say such provoking things, if your aim is to have me actually *like* you.'

'I only want to speak the truth to you. I could say all the right things, but that wouldn't be the correct thing to do. You need a little sense and honesty drummed into you.'

'Are you saying you could push my buttons if you wanted to?' she asked, leaning towards him, smiling mischievously. 'Because if you can, go ahead and do it – I dare you.'

They arrived at a small Thai restaurant in Palo Alto, where two men and a woman were standing outside waiting for them.

Before they stepped from the vehicle, Radley indicated the woman. 'That's Susan,' he said in a hushed tone. 'I can't stand her.'

'Why are you having dinner with her if you can't stand her?' asked Bernadette, mockingly.

'Because she's married to a friend of mine,' he said, as if pointing out the patently obvious.

The three friends greeted them uproariously, and Bernadette was introduced with much gesturing and back-slapping on the part of the single gentleman, whose name, she found out, was

Andrew. 'So good to meet you!' Andrew said loudly, grinning widely. 'We all know who *you* are! I read all about it. I have Radley Blake on Google Alerts. Ha, ha! The *marriage proposal*? I read it and I was like, no fucking way! I was like, I'm his best friend' – here he thumped Radley on the back – 'I'm his best friend, and there's no fucking way he's proposed to some random chick without telling me about it. And now you're doing an interview with him. That's cute. You're like a blogger, right?'

'I'm a journalist,' said Bernadette icily. 'I freelance, but—'

'Oh, you "freelance"! Riiight!' Andrew interrupted, laughing goofily, performing a dramatic physical parenthesis around the word.

'I freelance, but I have a monthly column in *Squire* magazine. Perhaps you've heard of it?'

'I don't read magazines,' said Andrew dismissively. 'They're full of shit.'

Susan's husband, a meek-looking man, held out his hand to introduce himself. 'I'm Carter,' he said, pleasantly, 'and this is Susan.'

'Big fan of your work!' said Susan, smiling a look-how-polite-I-can-be-by-contrast smile. 'And I love your shirt, that's just adorable.'

Bernadette had had quite enough of being put on stage, and she turned to Radley with cold eyes.

'Shall we go inside?' he suggested, allowing Bernadette and Susan to lead the way.

They were shown to a private room. The restaurant was busy and noisy. 'That's because it's the only place in Palo Alto that stays open until nine p.m.!' said Andrew, who spoke as if every utterance should be followed by an exclamation mark.

Carter was a nice enough man, Bernadette decided, although his only topic of conversation seemed to be the share price of his investments. Susan was extremely annoying, and had the habit, common to older women, of treating Bernadette as if she were a stupid teenage girl, prefacing most sentences with 'You're too young to remember this', or 'I didn't think that way either when I was in my twenties'.

'She's so sweet, Radley!' Susan said across the table for all to hear, and then, turning back to Bernadette, 'You're really mature for your age. That's so *refreshing.*'

Usually Bernadette would have retaliated by flirting offensively with her husband, but Carter was a chore even she didn't feel up to.

'I'm single!' said Andrew loudly – he seemed incapable of saying anything quietly. 'I could do with a nice lady to treat me well. You got any hot young friends, Bernadette? Anyone you could hook me up with? You've got your claws into this one here.' He banged Radley heavily on the back again. 'Do you realise you have one of the greatest men of the twenty-first century wrapped around your finger? Good for you, I say, that's awesome. Do you know how long I've known this guy? I knew him before he got funding. That's how long. This guy is my best friend.' He slung his arm around Radley's shoulder and squeezed with proprietorial affection.

'Yes, so you keep saying,' said Bernadette, impassively.

Andrew managed to keep up a never-ending stream of one-sided conversation throughout dinner, mostly espousing love and loyalty to Radley, who seemed largely unmoved by the demonstration, just nodding acknowledgement whilst forking up his Pad Thai. Occasionally he stole a glance at Bernadette and smiled to himself. It was odd how very removed he seemed from everything going on around him.

It annoyed Bernadette the way everyone at the table assumed she must be as enamoured with Radley as they were. Andrew in particular acted as though she had won a great prize. 'You take care of this guy,' he said as they left the restaurant after a painful couple of hours. He grabbed her by the shoulders. 'Look me in the eye and tell me you'll take care of him.'

Bernadette removed herself stiffly from his clutches. 'He doesn't need anyone to take care of him. Excuse me, I'm sure you mean well, but I do not answer to you. I don't know you.'

'Feisty!' said Andrew, nodding sagely. 'I'm impressed. I like that! Yeah!'

Bernadette shuddered and turned to say goodbye to Carter and Susan. The older woman leant in with a confiding air. 'You know, this crowd of guys can be a bit of a trip. If you need anything, call me! Us girls need to stick together, you know what I mean?'

'You're very kind,' Bernadette murmured.

The short drive to the Four Seasons allowed Bernadette just enough time to vent in agitation. 'How can you put up with that?' she demanded of Radley, who sat placidly by her side. 'How can you stand anyone claiming ownership of you? It was shameless! The false feeling, and the gaucherie, it made me feel ill.'

'Don't hold back, will you?' he said with a droll smile.

'But honestly! Why do you allow it? You must know they're all trying to get something from you.'

'This is the problem with manipulative people. You assume

the rest of the world must work as you do. Not everyone has an ulterior motive. They're my friends.'

Bernadette rolled her eyes. 'Well, no wonder.'

'No wonder what?'

'No wonder you came looking for me.'

Radley allowed a pause, his head cocked to one side as he regarded her inquisitively. 'Isn't that a quote from *Pretty Woman*?' he asked. Bernadette scowled.

The male receptionist recognised Radley, and had a suite made available to them immediately. 'Would you like help with your bags?' he asked.

'We're fine, thanks,' said Radley.

Bernadette felt keenly the lack of an overnight bag. She wondered what impression the receptionist had formed about a couple demanding a room late at night, with no luggage.

Her heart was beating fiercely in her chest, her breathing shallower than it should be. She was painfully aware of Radley's every movement, and it seemed suddenly that he was acting in a deliberately suggestive manner, his body turning to hers full of promise for the night ahead. He took her hand and led her across the lobby, past the restaurant, to a row of burnished elevators. He called the elevator with his free hand and pulled her to him.

'You are like a girl from a storybook,' he said.

Bernadette thrilled as he gazed sincerely into her eyes. It was the type of compliment that suited her exactly, the kind of thing she had always longed to hear someone say. Bernadette placed great stock in storybooks.

Radley laughed at her dreamy expression. 'See?' he said,

rather mischievously. 'How did you like that? That was me pushing your buttons. I told you I could . . .'

Bernadette snapped from her trance and frowned. 'Good work while it lasted. But can you keep it up without requiring praise for every punch that lands?'

They entered the elevator and Radley pressed the button. 'It is strange,' he said, as they ascended, 'to be riding in an elevator with you and not have it stop mid-journey.'

'We don't need it to,' said Bernadette. 'There's a bed waiting for us.'

They arrived without incident on the top floor. Radley found their room, Bernadette trailing behind, enjoying the deliciousness of anticipation. He managed the key card without any fumbling, pulled her into the room behind him, and shut the door firmly.

7

Once the door to the hotel room had shut behind them, Radley was all movement. Bernadette wasn't given the luxury of inspecting the grand suite with its many sofas. Radley pulled her urgently through to the bedroom, where a huge white bed was not allowed to be an elephant – he didn't give it time.

Instead, he pushed her rather roughly on to the smooth linen, her legs giving way easily, and then lay with his full weight on her prone form. It was everything she had expected, and her mind was quiet, finally, as limbic impulse took over. She was quivering, half afraid, of herself more than him, and half exultant.

'This is what you want, isn't it?' he said, searching her eyes for a response. She nodded as he pushed himself harder on top of her, so that the bed springs coiled in anticipation. She could feel his body through his clothes, and the chemical desire coursing through her own body made her vision blurry. She looked up at him through grey clouds, and was only slightly aware of the intensity with which he was returning her gaze.

He was watching her every move. She closed her eyes and lifted her mouth to be kissed.

Instead she heard him moan, an almost painful sound of longing. Her eyes opened as he ran his hand gently down her throat, dragging the tips of his fingers across her pale skin. Then suddenly he looked away. 'I can't,' he said hoarsely, pushing himself up to standing and moving from the bed.

'What?' she cried, aghast.

'I never intended to.'

'*What?*'

'I don't want you like this,' he said, as if that was enough of an explanation. He walked into the adjoining bathroom, out of sight, and Bernadette could hear him running a tap. When he returned, she noticed he had splashed water across his face and wrists. 'I don't appreciate being used, by you or anybody. I'm sorry that you've been hurt in your past, and I don't want to take advantage of a vulnerable person, but equally, I don't want *you* to take advantage of *me*. What you said in the elevator today made me determined not to sleep with you.'

'I'm not using you,' said Bernadette, trying to stop her breath coming in ragged gasps. 'It's mutual.'

'But it isn't,' he said, shaking his head with shining eyes. 'It isn't mutual at all. I want you more than I've ever wanted anything.'

'So have me!' she cried impatiently, wondering why most of her romantic encounters ended in debate rather than debauchery.

'I won't have you unless I can have all of you. Can you please get that idea lodged firmly into your pretty head?'

'But in the elevator, at your office – you said . . . you agreed that we would spend the night here.'

'I'm proving a point. Heavy-handedly, no doubt, but I am trying. You think all men are idiotic charlatans who can't resist you. But here I am, refusing to budge. My body is hurting with the denial, but I will not move. The reason you're so enamoured with Tim is because he won't let himself fall down the fucking rabbit hole. But I am a good man too!' he said, his voice a notch higher than usual. 'I am a good man. And I won't give in to the temptation. I want more. I admit it. Make of it what you will.'

'You're not a good man, you're horrible!' she cried, leaping from the bed and storming into the sitting room, banging the interconnecting door loudly behind her.

She threw herself down on an obliging sofa and indulged in a good, loud cry. She had been enjoying Radley very much, and the pain of interrupted titillation, the end of the frottage, had been an unexpected drop from heaven.

He had tricked her. He had purposely aroused her desire knowing that he was going to deny her satisfaction. He was pretending to be like Tim – he was trying to wrench feeling from her by force. She considered writing it all in her article to show the world the real nature of the 'reserved' Radley Blake. But her own involvement made it difficult. She would have to explain how she had demanded they spend the night together. How she had been prepared to sleep with him while on assignment. How Radley Blake had refused the Man Whisperer, while she lay whimpering with ardour beneath him. Glowering, she went in search of the minibar.

She woke the next morning in the large white bed, her clothes folded neatly on a nearby chair. Radley was lying next to her fully clothed, checking emails on his iPhone.

'What happened?' she said, sitting up slowly.

'I carried you through. You'd fallen asleep on the couch.'

'You undressed me?'

'I left your underwear on,' he said, casually.

'Did we . . . did we . . .?'

'My dear,' he said, slowly, 'if I wouldn't touch you when you were conscious and demanding it, is it likely that I would touch you when you were passed out and drooling?'

'You could be that kind of pervert,' she said. 'I wouldn't put it past you.'

'Nope,' he replied, cheerfully, 'I'm definitely into consensual acts of a sexual nature. I'd like to hear you panting my name.'

She took a pillow from behind her head and whacked him with it. 'I hate you. You've humiliated me.'

'Let's not exaggerate,' he said. 'I heard you crying last night and it very nearly broke my heart. But you have nothing to cry about. Last night I made it very clear that I wouldn't sleep with you until you gave me proof that you'd be willing to have some kind of meaningful relationship with me. I will not be used as a sexual toy to help you get over your feelings for Tim, although' – he shrugged with false modesty – 'I'm fairly certain you would forget about him pretty quickly.'

'Would not,' she interjected.

'Be that as it may, all that happened last night was that a man who desperately wanted you – who pushed himself to the very limit – refused to take you in search of higher pleasure. That's not really all that bad, is it? You should be flattered.'

'You should have taken what you could get,' she said, meanly. 'Cheap physical affection is all you're worth.'

He made no sound and she turned, scared, in case her words

had affected him too deeply. Words sometimes sprang from her lips before she could check them, her reputation as a bitch well earned from such outbursts. He smiled at her bravely. 'I guess I deserve that. It was a rotten trick.'

They flew back to Los Angeles in a haze of sadness and mistrust. Bernadette realised she should be taking more notes for her article, and the Dictaphones sat boldly on the table between them. They blundered through some simple question-and-answers, but neither heart was in it.

It was strange how arriving back at Radley's house seemed like coming home, and how despite the fact that it had only been twenty-four hours, their trip to the Bay Area had felt like a long journey.

'Elizabeth is coming over in a bit. Do you want to watch a movie until she gets here?' Radley asked. Bernadette was struck by the simple, domestic nature of the question.

'Okay,' she said. Her manner had been all gentle compliance since boarding the plane. She was tired, and confused in herself, and Radley seemed at a loss too.

She followed him down into the basement, neither of them having the energy to make a joke about sex dungeons or similar. The basement of Radley's house was not like the basement of a normal person's house. It was a full-on movie theatre, with thick black silk carpet, silk acoustic panels lining the walls, a tasteful LED starry ceiling, and specially designed velvet couches facing an enormous screen. Radley served her popcorn from a professional machine, and she helped herself to pick-and-mix from rows of glass candy jars behind a black lacquered bar.

They settled themselves on the middle couch, and Radley

started up the screen. He had chosen *Pretty Woman*. 'I know you've seen it before,' he said, 'but I don't know that we're in the mood for anything that requires much brainpower.'

Bernadette put her bag of sweets on the floor, tucked her legs up underneath her, and leaned against Radley with a confiding air that touched his heart. He put his arm around her. 'I'm sorry,' he whispered.

'It's okay,' she whispered back. 'I'm fine. I don't fancy you *that* much.'

They watched the familiar movie in companionable silence, with Bernadette snuggled under his arm. She tried to focus on the film, but the feel of Radley so close to her was distracting. She thought about the impressive Clarion Molecular buildings, and what an enormous undertaking the whole enterprise must be. Radley Blake *was* a genius after all.

But his behaviour towards her had been very ungentlemanly. He had premeditated a situation designed to hurt her, like a sadist would. She must not fall for him. The MP had been trauma enough, a romantic entanglement that had changed her whole personality and left her a wreck of her former self. Radley would guarantee her demise in entirety.

Just before the end of the film, a door at the back of the room opened, letting in annoying light, and Elizabeth's voice called out a hesitant 'Hello?'

Radley and Bernadette sprung apart as though caught doing something untoward. 'Am I interrupting?' continued Elizabeth, quite hopefully, as she peered into the darkened room.

'No,' said Radley, moving to greet her. 'We were just waiting for you.'

* * *

It had been Bernadette's idea to go to the Hollywood Bowl. She had demanded that Radley do something sophisticated, so that she could write about it in her article. 'Watching *Pretty Woman*,' she said, 'does not cut it.' So Radley had scored them three last-minute tickets to an Elgar concerto, and his chef had spent the afternoon preparing a picnic. Bernadette went home briefly to change her clothes, but was back at Radley's in good time.

Elizabeth was in excellent spirits as they arrived at the Bowl, streaming in with the large crowd. 'This is so cool!' she giggled. 'I don't do anything last-minute. I never even think about it. It must be wonderful to be like you, Bernie, so free and experimental.'

'I'd hardly call Elgar experimental,' said Bernadette, elbowing people aside as she made a beeline for their allotted seats.

Elizabeth carefully unpacked the picnic basket that Radley had been carrying, and Bernadette pulled out a Dictaphone, which she thrust under Radley's nose. 'Give me a quote about Elgar,' she demanded.

'I like Elgar. He was English, like you. And he was a self-made man, like me. Elgar could be our nineteenth-century love child.'

'Good enough,' said Bernadette, clicking off her Dictaphone, her work done for the evening.

She enjoyed the spectacle, the large outdoor amphitheatre alight with candles, the stirring music reminding her of home. Radley sat with an arm around each of them, and they shared a warm blanket, munching on dainty sandwiches and chugging ice-cold beer.

'We were thinking of doing a joint bachelor and bachelorette party,' Bernadette said suddenly. 'It was Radley's idea.'

Elizabeth looked beyond thrilled. 'That's an amazing idea!' she said. 'I'd love it.'

'We were thinking Vegas. You know, make it a traditional bender?'

'Vegas was Bernadette's idea,' said Radley, hastily. 'I wasn't sure you'd be up for that, but we could—'

'I want Vegas!' said Elizabeth, tugging at Radley's arm. 'I want whatever Bernadette thinks. I know you guys will make it so special. You're the best.' She rubbed her head affectionately against his shoulder, like a golden retriever.

'This had better be the party to end all parties,' Radley hissed to Bernadette.

'Just give me a budget and I'll see to it,' she said, under her breath.

'There is no budget,' he whispered. 'The limit is your imagination.'

Bernadette raised an eyebrow. 'I'll hold you to that.'

Bernadette dumped David, gently, a few days before the joint bachelor party. He was no longer necessary, a layer of skulduggery too deep, an added complication that was in no way forwarding her case with Tim. And he was annoying.

David did not react well to being discarded. He made it quite clear to Bernadette that she would never find another man who would treat her as well as he would. She thanked him politely for his concern, but said she was willing to take her chances.

She had seen very little of Tim in the run-up to the party, and had instead been spending copious amounts of time with Elizabeth, whose wide-eyed goodness was somewhat captivating. Bernadette hadn't realised that female company could be quite so satisfying.

Radley had kept his distance, allowing her uninterrupted time to write up her article. They had had a cordial email exchange during the arranging of the party, with Bernadette taking on the role of chief planner, and Radley that of financer.

The guests milled about on the tarmac by Radley's jet, waiting for their leader. Bernadette arrived fashionably late, dragging a rolling case behind her. She insisted they take the obligatory jet-setters' photograph, smiling in the LA sunshine, and managed to insert herself prominently between Tim and Radley. Radley's arm around her waist was heavy and comforting, and made her efforts to seize Tim around *his* waist all the more titillating.

The group was a select one. Lauren Paul, she of the Pinterest hair, seemed to be watching Bernadette with unusual engrossment; every time Bernadette looked across at her, Lauren would be staring back. Stephanie and Mason had arrived in colour-coordinating outfits, T-shirts in an overused shade of Tiffany turquoise, and ill-fitting jeans. Unforgivably, Stephanie was also wearing a fanny pack. Gina and Chris were physically more presentable, but seemed incapable of being civil to one another.

They boarded the jet, climbing the steep staircase into the cabin in a tight row, like animals boarding the Ark.

'This is something else!' breathed Mason, as he stepped aboard. Chris followed, and swore under his breath at the sight of the plane's interior. 'This thing must be a babe magnet!' he said, turning to stare in admiration at Radley.

'Yes, as far as women are concerned, billionaires are the new vampires, thanks to popular erotic fiction. *Fifty Shades* did wonders for my love life.' Radley smirked. 'I have a jet, therefore I am a misunderstood romantic.'

'You *are* a misunderstood romantic,' Bernadette muttered, pushing past him.

The short flight was a happy and riotous one. Bernadette was pleased to see Radley. She had spent the past weeks writing up her article, and reliving their eventful time together. She regarded him fondly, and this amatory tenderness was marred only by the occasional bout of sexual longing, which overtook her when she glanced at him, or when he stood too close. She swore to herself that she would not pretend to fall in love with him just so that he would kiss her, so that she could finally feel the sensation of his lips against hers. It was disconcerting, though, how much brain space he was taking up, compared to Tim. The ratio was strangely in Radley's favour, and Bernadette tried to consciously squash thoughts of Radley and focus on her true love.

Tim and Elizabeth sat enthroned at the centre of the group, sipping champagne. At one point Tim locked eyes with Bernadette and they both smiled quickly, acknowledging that they were searching for each other.

Lauren was fixated on Radley, laughing sycophantically whenever he said anything even remotely funny, and nodding in agreement at all other times. She kept eyeing Bernadette in an almost predatory fashion, noting every detail of her outfit and styling.

It was odd, Bernadette thought, that someone as sweet as Elizabeth could have such obnoxious friends. Perhaps diversity was the key to happiness, but it seemed to her that Elizabeth should be surrounded by Amish-type women, hard-working and make-up-free. Instead, she was comfortable with the likes of Lauren, who was frivolous and fake-tanned.

Bernadette was beginning to feel quite protective of Elizabeth, who had clearly been born lacking the necessary wiles. She came at the world with a sanguine belief in the goodness of all mankind that Bernadette had at first suspected of being fakery, but now believed to be the fault of a biochemical imbalance.

They had a bumpy landing in Vegas, where two stretch limos, one for the girls and one for the boys, were waiting to take them to the Bellagio.

'This is magic,' Elizabeth said to Bernadette as they climbed into the ridiculous vehicle.

'This is nothing,' Bernadette said, with a cat-like gleam in her eyes.

The six-bedroom penthouse was big enough to house the whole group. It was insanely luxurious, with all the obligatory Vegas paraphernalia: an overstocked minibar, several hot tubs, blackout blinds, and a twenty-four-hour butler service. There were gasps of appreciation as they were shown round. Bernadette had arranged for flowers to be strewn everywhere, and the florist had outdone himself. Long-stemmed roses of every hue sat in buckets and vases, and a rainbow of petals covered the beds and floated in filled bathtubs. The suite was an extravagant den of cream marble and pastel silks. Windows, and a terrace, looked out over the famous Bellagio fountains.

'I've never seen anything so amazing. Nurses' salaries do not cover shit like this,' exclaimed Gina, who worked with Elizabeth at Cedars-Sinai.

Some confusion arose over bedroom allocation. The rooms were of different sizes, and some were interconnecting. The largest room had been tactfully reserved for Tim and Elizabeth, but Elizabeth caused a stir by suggesting that she share with Bernadette. 'It's a bachelorette weekend after all,' she explained gently. 'I'd like to spend time with my girlfriends.'

'Oh goodie. A sleepover,' said Bernadette drily, although she wasn't entirely against the plan. In the end it was decided that Bernadette and Elizabeth should share the largest room, with its grand four-poster bed. Radley and Tim were to have the two smallest rooms, which were linked by a larger room for Lauren in the middle.

'I'd lock the adjoining door if I was you,' said Bernadette in a whisper to Radley. 'I bet Lauren's thrilled at the idea of easy night-time access.'

'Jealous?' asked Radley, grinning.

'Don't be stupid. I'm just warning you. As a friend.'

'There are too many doors in this place. It's like being in *Noises Off*.'

Bernadette had a faraway look in her eye. She was wondering if it would be possible to get Elizabeth very drunk at some point. If Elizabeth were to pass out in their room, Bernadette could escape to Tim's room and accost him. 'Quit wool-gathering and give us our instructions,' said Radley, stopping her mid-plot.

'Okay,' she said, snapping out of it. 'Everybody!' she called. 'We're here for two nights. Now, as a Vegas regular, I must advise you: as tempting as it is, do not go all out on the first night!' The group had gathered around Bernadette, laughing and at ease. She was quite enjoying being the centre of attention, and the way Elizabeth stared at her with such admiration was particularly flattering. 'The key is to pace ourselves. In fact, to avoid a *The Hangover*-type situation tonight . . . we're not going to be in Vegas at all!'

'What?' cried several members of her audience. 'But we've just got here! Where are we going?'

'It's a surprise,' she answered, shushing them all. 'Ladies, dress fancy, but bring something very warm . . .'

Two helicopters sat like fat black bumblebees, quivering and ready to ascend. The party swarmed to the gigantic machines, whipped to a frenzy of excitement by the whirring blades and the potential for serious adventure.

'Bernadette! Sit with me!' cried Elizabeth above the noise, taking Bernadette by the hand. It was childish for two grown women to hold hands like schoolgirls, but there was something so trusting and true in the gesture that Bernadette didn't shake her off.

'Okay,' she said grudgingly. She could afford to spend time on Elizabeth for one evening. The following night would be the moment to go all out for Tim, the right time to cause mischief and mayhem. This night was made for being the perfect bridesmaid.

Once everyone was seated, the helicopters rose straight up into the air – and they were off! It was a thrilling ride over the bright city. The lights were unlike anything else on the planet, a man-made borealis that glowed with the fullest colours of sin. Bernadette loved skylines, and neon, and looking down from great heights, and even though the sun had still not set, the effect was such that it might have been the dead of night.

Elizabeth was smiling like a child with ice cream, her enjoyment so full-bodied and unsullied that it was envy-making. Bernadette wished for the peace of mind that allowed such happiness.

The flight was all too quick, and when the Grand Canyon came in sight, Elizabeth cried out, 'I knew it!' – a fifth-grader with perfect marks on a test. They landed at the top of a sheer canyon face, in a feat of aerial manoeuvring that made even fearless Bernadette pale slightly. The pilots cut the engines, and the whirring noise that had become so familiar lessened suddenly. Everyone removed earphones and undid seat belts in merry uproar. They were escorted safely beyond the reach of the propeller blades, and gathered at a scenic point to admire the view. Only Lauren hung back, looking green. 'I'm afraid of heights!' she said, quavering.

'What do you mean, you're afraid of heights? You were just in a helicopter,' pointed out Bernadette crossly.

'I'm not afraid of *flying*, I'm afraid of *heights*. It's a completely different phobia,' said Lauren, starting to get hysterical.

'Well I don't see how it can be a real phobia if you're fine to go up high in a helicopter. It just doesn't make logical sense. You're going to ruin the whole evening,' Bernadette said. 'Don't be an idiot.'

Radley and the others had approached. 'She says she's afraid of heights!' Bernadette said sarcastically, appealing to the group for support.

'Well if she says she is, I'm sure she is,' Radley said in a mild tone, giving Bernadette a stern look. He went and took Lauren gently by the arm, leading her away from the canyon edge.

'Don't be upset, sweet girl,' whispered Elizabeth, putting her arm around Bernadette's waist. 'This is the best surprise. I love it! Nothing could ruin it.'

'People can ruin anything,' Bernadette replied, scowling at Lauren's back.

'I know you don't mean that,' said Elizabeth, softly.

Radley appeared to have magically calmed Lauren, and the two of them came back to the group all smiles. 'Lauren is going to be a good sport,' Radley said, beaming round. 'She's going to stick with me and we'll face the fear together.'

'Isn't that convenient?' muttered Bernadette. Elizabeth heard her and giggled.

'Radley wouldn't be interested in Lauren in a million years,' she whispered. 'And trust me, she wouldn't be into him either. She's—'

'Don't you believe it,' said Bernadette maliciously, cutting her off. She broke into a grin when she thought of how Lauren would react to their dinner reservation. On cue, a couple of guides popped up from a hidden pathway down the canyon side.

'Hi!' said Bernadette, moving to meet them with a wide smile. 'Are you ready?'

The older of the two nodded. 'Sure, we're here to show you around. Ladies and gents!' He addressed them all. 'If y'all just step back in the helicopters, it's only a short hop to your next stop.'

The friends hurriedly snapped pictures of the amazing view, with the sun setting in transcendent fashion over orange rocks. 'What kind of work are they doing down there?' asked Chris, pointing to a crane far below on the valley floor.

'Follow me to the helicopter, and I'll show you,' said the older guide, pointing his thumb at the patient machines.

There was a scramble to get back in the transport, everyone ducking low, wary of the moving air only a few feet above. 'Bernadette's fucking magical mystery tour,' said Lauren, ungenerously, as they took off.

The helicopters dropped them right down on the canyon floor, about a mile away from the forty-metre crane Chris had spotted. The guests were taking guesses as to what could be in store. 'If it's bungee jumping, you can fuck off,' Lauren said loudly.

'It's not bungee jumping,' Radley soothed her.

'How do you know?'

'Because I helped Bernadette arrange this,' he said. The statement seemed to have a mollifying effect on Lauren, who was observed to complain less from that point on.

Suddenly Gina shrieked, 'Donkeys! Oh my God, no way!'

They all turned towards where a group of gentle-tempered donkeys stood, completely unperturbed by the helicopters and the screeching humans. They were saddled and ready to mount. Bernadette confidently followed the two guides, and climbed effortlessly on to the nearest beast.

'Are you insane?' Gina asked. 'Why the hell didn't you tell us to wear sensible shoes, at least? Or pants? I'm in a short skirt here.'

Bernadette shrugged, looking down from her mount as if she were Lady Godiva on a white stallion. 'So am I. What else would you wear to ride a mule down the Grand Canyon?' Gina blinked, nonplussed, but Lauren pushed forward, eager to prove herself.

'Easy!' she declared, allowing the younger guide to help her mount. Elizabeth followed suit, giggling uncontrollably, and everyone else did likewise.

'Too late to turn back now,' said Mason.

The mules ambled along at an easy pace, allowing the humans to admire the towering canyon walls in the fading light.

'Bernie, this is already an unforgettable experience,' said Tim, pulling his donkey next to hers. She smiled at him, and noted that every physical marvel, every wonder of the natural world, was contained in his face alone.

'I just want Lizzie to have a good time,' she said, playing her part to perfection.

Tim looked at her gratefully. 'I can't tell you how happy that makes me. You're great, Bernie. No one but you could have thought of something like this. You're crazy! *It's* crazy . . . but it's great.'

Bernadette felt the familiar stirring of concern. It was very difficult to predict the reaction of other human beings. Why did people so often call her crazy? She didn't feel crazy at all.

Tim noticed her reverie, and, giving her a nod and a smile, trotted his animal forward. Radley replaced him, looking like an old-time cowboy.

'Sometimes I feel like the last bastion of sanity on earth,' Bernadette said glumly.

'And you call me a narcissist!'

'You're too big for that poor creature,' Bernadette said, ignoring him and pointing to his donkey. 'Your vast weight is squashing him. Look how he's struggling! He can hardly breathe.'

'Why do you feel like the last sane person on earth?'

'Because everything inside my head makes so much sense. I'm very logical. I reason from first principles. And yet people call me crazy!'

'Hmm, tricky,' said Radley, smiling at her affectionately. 'Would it help if I told you that right now, you are at your most attractive? Speculative, and grumpy, and riding that donkey like it was nothing at all.'

'No, that wouldn't help,' she replied. 'That would just put

you firmly with the insane masses.' She stole a glance at him from her tawny eyes, which were turning golden to match the sunset. 'I thought we had got away from all that.'

'Away from me wanting you? Never. Look at this place, isn't it romantic?'

'*It* is romantic, yes, but *we* are not,' and tapping her mule smartly in the sides, she trotted ahead to catch up with Tim. They were fast approaching the looming crane, and the group was straining its collective neck to see what lay ahead.

'Tim!' called Bernadette as she jogged alongside him. 'Do you like the crane?'

'It's pretty big,' he admitted. 'What is it?'

'It's a surprise!'

'How did you come up with all this? It isn't even your kind of thing, is it? Trekking across canyons and the like?'

'Oh no, it is absolutely my kind of thing! I love trekking, and hiking, and camping, and all that stuff. Really,' she lied, 'I'm quite outdoorsy. What makes you think I'm not?'

'Because of the way you look right now,' said Tim, laughing his rare, clear laugh. She laughed with him, despite being a little hurt.

When they were within five hundred metres of the base of the crane, the canyon round about them suddenly lit up in riotous colour, a spectacular display that threw reds and golds and oranges up the side of the crevasse, showcasing rock features and making it seem daylight again. It was like nothing they had ever seen, and the whole group, guides included, was awestruck and silent. The unlit part of the landscape was made darker, and it was as if they existed within a bubble of beauty, surrounded on all sides by an impenetrable inky blackness.

'Oh Radley,' Elizabeth whispered after she had looked her fill. 'This must have cost a fortune.'

'Never mind all that,' said Radley. 'It was Bernadette's doing.'

'Thank you to both of you for making it possible.'

'You're a great woman, Lizzie,' said Radley, in his softest voice.

The guides helped the group to dismount, and then rounded up the mules, who had played their part for the evening and done it well: not one of them had spooked or bolted. The nine human friends moved toward the giant crane, trying to comprehend what they were seeing. A dining table stood there laden with cutlery and glassware, the scarlet tablecloth a jaunty, lipstick-like slash of cheer.

'Here's the deal,' said Bernadette, turning to them all and grinning. 'We sit down, we get strapped in, and that crane,' she waved up above her, 'winches that table,' she pointed to the scarlet slash, 'high up above the canyon floor. And that is where we dine.' Elizabeth screamed with excitement and threw her arms around Tim's neck.

'Actually, that's pretty cool,' said Mason, looking to Stephanie for approval. Stephanie nodded her assent.

'No. Fucking. Way,' said Lauren, gazing up at the crane in terror. 'There is no way you're getting me up on that thing. Are you crazy? Didn't you think to check if any of us had a fear of heights?'

'No, I did not,' said Bernadette, bristling. 'I imagined that if you'd made the plane ride here at thirty-five thousand feet, and the helicopter tour over Vegas, you would be able to handle a forty-foot dinner reservation.'

'I'm sure there's provision for you to eat down here,' said

Radley smoothly, draping a large arm around Lauren's shoulders. 'You'll still be able to appreciate the beauty of the lit canyon from ground level.'

Lauren looked annoyed, as everyone else seemed relieved with this solution. 'Well that's going to be a great night for *me*,' she spat. 'Alone at the bottom of the Grand Canyon.'

'You could always try coming up with us first, and see if you like it,' Radley continued artlessly. 'Why don't you try sitting by me?'

Noting that her audience's patience was wearing thin, Lauren allowed herself to be speedily cajoled. Radley took her to inspect the chairs and the harnesses.

'This is so unlike Radley,' said Elizabeth, quietly, to Bernadette. 'He doesn't suffer fools gladly. Normally he would leave Lauren alone. I think this must be for your benefit. You're softening him.'

'It's nothing to do with me,' said Bernadette. 'I've never seen him be anything other than completely attentive. He's particularly kind to the weak, I've noticed.'

Elizabeth laughed. 'That explains why he's so good to me, then.'

Bernadette found herself putting protective arms around Elizabeth and hugging her tightly. 'Don't say you're weak. You're not. You're so much stronger than Lauren, or those other women.' She was not given to impulsive hugging, and she wondered at herself. But she disliked hearing Elizabeth talk nonsense, disliked the idea that she would have a low opinion of herself when, clearly, she was a being far superior to her awful contemporaries. Bernadette subscribed to the philosophy that the more innocent the victim, the more heinous the crime.

And Elizabeth was so innocent and natural, it seemed any crime against her was a truly monstrous thing.

The process of being harnessed to a chair bolted to a table and winched high into the night sky was a unique one. Bernadette enjoyed the giddying feeling, the rush of blood to body parts, and the quick tattoo of her heart. Three chefs on a platform in the middle of the table began serving appetisers even before the contraption moved upwards. Lauren, who was sitting next to Radley, could be heard saying loudly, 'Bernadette has a theatrical bent, hasn't she? Knows how to put on a show!'

Chris smiled across at Bernadette. 'This whole thing is completely crazy, but really cool. It's eccentric, you know. You're an English eccentric! The helicopters and the donkeys and the whole levitating table thing. Feel sorry for your boyfriend; you must be exhausting!' He meant it good-naturedly, but Bernadette, not noted for her social graces, was unable to let it pass.

'I don't have a boyfriend, but thank you so much for bringing that up.'

'Chris!' moaned Gina. 'You douche. You're so insensitive! Obviously she doesn't have a boyfriend. Do you see one here? She's *alone*.' The couple maintained a continuous squabble as the table was lifted higher, whilst Bernadette kept her lips pressed firmly together, a wounded martyr.

The canyon floor dropping away below looked like it was awash with flame, as though an artist had taken watercolour paints and tried his hand at a great inferno. 'I don't think I can do this!' Lauren cried, clutching Radley's hand. 'What if something goes wrong? What if there's a screw loose?'

'*You've* got a screw loose,' muttered Bernadette to herself. But finally they were up and settled, and Lauren seemed to have calmed down. The warm night air puffed gently past them, and the table did not budge. They dined grandly in the French style: a crisp salad, excellent sole, *blanquette de veau*, a fruit tart, and a large selection of cheeses, all accompanied by superb wines. As they were finishing, drinking strong coffee and talking loudly, an incredible pyrotechnic display lit up the air above them, causing gasps of delight. It looked as though the sky were raining coloured stars all around them.

'Who's a clever girl?' said Radley, turning to smile at Bernadette.

She smiled back at him and shrugged. 'Thanks for forking out all the cash.'

'It was money well spent,' he replied, turning to look at Elizabeth, who was laughing, the colours of the night sky reflected on her shining face.

The next day was dedicated to spa treatments for the girls and a trip to the gun range for the boys. 'Sweeping gender generalisation,' said Lauren to Bernadette. 'I would have thought *you* would have known better.'

'What do you mean?' asked Bernadette suspiciously.

'The guys get sent to the gun range while we sit around and have manicures? Really? Wouldn't you rather be there pumping lead with the menfolk?'

'No,' said Bernadette. 'Absolutely not. I abhor violence.' She looked around the spa at the three other women. Elizabeth was having a shoulder massage whilst someone painted her toenails, and Gina and Stephanie were deeply engrossed in conversation over their respective manicurists.

'Ladies,' said Bernadette, loudly, 'would any of you have preferred to go to the gun range?'

They looked up at her blankly. Gina shook her head firmly and said, 'No, duh,' before returning to her conversation.

'I think I called it correctly,' said Bernadette, turning to Lauren with a supercilious smirk.

'I just didn't think *you* would be so generic,' said Lauren, emphasising some meaning of her own.

The group re-formed, both genders, for lunch at a poolside cabana. The dynamic had been established the previous evening, and conversation was quick and littered with easy laughter. They drank a lot of white wine. Radley looked dashing in an open-necked white shirt and taupe slacks. Bernadette felt bubble-headed and hot.

'A toast,' said Radley, as they neared the end of lunch. 'I'd like to make a toast to my darling Elizabeth.'

'Whoop whoop!' cried Chris, who was immediately silenced by a stern look from his wife.

'Elizabeth,' Radley continued, addressing her with a raised glass, 'it is clear to anyone who knows you what an incredibly unusual human being you are. You represent everything I most admire—'

'Rad!' Elizabeth interrupted, laughing and blushing to the roots of her hair. 'Cut it out!'

'I'm serious, Lizzie. Your empathy and sobriety are unsurpassed. Your goodness of heart is almost unbelievable. It is your quiet guidance that has kept me safe all these years, my dear, and I thank you sincerely from the bottom of my heart. And now you are to be married, and I don't think I can imagine any person better suited to the institution than you—'

'Okay, okay,' cut in Bernadette, unable to cope any longer. 'I guess I'd better say something good about Tim too. A wedding isn't just about the bride, you know!' she said, turning and hiccoughing in Radley's direction.

'Thank you,' whispered Elizabeth, visibly grateful to Bernadette for coming to her rescue and saving her from too much unwanted attention. Radley, however, glowered menacingly, unconvinced that her motive was quite so selfless.

'Tim,' Bernadette went on, undeterred by Radley's dark looks, 'Tim, Tim, Tim. What can I say?'

Tim began to look a little apprehensive. 'Bernie, you've had quite a bit of wine there. You don't have to say anything . . .'

'No, no. I *want* to.'

'Okay.' He gulped nervously.

'Tim. You are great. That's it, really . . . You'd think I'd be more eloquent, given what I do – but I'm not. That's it. You're great. So great that words don't work for me any more. I just look at you, and I'm speechless.'

Stephanie giggled. Mason giggled too. Bernadette bowed solemnly and sat down. 'Speechless!' she added, for emphasis.

'That's quite enough of that,' said Radley, removing Bernadette's wine glass from her hand as she tried to take a swig.

'Thank you,' said Elizabeth, leaning over to speak quietly to Bernadette. 'You're so sweet. I hate it when everyone's looking at me – and I know Tim can feel a bit overwhelmed by all this wedding chat. And Rad can be intense!'

Bernadette nodded sagely. 'You're welcome.'

It was decided that after lunch they should retire to the penthouse and rest, in preparation for the long night ahead. A languor had overtaken the whole party due to the copious wine and the oppressive heat of the midday sun, and they retreated with relief to the joys of the air-conditioned mega-suite. Stephanie and Mason made their way out to the hot tub on the terrace, Mason grumbling that he would rather have gone to have a lie-down and watch the golf. Gina and Chris soon joined them, and the two couples splashed and frolicked at an affable low tempo, sipping from rum cocktails.

Elizabeth went to have a nap, and Bernadette decided to do likewise. The two of them slipped out of their dresses to lie on the queen-sized bed in their underwear, Bernadette quietly rejoicing at her own flat stomach and unlined thighs.

'Can I ask you something personal?' Elizabeth murmured.

'All right,' said Bernadette, cautiously.

'Why don't you love Radley?'

Bernadette stiffened at the question, and Elizabeth quickly continued, 'I'm sorry, sweet girl, I don't want to push you. But I just find it so hard to understand.'

'Radley isn't in love with *me*,' said Bernadette, choosing her words carefully, 'so it's a somewhat moot point.'

'He *is* in love with you!'

'No, he *thinks* he's in love with me. There's a difference. Trust me, I know. Everyone thinks they love me, at first.'

'Is that the only thing holding you back?'

'No. But I can't tell you the other thing, so please don't ask me.'

'Of course,' said Elizabeth, thoughtfully. 'I didn't mean to upset you. I just care for you both, very much.'

'I know.'

Elizabeth tactfully turned on her side, and within a very short time she was asleep, dreaming peacefully. Bernadette lay restlessly on the large bed, her legs tangled in the sheets and her brain busy with hope and speculation. It was impossible to sleep after all; her mind would not allow it, despite the heat and the soporific effect of the alcohol.

She dressed quietly, and tiptoed round the bed to stare down at Elizabeth's face. She looked so peaceful and pretty in this dim, artificial environment, with the blush of sleep upon her and the air-conditioning blowing strands of her hair back from her face.

Bernadette exited the bedroom, with no definite plan, although a vague sense that she might seek out Radley. She padded softly across the marble floor into the main living area, but stopped short when she saw Tim, sitting alone.

'Hi,' she said.

'Hi.' He looked distracted.

'Anything wrong?'

He looked around. The two playful couples were still in the hot tub; they could be seen through the sliding glass doors, the splashing at a minimum but the drinking still going strong. Lauren and Radley were nowhere in sight.

'Do you want to take a walk?' Tim asked.

'Sure,' she said, surprised.

Tim had a key and Bernadette said she didn't need to fetch anything, so they set off immediately, exiting the suite without telling anyone where they were headed.

Bernadette could tell something was afoot, and she kept pace with Tim in silence, not daring to break the spell that allowed her this unexpected tête-à-tête. They went down to the lobby and snaked through the gaming machines, before emerging into the Vegas heat. Tim found a bench by the lake and sat down.

Bernadette hovered for a moment, and then decided to sit next to him.

'Are you okay?' she asked.

'I'm just . . . I'm having doubts.'

Bernadette's heart leapt into her throat. 'Doubts about the wedding?' she asked, trying to keep her voice neutral.

'I guess. I mean, nothing too serious.' He smiled ruefully. 'Nothing catastrophic. I just . . . Something doesn't feel right.'

Bernadette was paralysed with terror. She knew exactly what to do in theory: she should lean in now and kiss him. It would be the most natural thing in the world, and she could tell it would not be unwelcome. But she couldn't do it.

'I'm sorry, I know I shouldn't be saying this – to you of all people!' he continued.

'I think you've chosen to tell me precisely because it's me,' she said softly.

He looked at her, his clear blue eyes framed by the palest lashes, his glasses gleaming in the sun. 'You're right,' he said. 'I should have known better than to try and pull one over on you, the Man Whisperer! Something just doesn't feel right . . . and it was you I wanted to tell.'

'Why?'

'That part I don't know. I'm sorry, Bernie. I'm a royal fuck-up.'

'You're not a fuck-up,' she said, cautiously reaching for his hand. 'You haven't done anything . . . yet . . .'

She let the last word trail into nothingness, dancing with possibility around them. He didn't correct her, nor did he try to pull his hand away. His hand was big and cool despite the heat. His long fingers grasped hers and held on tightly.

223

'I don't know what to say,' Bernadette whispered.

He turned to her almost accusingly. 'I thought you would. I thought you would know,' and then he stopped himself, inhaling quickly. 'I'm sorry! This is so wrong of me.'

She realised that he was floundering, too scared to initiate anything irrevocable. He wanted her to take the lead. Usually these things came so easily to her, but she felt as though her body and brain were being controlled by some greater force. 'You don't have to make any quick decisions,' she cooed, as if talking to a frightened horse. 'You've not said anything wrong, or done anything wrong. Everyone gets nervous before their wedding.'

'Yes,' he said, dejectedly.

She knew he was disappointed. He had given her enough of an opening, and had expected her to pounce immediately. But she could not. 'This isn't the time—' she continued.

'I know!' he interjected. 'I know! Shit. I'm sorry. I don't know what I'm doing.' He stood, his shoes scuffing gently on the pink gravel path, 'I knew you wouldn't really want me. Not when it came down to it.' He smiled and shrugged, hurt with a hint of anger.

Bernadette was nearly speechless. 'But it's *you*,' she said. 'Of course I want you!'

Tim looked hard at her, blinking in the sunlight, and then turned and walked away, back to the hotel, a mirage on the near horizon. She couldn't follow him. Instead she stared out across the artificial lake, wondering what unseen force had suddenly prevented her from taking what she wanted.

At eight o'clock that evening, the group was assembled and ready to go. The guys looked handsome, and the women looked like exaggerated versions of themselves, with outlined eyes, coloured lips, and clothes designed to entice. They ate at the hotel restaurant and Bernadette gorged herself on steak and red wine, careful always to avoid Tim's eye. For his part, Tim was being overly attentive to Elizabeth, who basked in his affection like a cat in the sun.

Radley was seated next to Bernadette, and at a noisy moment he shifted so his hand was on her bare knee. She gasped at the contact. He leant in close to her and whispered, 'Doesn't Vegas inspire you to be your very naughtiest self?'

'Not at all. In fact, quite the contrary. I seem to be most reserved in Vegas.' She smiled a secret smile, and Radley looked at her thoughtfully, removing his hand.

It was at the nightclub, where she danced with abandon, her senses dulled by too much drink, her balance affected by absurd high heels, where she tottered and swayed, and laughed without reason, that Bernadette discovered the true reason for Lauren's animosity.

Lauren had been hanging off Radley for most of the evening, but Bernadette had become accustomed to the sight and wasn't rushing to his rescue. When she excused herself from the group and headed to the restroom, Lauren followed her, and, catching up, slyly slipped her hand into Bernadette's.

'We're not friends,' said Bernadette, looking to pull her hand away, but Lauren was surprisingly strong, and wouldn't let go. Bernadette was stopped from further reaction by Lauren suddenly kissing her full on the mouth. It was a fine kiss, as kisses go, but Bernadette was too confused to register much of it.

'God, you're hot,' Lauren breathed, pulling back to look Bernadette in the eye.

Bernadette couldn't respond, and Lauren laughed, moving to kiss her again. Bernadette was more sensible of the experience the second time round, and noted Lauren's firm, thin lips and slender jaw.

'I thought you wanted Radley. You can't take your eyes off him. Or your hands,' she said, suspiciously.

'Radley Blake is a fucking genius! He's super fucking famous! Of course I can't stop staring at him. Why, are you jealous? It's you I want to fuck.' Lauren went to kiss her again, but Bernadette put up a warning hand.

'I'm not attracted to you.'

'You're not gay? But Radley said you were bored with guys.'

'I *am* bored with guys, but that doesn't mean I'm attracted to you.' She couldn't help adding, 'You're not my type.'

'What, a woman?' asked Lauren.

'A bitch,' clarified Bernadette.

Once the group had tired of the club, in the early hours, a cab dropped them back at the hotel in time for one of the quarter-hour lake shows, with dozens of dancing fountains slipping across the water in an impressive aquatic display.

'Oh look!' cried Bernadette. 'It's beautiful!'

They all ran to the railings and leaned over, enjoying the lights and the music and the falling water. But looking was not enough for Bernadette. Before anyone could guess what she was about, she'd climbed over the railing, skidded down a garden slope and leapt into the lake. She gasped as the water hit her. It came up to her knees and was colder than she had expected. She began to wade further out towards the fountains.

Her friends left behind were speechless. The wider crowd of strangers gathered to watch the fountain show had spotted her and were cheering her on. Camera flashes exploded around them, and Bernadette turned to wave.

'That chick is *insane*,' said Mason, shaking his head, dumbfounded.

'Totally,' added Lauren bitterly.

Within seconds, hotel security – two guys in dark jackets with 'Security' emblazoned across the back – was upon them. 'Is that lady a friend of yours?' asked the leaner of the two guards. 'She belong to one of you?'

'Yes,' said Radley. 'She's mine. If you'd be so kind as to hold on one moment, I'll go and get her,' and with that, he too hopped over the railing. The security officer sighed a heavy sigh.

Radley slid nimbly down the slope in three bounds, and jumped into the water. 'Fuck! It's cold!' he exclaimed. Bernadette turned at the splash and stood still, allowing him to wade out to her.

'It isn't working, you know,' said Radley as he got close. 'This kind of display. Making a spectacle of yourself. It isn't Tim's kind of thing at all.'

As he reached her, he noticed she was shivering. He wrapped his arms around her and pulled her against his warm body. The watching crowd cheered.

'You're turning him off, if anything,' Radley continued, 'And you drink too much, do you know that?'

Bernadette looked up at the sky and then kissed his chin affectionately. 'The part about the drinking is probably true,' she acknowledged. 'Given my current predicament. The cold

227

water sobered me up pretty fast, but it seemed like such a good idea. Romantic, you know?'

'*I'm* the man around here that enjoys theatrics. But it isn't me you're trying to impress, is it?'

'No,' she said, staring deep into his eyes. 'It isn't.'

8

Bernadette had a special relationship with New York City. She loved the romance of the place. New York was a crossroads for the world, an ever-changing metropolis with the weight of history behind it. It was the American city she found most comparable to London, and in that sense it was home. Unlike LA – the sprawling sunny suburb of a city – New York was a proper urban land, with an unrivalled cityscape of jagged modern spires and glass-and-steel powerhouses. Its lights were beacons, the shapes of the tall buildings against the night sky could be observed by all five senses, and the tap of her heels on the sidewalk marked her as the owner of it all. It was London, but more. It screamed louder, smelt stronger and felt hotter. The extremes of temperature and of mindset matched her own mercurial personality. And the city's acceptance of neurosis – with an ever-present Woody Allen voice-over – made it the only place in the world she felt sane. Her Irish blood was stirred by the thought of her Celtic ancestors coming ashore here, and her green eyes shone brighter in the New York sun.

She wasn't even nervous about her second speaking engagement as the Man Whisperer. In fact, nothing could dim her ebullient joy, because finally Tim was taking charge and had admitted his true feelings.

A week after the Vegas trip, he had texted her an apology: *I'm sorry for putting you in that position.*

I loved being put in that position, she had replied. *I want you to put me in every position. I do want you.*

New York, was his response. *We should talk in New York.*

We should do more than talk . . . she flirted.

And then the texts had come fast: *Okay. We can. I'll arrive Friday. 4 p.m.*

I'll be waiting.

Okay.

I can't wait to see you. I want you so badly.

I want you too, Bernadette.

And that was that. Her life had changed with one text. Suddenly everything seemed possible. It would be hard for Elizabeth, of course, and Bernadette was quickly filled with an overwhelmingly charitable feeling towards the other woman. They would make sure Elizabeth was hurt as little as possible. They'd look after her, always. It would be easy for her to find a good man, because she was a good woman. Elizabeth would have a happy future too, even if Bernadette had to engineer one somehow.

It was easy to imagine a happy future for Elizabeth in the removed environment of New York City. New York existed only to serve as the backdrop to the culmination of Bernadette's romantic life. Tim would kiss her (and more) in New York. It was the city of their weekend getaway, their *ville de l'amour*, the scene of many previous such crimes, with every possible monument to romance.

She had been in the city a day and was already imbued with the adventurous spirit of it. Safely ensconced at the Crosby Street Hotel, she ventured out alone in the afternoon heat with no particular idea or intent. She wandered pavements, dodged bustling bodies and looked up a lot. It was nice to have an extra dimension filled once more. In LA she had grown accustomed to everything being low-level and earthquake-proof. In New York, buildings towered above her and bore down upon her, threatening to block out the sky. It seemed as if the whole world was man-made, and nature was an afterthought on the outskirts of vision and memory.

She passed hot-dog stands and retail stalls, from where Radley Blake's face, multiplied a hundred times, stared at her with calm indifference. *Squire* magazine had published her article on Radley, and his face was on the cover. The newsstands were plastered with him and his handsomeness. She smiled to see him there, and thought it strange how familiar he was to her now, like an old friend.

The article had garnered much interest, mostly about the man himself, who was a new and fascinating character to the wider public, a man of mystery, rare in these degenerate, tell-all times.

But some opinion had also been expressed on Bernadette's writing. One columnist pointed out that Radley Blake was the only man Bernadette had ever been sympathetic to and seemed to actually like, and there was much noise in the blogosphere speculating on a romantic relationship between the two. Bernadette didn't care. She believed her piece to be a just and unbiased account of a rather remarkable man, a man not only incredibly successful in his professional and academic life, but on balance, a *good* human being. It was much harder to be good than successful, and she wanted to laud him for this. 'Gushing', one snide reader had called it, in the comments section. Bernadette had never before been accused of gushing, and she was revolted by the word. Gushy girls were the lowest of the low.

Bernadette had been honest in her reporting, even going so far as to admit that the Hollywood Bowl had been her idea, and that Blake would have been happier watching a movie at home with friends. She had carefully researched the science behind Clarion Molecular (aided by the sweet Sam, who connected her with all the right people), and had admitted some disparity between the way Radley was described by friends and colleagues, and the way she experienced him. As one particularly bitter rival commented:

The Man Whisperer is so enamoured with her own sway over the unenviable Radley Blake that she dedicates time to detailing the way he speaks to her *as opposed to anyone else; apparently he's funnier, more relaxed and more charming in her company – and doesn't she delight in the difference! It turns out the way to secure a good write-up from the lady journalist is to propose marriage in a public place. A step* this *reporter is not willing to take!*

Radley had contacted Bernadette as soon as the article was published. She hadn't let him read it beforehand, and he hadn't asked to see it, but when the magazine came out, he sent her a text – *You do love me after all!* – to which she didn't reply. Undeterred, he followed it up with *I'm flattered, to be sure* and *You have no idea what this has done for my personal life* – suddenly *I'm popular!* and finally, *Can we meet to discuss your excellent writing?*

We can't meet right now, she had texted back. *I'm in New York to do more whispering.*

The whisper that was heard across the world! he texted jovially.

She hadn't replied. She felt she had done more than enough for Radley Blake, had compromised her whole writing style, in fact, and therefore could put off his romantic ministrations without guilt. She was determined to thoroughly enjoy her time in New York, remorse-free, without reference to Radley, or Elizabeth, or anyone else who might make her feel bad. The only slight hiccough was that Rose was arriving that evening. It had been arranged a while ago, when the New York tour date had been confirmed. London to New York was a much easier flight than London to LA, and so it seemed logical that they should combine business with pleasure. Rose was coming to hear Bernadette speak, and then they were planning to spend a couple of days touring the city, enjoying each other's company.

It was unfortunate, but it couldn't be helped. Bernadette was usually overjoyed at the thought of seeing Rose, but in this instance, with the awkward timing – a sin being committed in such close proximity to her moral mother – she felt somewhat uneasy.

She had arranged for a car to collect Rose from JFK, and was planning on calling her and feigning tiredness that evening. Because Tim was due at her hotel room at 4 p.m.! Heavens above!

She absent-mindedly purchased another copy of *Squire* from

a friendly vendor (she already had five of this issue at home), and stopped to flick through it, sitting on a park bench. The photos of Radley that accompanied the article were particularly flattering. She hadn't been present for the shoot, but had heard from a third party that he had been utterly obliging, quiet and efficient. The results were very pleasing. His unusually strong features looked ridiculously symmetrical, almost as if there had been too much Photoshop involved – although Bernadette knew for a fact that very little retouching had been required. His dark eyes challenged the reader to judge him, and the trademark smirk, as enigmatic as the *Mona Lisa*'s, seemed like a finger-up to the whole process. She was so absorbed that she lost track of time, and was only made aware of a sense of urgency when her cell buzzed with a text message at 3.10.

It was from Radley, and it said, *I'm in New York.*

Bernadette groaned as she gathered herself and hurried hotel-wards. It was just like him to muscle in unwanted at a crucial moment. Why couldn't he learn to take no for an answer? She texted back as she walked briskly, *I don't want to see you.*

Tough. Let me at you, he pinged back immediately.

I'll see you at the talk. 6 p.m. tomorrow @ the Plaza. Not before.

I will find you. Today.

Bernadette laughed. Good luck, in a city of eight million people, she thought.

When she arrived back in her room, she made quick preparations for Tim, drawing the curtains, and scattering rose petals across the bed and on the floor. Then she took a hasty shower. She was already smooth thanks to earlier depilatory efforts, but she rubbed her skin raw with a sugar scrub to further the cause. Once her body had been attended to, she washed her hair with sweet strawberry shampoo. She smelt a bit like a giant gummy drop once she was finished, but not too stripper-ish.

She lathered on coconut oil, adding a tropical fragrance layer on top of the sickly sugar products. Then she blew out her hair, going for a tousled beachy look rather than pin-up perfection, as she simply didn't have time to construct the latter. Make-up was easy: soft eyeliner, a swipe of grey shadow, a flick of pink blush and a thorough application of jet-black mascara. Her lips were cherry red of their own accord, so she slathered them with Vaseline and let them be. Her outfit was stupendous, La Perla's finest: a bustier and garter belt set in black silk, with the sheerest lace-topped stockings. She slipped into a pair of sky-high YSLs and managed to light the last candle just as there came a knock on the door. It was exactly 4 p.m.

Oh Tim, Tim! she thought, as she rushed to answer, her heart bursting with love and anticipation. He was always meant to be hers, and she had earned him, there was no doubt about that. Her love had been tested beyond human endurance and she had survived. She still preferred him above every human being she had ever met. He was still her childhood dream, the only man to even come close to it.

She opened the door slowly, allowing one stockinged leg to creep round the frame and give him a taste of things to come. Then she pulled it wider – to reveal Radley and Elizabeth staring at her in consternation.

Bernadette gasped, rendered speechless and utterly terrified. She didn't understand how Radley had managed to find her, nor did she know why he had brought Elizabeth with him. The only thing she could think about was that Tim would arrive at any moment, and they would be caught red-handed. She didn't move.

Radley hustled her back inside the room, dragging Elizabeth in with them, and shut the door. Elizabeth stared in confusion at the rose petals, her face bathed in flattering candlelight. The three of them looked at each other in the half-darkness. Bernadette couldn't speak. She could barely breathe.

'Darling,' said Radley, moving to her and kissing her hand, 'I'm sorry. When I texted, I should have told you I would have Lizzie with me.'

The signs of dawning comprehension on Elizabeth's face were not matched on Bernadette's.

'Look,' continued Radley, 'you've even set out our magazine. How sweet.' He pointed to the copy of *Squire* thrown down on a nearby coffee table. The two women looked at it. Elizabeth blushed and giggled.

'Oh my God, I didn't know!' she said. 'I wouldn't have come up.' She put an arm around Bernadette, and an arm around Radley, and pulled them both into a giant hug. 'You guys!' she laughed. 'You didn't say anything!'

'There's nothing really to tell, as yet,' said Radley truthfully.

Bernadette sat down heavily on a sofa. 'Where's T—' she began, but Radley cut her off.

'I've made reservations for the three of us at Blue Hill tonight.'

'For three?' asked Bernadette, springing back up to a standing position, her head spinning.

'It's great food. They have their own farm,' Radley continued. 'It's a shame Tim couldn't make it out of LA, but now I have my two favourite ladies to myself.'

Bernadette was mortified. She couldn't quite grasp the detail of what had occurred, but she knew that Radley was communicating one simple fact: Tim was not coming.

'I should leave you two alone,' said Elizabeth, grinning. 'Just wanted to check in. I'm sorry I spoiled the surprise.'

'Oh, you didn't,' said Radley. 'Bernadette will make it up to me, won't you, *darling*?'

'Yes,' Bernadette said dully, 'I'll make it up to him.'

'Don't worry about me knowing,' reassured Elizabeth, distressed by Bernadette's sad face. 'I won't say anything to anyone, I promise!' She moved to give her friend a hug, but Bernadette couldn't bear it, and stepped smartly backwards out of reach.

'Please don't hug me when I'm half naked.'

'Sorry!' said Elizabeth, incorrectly ascribing Bernadette's coldness to modesty. 'I'll see you guys later?'

'See you in a bit,' said Radley cheerfully, ushering her from the room.

When Elizabeth had gone, Radley turned back to Bernadette, who was standing with her arms wrapped round her body. He picked up a soft throw from the couch and draped it over her.

'I don't understand,' said Bernadette shakily.

'I only understand part of it,' said Radley. 'But perhaps you'll enlighten me as to the rest.'

'How did you find me?' she asked.

'I flew up today with Elizabeth. When I texted you to say I was in New York, we were en route from JFK. Elizabeth said she was to meet you at four o'clock in your hotel room, on Tim's instructions. I thought I would join her and surprise you. Clearly you were surprised.'

Bernadette began to cry.

'Save your tears!' said Radley, quite harshly. 'And tell me what you're up to.'

237

'Tim said he would meet me here. At four,' Bernadette said, her voice a little wobbly, although she didn't dare continue crying.

'His plans changed. He sent Elizabeth as an emissary. And he didn't tell you?'

'No,' she said sadly.

'Was he expecting you to be dressed up like a dog's dinner, or is this all your own doing?' he said scathingly, glancing round at the petals and candles, and running an appraising eye over the La Perla ensemble.

'He didn't know I would be dressed like this,' said Bernadette. She didn't tell him that Tim had implied – had thoroughly implied – that this rendezvous would be the start of an affair. She just hung her head in shame and distress.

'You're hellish, you know that?' said Radley, clearly appalled. 'Leave him alone, why can't you?'

'Why can't you leave *me* alone?' cried Bernadette. 'Just leave me alone!'

He was over to her in two strides and holding her against him as she sobbed.

'I'm sorry,' she said, between hiccoughs. 'I didn't mean that.'

'I know,' he said, rubbing her back patiently. Eventually her weeping subsided and she stared at him with watery eyes. 'You do look a mess,' he said, not unkindly. 'Go and clean yourself up, and for God's sake put some clothes on.'

Bernadette washed and changed in the bathroom. 'My mother will be here tonight,' she called through to him. 'She lands in an hour or so.'

'Why didn't you say so? Who's meeting her at the airport?'

'A driver.'

'Oh no,' said Radley. '*I'll* be there to collect her.'

'Thanks, but you'd never make it to JFK on time. It's rush hour.'

'My helicopter is on standby. I'll chopper her into the city.'

'Your helicopter! Of course! Why didn't I think of that?' she asked sarcastically.

She listened for his response, but there was none. 'Of course I'm grateful,' she added hastily. 'I had meant to meet her myself, but . . .'

She fell quiet, gasping silently with the pain of missing Tim, with the thought of what might have been. She clutched at the sink, trying to catch her breath. Why hadn't he texted to let her know he wouldn't be coming? Why had he told Elizabeth to meet her when he knew she would be expecting him? It didn't make any sense.

'I'm going to head out right now, in order to catch Rose,' Radley said, knocking at the bathroom door and opening it in time to see her in an agony of despair. 'He's not worth it, Bernadette,' he continued grimly. 'The sooner you realise it, the better. I mean it as a friend.'

Bernadette reached out for Radley's hand, clutching desperately for support. He allowed her to lean against him. 'Sometimes I want to shake you until the bones rattle in your body,' he said, mumbling into her hair. 'You have so much potential, masses and masses of potential. And you waste it all by being silly over some mediocre man.'

'I can't help it,' she whispered.

'Well please try.' He carefully removed himself from her grasp and balanced her against the sink. 'Pull yourself together. Where is Rose staying while she's in town?'

'Here . . . In a different room.'

'Okay. If she's up for dinner, we'll meet you at Blue Hill. If not, I'll settle her in her room and join you and Elizabeth later.'

'Thank you for being so good to me. And my mother.'

'Of course.' He didn't smile, but the intensity of his eyes communicated deep affection. She felt the loss of him when he left.

Bernadette and Elizabeth sat facing each other across a round table. Blue Hill was a charming and discreet place with flattering lighting. Elizabeth looked almost pretty. Bernadette wondered how long it would be before Radley and her mother arrived. It would be a difficult tête-à-tête.

'Thank you for coming to support me,' she said gamely, smiling a winning smile. Elizabeth beamed back.

'I wouldn't miss it! I love it when you speak. The way you say things is kind of special. You're an inspiration. I wish I could be like you.'

'What do you mean?' asked Bernadette, bemused.

'You're just so . . . ballsy and honest. You don't care what anyone thinks of you. You just say what you think – you say out loud the things the rest of us think in our heads!'

'I *do* care what people think of me.'

'That's only because you're kind. You try not to hurt other people's feelings. I know you think I'm stupid and awkward and slow sometimes. I can read it in your face – you're so open! But you're patient with me even so. That's why you and Rad are so well suited. You're like these good-looking, intelligent, charitable super-humans!'

Bernadette was not given to bouts of modesty, nor was she

easily embarrassed, but Elizabeth's unexpected little speech had left her feeling quite discomposed, and she fell into a fit of self-reproach. 'You're not awkward,' she mumbled, wishing with all her might that something would happen to get her out of this uncomfortable situation.

At that exact moment, the middle-aged maître d', who was passing their table with a bottle of red wine, collapsed on the floor, dropping the bottle, and proceeded to have a heart attack.

'Bernadette, call an ambulance,' said Elizabeth quietly, before Bernadette even had a chance to register what was happening. She looked round in a panic. Several of the other diners were dithering too, fumbling for cell phones, but a quick-thinking waiter was already dialling 911 from the restaurant telephone.

Elizabeth was kneeling on the floor beside the man, talking to him calmly. She looked up at Bernadette, who was in shock. 'Bernadette, get some aspirin please,' she said in the same quiet tone, before turning her attention back to her patient.

'Does anyone have any aspirin?' Bernadette asked loudly, appealing to the other diners. Someone found some and passed it over, and Bernadette thrust it at Elizabeth, her hands shaking. Elizabeth had wrapped her own coat around the man to keep him warm, and was asking him questions about his daughter. Bernadette wanted to cry, it was so unexpected and awful. Bile and panic rose in her throat, and she huddled back, feeling like an intruder on what should be the most intimate moment of a person's existence.

'She's a doctor,' she announced to the watching room, pointing at Elizabeth as if she were a movie star. 'She's a doctor.'

The ambulance arrived after what seemed like a lifetime, and

Elizabeth quickly filled the paramedics in on what had happened. The poor man was clutching at her hand, tears in his eyes.

'Would you like me to come to the hospital with you?' she asked, and he nodded gratefully.

She quickly gathered her belongings while Bernadette stood uselessly by, feeling like a child being abandoned by its mother.

'What about—' Bernadette began, but Elizabeth gave her a quick hug before turning to leave. 'I'm pretty sure he's going to be fine,' she said. 'Try not to worry, sweetie. I'll text you as soon as I know anything. I'll wait till his family can join him, maybe a bit longer. See you tomorrow. Get some sleep!'

And she was gone. Bernadette slumped heavily at the table, replaying her own part in the scene. She had been powerless to help, and Elizabeth had been wonderful. There is nothing more defeminising than being faced with an opportunity to care and minister, and realising you are completely redundant. Elizabeth had won all the glory and Bernadette was a blithering idiot, a waste-of-space cotton-headed dawdler. And she was selfish now, to be thinking only of her own performance rather than focusing on the man at the centre of the tragedy.

It was odd, she noted, how she had wanted rid of Elizabeth, wanted to be free of the awkward dinner, and now here she was all alone. The universe often conspired to help Bernadette, and rather than be grateful, she resented it. What a cruel thing the universe had done this time – she must be more careful what she wished for. It was in such an introspective reverie that Radley found her.

'What's the matter?' he asked. He had appeared over her, and was glancing around the restaurant, overtaken by the odd feeling of ruinous aftermath. She gaped up at him wordlessly.

'Your mother, wonderful woman that she is, is resting at the hotel. She said she would see you in the morning. Where's Elizabeth?'

Bernadette didn't quite know where to begin. A waiter approached them. 'Your friend was incredible,' he said to Bernadette. 'I guess she's not coming back? Do you two want to order?' He glanced appreciatively at Radley. 'Your meal is complimentary, of course. We're so sorry for the upset.'

'I can't eat,' said Bernadette. 'But thank you.'

The waiter nodded understandingly. 'Please thank your friend from us. She was amazing. Any time she wants to come back and dine, we'll arrange something special.'

Bernadette smiled weakly, trying to look extra pretty to make up for her own lack of heroism.

'What on earth did you do? Where's Elizabeth?' asked Radley, deeply concerned now.

'I didn't do anything!' she cried indignantly. 'Let's just go.'

They exited the underground restaurant and were hit by the thick New York night. The air was heavy with heat and scent. Bernadette took Radley's hand in a natural fashion and began walking up the quiet street. His questioning halted by the good fortune of hand-holding, they managed to walk silently for almost half a mile before he began again.

'All right, out with it. Why are we wandering aimlessly across the city? What did you do to Elizabeth?'

'Will you stop accusing me? I didn't do anything. A man almost died, right in front of us! He may be dead now, for all I know. And Elizabeth went with him to the hospital.'

Radley stopped abruptly and hugged her tight. Bernadette felt obliged to cry, as the situation demanded, but was unable.

243

She cursed herself. She had collapsed weeping in Radley's arms earlier in the day when confronting her own disappointment, but now, when facing someone else's life-and-death situation, she couldn't produce even one salty tribute. She was a bad woman. She tried scrunching her face and sniffing a little into his lapels, hoping that would suffice.

He let her go and reached for his iPhone, tapping out a text to Elizabeth. 'Why don't you and I go for a stiff drink?' he said, looking up at Bernadette with dark eyes, and smiling with his least offensive smirk.

'I've stopped drinking,' she said.

'Since when?' he asked, surprised.

'Since . . . For a while,' she murmured vaguely, wringing her hands and looking blindly down the street.

'Then let's keep walking,' he said quietly, taking one of her hands and tucking her arm under his, pulling her close to his side. They moved briskly, marching almost, dodging piles of trash and other sidewalk hazards without skipping a beat. Their rhythm was a good one, and Bernadette welcomed the physical movement. When she couldn't bear to think, she needed to move. She came at the world with her head high and every muscle braced for action. The flight instinct was strong in her, and each internal demon triggered a reaction.

Radley had sensed the distress in her and guessed at a remedy. They covered ground, him steering them without seeming to, so that Bernadette could remain in her purposeless state. It wasn't until she was properly panting that he slowed. They were in the middle of a tourist area, brightly lit kebab shops and pizza joints all around. Their two cell phones buzzed simultaneously, and both reached for their respective lifelines.

He is fine, Elizabeth had group-texted them. *Will make a complete recovery. Family is with him. All okay. Love you both x.*

Bernadette and Radley looked from the screens into each other's eyes, their vision blurring slightly at the sudden change in the light. They were both smiling, and Bernadette realised with some relief that she had been genuinely concerned for the poor maître d'.

'Are you hungry?' asked Radley. 'Pizza?'

'Sure.'

She perched on a sticky high stool at a greasy Formica counter, while Radley ordered slices from an Italian-themed tourist trap. He pulled a wad of hundred-dollar bills from his pocket.

'Hundreds? That's very gangster of you,' Bernadette observed as he paid.

'Sam withdraws for me,' he shrugged.

'Your assistant withdraws your cash? You're too important to use the ATM? That's disgraceful!'

'Not important. Time-constrained.'

'Well I'm honoured that someone so constrained should waste so much of his time eating pizza with little ole me.'

'I don't consider this a waste. I'm very careful with time, and with money.'

He came to sit next to her, their knees touching as they balanced, preferring to rest the paper plates on their laps rather than the counter top.

'You're careful with a lot of things,' she said. His look was a question mark. 'You're careful with your heart, for instance,' she continued. 'You won't be tempted from the path of right-eousness, in search of baser pleasures . . .'

'Not by you,' and he bit fiercely into his pizza in a manner that discouraged her from continuing.

She wished they were sitting under more flattering lighting, dreading to imagine the strange shadows cast by the bright down-lights, and shuddering at the close proximity of Radley's penetrating eyes to her open-pored, freckled face.

'Elizabeth was quite impressive,' she said speculatively, though a mouthful of margherita.

'That doesn't surprise me.'

'I, of course, was useless. But let me guess, that doesn't surprise you either.'

'It was a scary thing to witness,' he said gently. 'No one knows how they're going to react in situations like that. Elizabeth is practised at such things, being a doctor. You are not.'

Radley leant forward and brushed his fingers lightly over her cheek, tucking a wayward strand of hair behind her ear. Bernadette pulled back from his touch. It wasn't that she disliked it – quite the contrary – but she had been keeping as much of her hair over her face as possible, using it as a shield from his keen gaze. She hated it when romantic gestures went wrong. So often she had pulled away from a man because he was trying to hold her hand when her skin was dry, or kiss her when she'd just eaten garlic, or pull her hair back from her face when she was trying to hide a pimple behind the dark curtain. Every time she would withdraw coyly, and leave him to guess at the reason for the rejection, rather than communicate her vanity like an adult.

'Do you think life is real?' she asked.

'What?'

'Do you think there is anything *more*? Sometimes I feel quite certain that what we feel is true is actually a great big trick. You know, my experience of reality is that my *feelings* – my thoughts and emotions – are the truest things about me.'

'Yes,' said Radley. 'You make that quite evident.'

She wrinkled her nose at him and smiled. 'I'm being serious! Physical reality seems like the less real and less important thing. Maybe we're all just brains in a jar somewhere.'

Radley munched on his pizza, stopping to lick some tomato sauce from his wrist. 'Life is a mathematical projection.' He shrugged.

'That can't be right!'

'I hate to break it to you, but no one gets to know the secrets of the universe, Bernadette, not even you. Maybe we're all stuck inside a complex simulation – but if we are, we'll never know it. Accept it as something beyond your reach.'

'Never,' she said stubbornly, rising from the table with an imperious look. He laughed and took her hands (she had moisturised recently, so she let her little paws rest lightly in his great palms).

'Would you like it if I told you that our having pizza in New York right now was written in the stars? Predetermined by weeping angels, who wrote the date across the firmament in an everlasting constellation?' he said, with muted drama.

She raised a sceptical eyebrow. 'Why are the angels weeping?'

'That,' he said, 'is the first happy thought you have had all night, and I'm going to take it as an excellent omen for us. Why are the angels weeping indeed?'

They soon resumed their walk up the wide avenue, their previous frenzy replaced by a delicious pizza-fed languor. 'I think perhaps this *is* a simulation,' Bernadette mused. 'A giant

247

video game. You are being controlled by a skilled gamer. Mine is a little more amateurish, a weekend player.'

'As a biologist, I would like to point out how difficult it is to correctly simulate even the most simple life forms—'

But Bernadette had cut him off with a cry, pointing towards a neon sign in a black second-floor window. 'Look!' she exclaimed.

'Fortune-teller?' he read, looking at her in surprise. 'You didn't strike me as the type.'

'I'm not,' she assured him. 'But tonight I feel like it, for some reason. After all your talk of angels, it seems like The Thing To Do.' She spoke the last in obvious capital letters, and Radley grinned indulgently.

'I'm not one to argue with destiny. It seems like An Idiotic Idea to me. But if you really want to . . .' He indicated that she should enter the building.

Bernadette felt unaccountably excited; alive with good humour, as though the maître d's recovery had given her a shot of new life as well. She turned coquettishly to Radley as she pushed open the glass door. 'Of course, I don't believe in any of this kind of tosh. Fortune-telling, like horoscopes, is a lie designed to please women. But since so many things fall into that category, it seems rude to ignore them entirely. Let's waste some money and have some fun.'

'I don't like to waste money, remember?' he said.

The door opened immediately on to a narrow stairway that smelt strongly of Chinese food. Bernadette climbed the stairs between two white-painted walls, conscious that Radley was following close behind. At the top, she had the choice of turning right into a tattoo parlour, or entering a door on the left that promised palmistry, tarot and fortune-telling. She stopped on the top stair, Radley just below her.

'Perhaps we should get something pierced instead?' he asked, looking to the tattoo parlour. 'It might be less painful.'

'Don't be dull. This is going to be fun! It'll be something we always remember.'

'I like that. I appreciate the idea of permanence it suggests.'

'We can remember it separately,' Bernadette clarified.

Radley looked like the patient general of a forgotten army, his athletic frame relaxed, one foot resting a stair higher than the other, as though about to mount a waiting steed. 'Well go on then,' he prompted as she stared. 'Or are we to stay in this stairwell all evening?'

She hastily pushed open the door on the left, glancing back over her shoulder to wink at him, full of mischief, and most pleased with their endeavour.

'I'm closed!' called a shrill voice from the depths of a dark room. It took a moment for Bernadette's eyes to adjust to the gloom. A huge moth-eaten Indian rug covered the floor. There were scatter cushions and hookahs littered around, clustered near low Turkish tables. The air was thick with patchouli, and the low light came from standing lamps covered with saris of various colours. In one corner a small woman was fiddling with an improbably old television set. She looked at Bernadette with dark, beady eyes. 'I'm closed,' she repeated, waving a dismissive hand.

Bernadette stopped in the doorway, cross. She didn't like her plans to be derailed by short women. And she expected more sympathy from someone supposedly in commune with higher powers. The fortune-teller was oldish, probably in her fifties, with an abundance of dark curls, and shapeless garments covering her thin body. Bracelets jangled at both wrists and large silver hoops dangled from her ears. It was cheap theatre, illusion-lite, and Bernadette was determined to have it. 'Couldn't you just squeeze us in?' she wheedled, smiling her most unthreatening little-girl smile.

'Who's us?' asked the woman. Her voice was scratchy and nasal with New York intonation. Radley stepped into the room behind Bernadette. The fortune-teller looked him up and down with some interest. 'I'm closed,' she said, but more amiably this time.

'Please?' Bernadette coaxed. 'It's very important.'

The woman shook her head and walked towards them, shooing them like they were poultry. 'I've finished for the day, hun. Why don't you try tomorrow? It's late. Take your man home. I was about to head out myself.'

'Look,' said Bernadette, standing her ground, 'we'll pay you well. Triple your rate. And I don't want long. Twenty minutes.'

The little woman stared up into her determined face and sighed heavily. 'Okay. Twenty minutes. What do you want? Cards? Palm?'

'Just a bog-standard fortune-telling.'

'For you? Or you want a joint read for the both of you?' she said, jabbing Radley in the stomach with a bony finger.

'We'll have a joint read,' said Bernadette firmly, before Radley could object.

'Take a seat.' The woman pointed to two of the larger floor cushions. Bernadette dropped gracefully on to one of them; Radley, sighing audibly, lowered himself carefully to the other, snorting disgruntledly. The fortune-teller settled herself on a third cushion, pulling her mass of hair back behind her shoulders and pushing the bracelets up her arms like a drunkard rolling his sleeves before a brawl. 'Okay, kids,' she said, beaming professionally at them. 'Where are you from?'

Radley opened his mouth to answer, but Bernadette whacked a restraining arm across him. 'Don't tell her anything specific,' she hissed, eyeballing the woman. 'That's how they do this. They take what you say and repeat it back to you, making you think it's magic.'

Radley blinked at her, nonplussed, rubbing his chest where she had hit him. The psychic folded her arms and arched a fuzzy eyebrow in a papery brow. 'Listen, girlie,' she said, 'if you're not going to talk, this is going to be a long twenty minutes. What is it you want to know? How can I help you?'

Bernadette shook her head vigorously, clamping her lips together. Radley and the fortune-teller exchanged an exasperated look. He shrugged apologetically.

'Okay,' the woman sighed. 'Here's how this works. We chat through what's going on in your life right now, and I give you some possible solutions for the future, okay? I need you to work with me here.'

'You're meant to be a psychic, not a psychiatrist,' said Bernadette. 'You should be able to divine my future without me giving you any information about myself.'

Radley scratched at his cushion, embarrassed. Bernadette continued to stare down the little New Yorker.

'All right,' said the woman. 'You want the truth? Let's do this.' She squinted challengingly at Bernadette and then shut her eyes, throwing her head back dramatically. She swept her arms out to the sides and cried loudly, 'Spirits! Come to me now!'

Radley jumped in alarm. The fortune-teller was swaying backwards and forwards, muttering to herself. It was difficult to catch her exact words, but Bernadette was confident she heard 'hocus pocus' in there somewhere. The woman's eyes snapped open and she stared at Bernadette meanly. 'You're obviously English. You grew up in the south of England. Your parents divorced when you were young. Your father was neglectful, and you lost contact with him years ago. You take pride in your appearance. You're unmarried. You're incapable of monogamy. You've had a series of unfulfilling relationships. You suffer because you hate yourself, and you despise anyone who would love you. You're too smart for your own good. You're motivated by love, not money. You have money of your own. You have exacting and unrealistic expectations of yourself and those around you. You have a reputation for being an ice queen, a bitch, a snobby English girl, yada yada. You're inconsiderate of other people's feelings and you have trouble with empathy. There you go.'

Bernadette's eyes were round and wide and she stared in consternation in the face of such abuse. Radley felt compelled to give the woman a round of applause.

'That was a cold read,' the fortune-teller said. 'Those are the things I can divine about you from the way you came in the room. If you'd answered my questions, it could have been a whole lot more illuminating. There's no charge. Now would you kindly leave me to get on with my evening?'

'That wasn't a fortune,' Bernadette whispered, her throat dry. She stood up, somewhat shakily, and Radley rose to his feet next to her.

'Remarkably accurate, though,' he said enthusiastically, stopping when Bernadette turned reproachful eyes upon him.

'It wasn't fortune-telling,' Bernadette repeated, making hastily for the door.

'You're a little madam,' said the psychic. 'Here's your fortune. You and him,' she jabbed Radley in the chest, 'you haven't slept together yet. You're not even dating. But you're going to end up together, marriage, bambinos, the works. You're going to live to a ripe old age and be very happy together. Got it?'

Bernadette shook her head triumphantly. 'Ha! You're totally wrong. I'm in love with someone else.'

'No you're not,' said the woman.

'You're really not,' Radley added.

'If you were in love with someone else, you wouldn't be here with him now,' said the dark-eyed mystic. 'I'm telling you, you're going to end up with him.' She jabbed at Radley again. 'It's written in the stars.'

Bernadette's mouth dropped open. 'In the stars?' she repeated.

'Written across the firmament in an everlasting constellation?' asked Radley hopefully.

'Exactly. Now goodnight, safe travels, it was a pleasure meeting you.'

Radley handed the woman a hundred-dollar bill, which she looked very pleased about. He had to drag Bernadette from the room, because she was suddenly rooted to the Indian rug, chewing on her bottom lip, deep in thought.

He started down the steep staircase and Bernadette followed carefully. Halfway down, she stopped. 'Radley?' He turned to look at her with expectant eyes. The fact that he was standing below her made their heads level. He was disconcertingly close. 'Do you think she's right? About us ending up together?' She asked the question in a clear voice, with no sign of flirtation or malice.

'I hope so,' he answered quietly, honestly.

Her eyes shone, and for once she wasn't trying to be seductive, wasn't batting her lashes, or pouting, or twitching an eyebrow. She had a sweet face when it wasn't animated with libidinous feeling, and her body was delicate and soft when not stretched in various artificial poses. She stood still, quivering like an alert deer, and slowly allowed her forehead to lean against his. He hesitated, his vulnerability unusually evident. They stayed like that, neither daring to move, their breathing becoming deeper and slower, their breath mingling, the shared air warming their mouths and signalling further pleasure.

Bernadette was almost unbearably aroused. She had never been more aware of her own breath, and it was a giddying rush every time she opened her mouth in small gasps to accept the air. She could feel a swirling in her stomach, a wonderful and unusual sensation, like breath where your breath shouldn't be. Her adrenalin soared, her heart beat faster, and she closed her eyes and kissed him.

It was like falling, an overpowering tumble into nothingness. She couldn't think; she could only feel. His lips were firm and soft against hers, and he moved carefully, as though she were a precious thing. His arms were around her, he was holding her so perfectly, and she leant her weight against him, entirely trusting. Behind her closed eyes she could see bright, flashing colours, a kaleidoscope of desire. He tasted good, and she pushed for more, her tongue finding his and exulting. It was too good, too good, too much and not enough, maddeningly effective. He had complete control of the kiss, as she had complete control of his heart. It was dangerous to be so enthralled, and her knees buckled with the thrill of it.

He guided her down until she was sitting on a stair and he was above her, kissing her all the while. His hands moved to her hair and his lips moved to her neck, and she gasped aloud with the pleasure. He drew away to look at her, to give her the chance to speak, to draw proper breath, but she pulled him back to her and they kissed again, harder and with more urgency.

They were so engrossed that they didn't hear the fortune-teller locking the door at the top of the stairs, didn't hear her until she was right on top of them. 'I told you so,' she said loudly, smiling with satisfaction at the couple writhing in the stairwell. Bernadette felt Radley laugh; it was entirely possible for him to kiss and laugh at the same time, which she thought was a great talent. He managed to keep kissing her while he reached in his pocket for the roll of hundred-dollar bills, and they were still kissing as he thrust all the money at the surprised psychic. The happy woman dropped the bills, and banknotes rained down on them, fluttering past them and landing like snow on the stairs – and still they kissed on.

9

Big Sur, the stretch of coastline north-west of Los Angeles, bursts with teleological beauty. Every flower and shrub, each white-tipped wave, towering cliff and expansive redwood, is perfectly positioned. Uniformly riotous, everything between heaven and ocean is designed for one purpose: to bring joy to those lucky enough to bear witness.

Bernadette was unmoved. She had been in an ornery fit since New York. Kissing Radley had been too wonderful and too terrifying. She hated to feel out of control, and the kiss had been most unnerving.

Afterwards, when they had emerged into the heat of the New York night, still giddy, and he had pulled her to him, looking down with the most pleasant expectation, she had taken fright. She was shy, and shaky, and wanted to cry with how much he affected her, and what it meant.

'I can't do this,' she said. 'I'm not ready.'

And he had, surprisingly, been incredibly compliant. He walked her back to her hotel and left her at the door, sensibly not even leaning in for a goodnight kiss, which would inevitably have led to so much more.

She texted to let him know that she didn't want anything to change between them, cringing at the platitude. And he had replied: *I still want everything. I want all of you. But I will wait. I will wait, indefinitely.* And somehow *he* avoided the platitude snag, and sounded sweet rather than corny.

She had been so shaken that she wouldn't allow him to see her for the remainder of the New York trip. The morning after their kiss, the morning of her speaking engagement, he had sent a package to her hotel room, because she had refused to let him hand-deliver it. Inside the large box was the sapphire-blue cocktail dress she had so admired in the Neiman Marcus window when they had been shopping for wedding dresses. She laughed out loud to see it. The wedding-dress excursion seemed so long ago, and it was impossible to trace the passage of feeling from then to now. She couldn't remember who she loved. She couldn't decide if she loved Tim any longer. When she thought of Tim, her head hurt. And when she thought of Radley, all she knew was the kiss.

She had laughed at the dress because she had already bought its duplicate for herself, and had it with her in New York. She took a picture of the two dresses, side by side, and sent it to Radley captioned *Haha!*

Who bought you the other? he asked, immediately.

No one, moron. I bought it myself. I don't need no man, she texted back.

Of course. Forgive me for being primitive.

It was strange for Radley to be so docile and manageable. She half expected him to burst through her door in an impassioned show of feeling, demanding a continuation of their carnal escapade. But he kept his distance, respectfully.

It was an odd moment for Bernadette, who was conscious of some change in herself. It was, unfortunately, not the provenance of some higher sensibility, a transformation towards a more stoic way of being, but something far more commonplace. Thoughts of Radley came unbidden at every moment: the feel of his mouth on hers, the luxury of his gentle arms encircling her body. She was not dreaming *only* of sensation, because now her emotions were more than they had been. She was no longer lecherous, but left more than anything desiring his good opinion. Suddenly she wanted his beliefs as her own, his good sense to guide her; she craved his respect, and wanted to be worthy of his friendship.

She was disgusted with herself, and couldn't understand how her old love for Tim had been so effortlessly eclipsed. And if love could be that easily transferred, what mattered love at all?

But her heart turned out to be as contrary a beast as her mind, and seemed to be overtaken by her perverse nature, for no matter how hard she tried to rekindle the ancient feelings, her love for Tim would not relight. Bernadette had not foreseen such an event, although her lust for Radley should conceivably have aroused some secret suspicion. And Tim's odd behaviour, the fact that he had treated her badly and given no reason, was unexpected. Perhaps her love for him had been a projection after all.

The other obstacle to complete happiness was that Radley Blake seemed, as he always had done, Too Good To Be True. Bernadette did not believe herself worthy of such opportunity. Radley, like the MP, like her father, was too charming, too debonair. He was a tender trap, and she must not fall again.

Surprisingly, Rose had seemed to know that something had happened. After the Man Whisperer's New York speech, she had taken Bernadette for a celebratory dinner.

'You spoke beautifully, my darling,' she said, as they faced one another over a damask tablecloth, lit by soft candlelight. 'It was quite inspiring.'

Bernadette's second speaking engagement as the Man Whisperer had indeed been something of a triumph. She had made an impassioned but well-thought-through argument for gender equality, without alienating her audience. It was the first time in her career that she had actually been both truthful and sympathetic. It was a liberating experience, and she felt weirdly connected to the roomful of women.

'Do you really think I spoke well? It seemed like I did. The audience didn't yell at me this time.'

'You were wonderful. Radley thought so too; I spoke to him afterwards. He's very proud of you.'

Bernadette stiffened. 'He doesn't really have a reason to be proud of me. We're not that close. We don't even know each other very well.'

Rose glanced at Bernadette, her beautiful face unfathomable. 'The way he speaks of you, he seems to know you very well. He has a great understanding of your character. When he picked me up from the airport the other day, we had such a good conversation. And it was all about you! I felt like I was learning things about you that even I hadn't realised.'

'Oh, Radley can be charming,' Bernadette said crossly. 'He's good at dominating conversation.'

'No,' said Rose, who rarely expressed a contrary opinion with such resolve. 'Your father could be charming. Charming men are not uncommon. Radley is more than that. Radley is a man of substance.'

Bernadette had been surprised by Rose's endorsement; it made the situation with Radley seem all the more significant and terrifying. Which was why, as she was driven up the beautiful Big Sur coastline towards Tim and Elizabeth's wedding destination, she was distinctly discomposed. There would be no escaping Radley at the celebration, as there had been in the intervening weeks.

Her discomfort was not the frantic kind; she didn't feel sick with nerves, she wasn't sweating and close to tears, nor physically uncomfortable. But there was an unseen tension that kept her feeling as though she was light as air, as though she could escape her body at any moment.

The fact that David was driving her did not affect her much one way or the other. She had asked him to the wedding as a platonic date, wishing, rather than believing, that he would be happy with friendship alone. She was trying to be as nice to him as possible, flattering him gently and encouraging him to talk. David would serve as an unmistakable sign to Radley that she must not be touched nor loved, a sign that she was clearly not yet of sound mind.

But as she gazed at the passing landscape, and the vivid, sparkling ocean, she felt a twinge of regret that she had not been brave enough to fend off Radley alone. She was using David again. When would she see people as people, and not as commodities with a certain value? It was a beautiful day, but she could not enjoy it. Nothing would break into her inner world; she was all emotion and consciousness, quite useless in objective reality.

They arrived at the Post Ranch Inn just as the sun was setting. Each room was stand-alone, and was either built high up in a pine, as a tree house, or was a sort of Hobbit hole cut into the cliff, suspending the occupants' above the heaving ocean below. David and Bernadette went to the main house to check in, and found Tim and Elizabeth there greeting arriving guests.

Elizabeth called out in delight when she saw Bernadette, running to her and hugging her hard. Bernadette had a mad-doggish reaction to seeing her friend, and was quite distracted by unaccountable joy.

'Bernie! Stay with me tonight!' giggled Elizabeth. 'Tim and I are in different rooms – you know, tradition before the wedding! I'd love for you to stay with me. What do you think?'

'Yes!' Bernadette grinned, and then whispered, 'It'll save me having to share a room with David!'

Elizabeth squeezed her hand in response, and the two women smiled conspiratorially at one another. Bernadette's breath caught in her throat as Tim came up behind her and gave her a welcoming bear hug. She startled, and skipped neatly out of his reach, grinning manically as though happy to see him, but unable to look him in the eye. He had only sent her a cursory text since their non-encounter in New York, apologising but giving no reason for his change of heart.

Elizabeth laughed at Bernadette's gawky behaviour, and took her by the hand. 'Don't scare Bernie, Tim! Creeping up like that! I'm taking her away to my room. We'll see you guys at the rehearsal dinner.'

David looked miffed and Tim appeared quite thoughtful as the women moved away.

The hotel grounds were set between the ocean far below and the forest, with the rooms stippled among the trees and along the cliff edge. A path wound through the middle, where the smell of the pine and the salt air mingled. The girls walked arm in arm in the fading sunlight, enjoying the slight breeze that worked its way over the nearby cliff.

'It's so beautiful here,' Bernadette sighed, leaning against Elizabeth as if fatigued by happiness.

'I feel like the luckiest person in the world!'

'And so you are. You deserve to be.'

The bridal suite was a tree house, and they climbed the long, rustic staircase into the leafy canopy. The room had a spectacular view of the treetops, and the walls were made of warm red wood, which gave a cosseting, womb-like feel to the place. There was a large bed covered with a blue bedspread, and an enclosed fireplace with a tin chimney. Everything was entirely sympathetic to the natural surroundings, and Bernadette felt that all architecture should be as ecologically sound, if it was also able to be so sumptuous.

Elizabeth lay down delicately on the bed and gazed up at the darkening sky through a carefully positioned skylight. 'Do you think Tim and I are a good match?' she asked, from nowhere.

Bernadette stared at her, moving to the bed slowly, taking time to think of an answer and instead asking a question of her own. 'What makes you say that?'

'Because I respect your opinion, of course!'

'Well it would be a bit late to do anything about it now, wouldn't it?'

'Not necessarily. I'm not the jilting type, but you never know. People can surprise you. It's always the quiet ones . . .'

Bernadette sat next to her and took her hand. Elizabeth looked up at her with such trust, a smile on her sweet face, her hair framing her head like a halo.

'Do you really want an answer?' asked Bernadette. 'Or do you just want to talk?'

'No, an answer! A real answer.'

Bernadette thought carefully. 'I think you are an excellent match. There could be no better choice of wife for anyone than you. You are the epitome of everything good and wonderful. You're kind-hearted, and honest, and intelligent, and fun, and attractive.' Here she twisted a lock of Elizabeth's sandy hair through her fingers. 'You see the best in others, you love fiercely, you're protective, and maternal, and – and Tim's great too.'

Elizabeth kissed Bernadette's hand. 'You're so cute.'

'Why do you ask, though? Are you not happy? You need to be happy! Tim needs to make you happy.'

'Oh, I'm always happy. Happiness comes from within. I'm not relying on him for that.' She sighed and stretched, and Bernadette noticed a more knowing look on her face than she had ever seen there before.

'You're not . . . you're not going to ditch him at the altar, are you?' she asked, afraid.

Elizabeth laughed. 'No, I'm not, don't worry. Now, let's call for your luggage, and get ready for dinner.'

The rehearsal dinner was in the hotel restaurant, a low building slung out over the cliff edge so that the view from the window tables was of the Pacific Ocean swirling far below. There was a festive atmosphere, with a jazz quartet playing well-known songs, and soft candlelight illuminating the *mise en scène*.

Entering with Elizabeth was helpful, as the arrival of the bride was distracting to the gathered guests, and Bernadette was able to slip into the room relatively unnoticed. She skirted around the dark edges of the place, observing with a scholarly detachment. There were many smiling, laughing faces. There was a large and appetising buffet laid out with delicious farm-to-table dishes. There was no seating plan, but round tables were clustered in friendly groups, each with a centrepiece of wild flowers. No one was seated yet, and more people were still arriving.

Bernadette ordered a sparkling water from the open bar, and wandered to the back of the restaurant, where a door led on to a large terrace. No one was in this part of the room, and in the low light it would be difficult to witness her sneaking outside. She already felt in need of some air. Not that the event itself was stifling, but she was still in a Radley-induced state, where closed spaces and casual conversation encouraged her mind to roam, and she would be assaulted by the memory of their kiss.

Escaping outside was no better, for when she heard the gentle crash of breaking waves on the rocks far below, and smelt the comforting scents of pine and damp heather, her body was enlivened and she ached for him. The terrace was much larger than she had imagined, with a pool, jacuzzi, several sunloungers, and a rock garden cut into the clifftop.

She walked out further along the terrace, and jumped as she noticed that a man was out there, too. It was Tim. He had been looking out at the ocean, but turned to her. 'I thought you were trying to avoid me,' he said, not quite sounding like himself.

'I didn't come out here to find you,' she clarified, blushing. 'I didn't know there was anyone out here.'

'So you *are* avoiding me?'

'No. Of course not. The reality is that *you* avoided *me*. And then gave me no explanation.'

They stared awkwardly at one another. It was difficult to see clearly, with the yellow light from the restaurant competing with the white light of the moon, and almost everything in darkness. Tim's face was half in shadow, and his blonde hair looked black.

'I'm struggling, Bernadette.'

'With what?' she asked, stupidly.

'With you! What do you think? I can't stop thinking about you.'

'But you didn't come to New York. You sent Lizzie instead.' Her voice broke a little at the memory, and he groaned in response.

'I'm sorry. Shit, I'm sorry. I messed up. I just . . . I didn't have the balls to do it. I'm not really that type of man. I thought I could be – in a way, I wish I could be. But I just couldn't do it. Can you forgive me?'

Bernadette, now falling in love with another man, was inclined to be generous. 'Of course,' she said, shrugging.

He looked at her keenly, and took several steps towards her, taking both her hands in his. 'You didn't mean it, did you? When you said you loved me. It was just some kind of flirtation. I'm one in a long line for you, right?'

'No!' she cried. 'I did mean it! I do! It's just—'

There were footsteps behind her, and she could tell from Tim's harassed expression who it was that was approaching. She was suddenly light-headed, and pulled her hands away from Tim quickly. She turned to see Radley advancing on them.

He was backlit as he emerged from the restaurant, an inky-black, clearly defined shadow, his expression obscured, nothing but the shape of a man.

'Well isn't this a romantic scene?' he said sardonically.

Tim laughed, a somewhat forced sound. 'You have a habit of saying inappropriate things, Blake.'

'*Blake?*' asked Radley incredulously. 'We're calling each other by our last names now, are we? What next? Pistols at dawn? Okay, *Bazier*, as you will. Out of the three of us, I doubt I'm being the most inappropriate.'

'I haven't done anything, Radley,' said Bernadette, in a small voice. Radley smiled at her briefly, his eyes softening as he looked at her with the air of a man whose every wish had been granted.

'You do talk such shit, Radley,' said Tim, excited past his usually even temper.

Radley took a step towards him, menacingly enough that Bernadette felt compelled to put a warning hand on his chest. It felt amazingly warm and firm under her palm.

'Let's be honest here,' he growled. 'Bernadette hasn't been carrying a torch for you all this time without some sort of encouragement. You thought you could love her from afar, but what good is it for her to be your muse? She gets nothing but heartache from that arrangement.' Bernadette's eyes were wide, and Tim seemed unable to speak, as Radley continued. 'You were content with a mild flirtation, hiding behind romantic gestures and words, convoluted and covert. Gestures that seemed to you poignant and sacred – but this girl cares nothing for subtlety! Look at her! She smashed through all your little tokens, forcing more from you than you can possibly give. You tried so hard to love her and balance on that ledge. But the trouble is, there's a fucking precipice on the other side of it.' Radley's arm pointed involuntarily to the edge of the cliff, at the swirling water a thousand feet below. He looked like a Spartan. 'Don't fall into that oblivion, or it will kill you.'

'You should know,' said Tim, deliberately. 'Look who's under the spell of the Man Whisperer.'

'And for God's sake stop calling her by that idiotic name!' said Radley.

Tim rolled his eyes. 'I'm going inside. Bernie, do you want to come with me?'

Radley smiled reassuringly at Bernadette and took her by the hand, as if helping a small child to cross a road. 'Stay here with me. Please.'

Bernadette nodded. She had no intention of going anywhere else. Tim walked past them towards the restaurant, taking long, nimble strides, a look of absolute loathing on his face. Abruptly Bernadette realised that he hated Radley. Which was a shocking revelation on two counts: firstly because Tim wasn't at all the kind of person to hate anyone, and secondly because Radley himself was so utterly lovable, she couldn't imagine him being the object of anyone's spite.

Once she was alone with the genius Radley Blake, she found herself unusually speechless. He smiled down at her intuitively. 'Lost your tongue?'

She nodded, and he laughed, pulling her closer to him, taking her under his arm to fend off the night-time breezes. 'Oh no you don't!' he said. 'You think that being in love is all breathless torture, and gasping-for-air anguish, and not having a mind of your own. I won't have you mindlessly mooning over me the way you did Tim. That sort of thing is just affectation; it isn't real, and it won't last. I see you are intending the transfer of your boisterous devotion from Tim to me, and I fear for my sanity and peace of mind. We won't pursue anything until this thunderstruck phase has passed, and you are able to be sensibly in love, like a normal person.'

'I don't want this phase to pass,' she said quietly, nuzzling into his chest.

Radley kissed the top of her head fiercely, several times, and then drew back, leading her to one of the sunloungers. He sat down and hauled her into his lap, where she curled up against him, her head resting on his chest. She tucked her legs in tightly, making herself into a cosy little ball, feeling the warmth of his large body beneath her. Physically she felt utterly safe, but her heart was screaming in her chest, warning her not to believe in the lure of corporeal comfort. Her emotions were too extreme, and dangerous.

'Now I'm going to tell you a story. It's a night of lengthy speeches for me,' said Radley, kissing her head again. 'Are you sitting comfortably?'

Bernadette laughed at his antics. 'Yes. Very comfortably,' she said, basking in the moonlight like a cat, rubbing her head against his chest and practically purring.

'Excellent. Now this is the story of our immediate future. Do you want to hear it?'

'Like a fortune?' she asked.

'Exactly like a fortune: something preordained, written across the stars in an everlasting firmament.'

'Yes!'

'Very good. Well, here's what's going to happen: we're going

268

to enjoy Tim and Elizabeth's wedding with a clear heart and a light conscience. Yes?' There was a warning tone in the way he asked the question that caused Bernadette to answer hastily.

'Yes,' she said, nodding fervently.

'And then when we get back to Los Angeles, you're going to take a little time to decide exactly what it is that you're feeling for me. Take as long as you need . . . except you mustn't take *too* long about it, if we're going to get married and have a whole parcel of babies, because I'm not getting any younger.'

Bernadette laughed again, enjoying his teasing, but her stomach tightened at the thought of being married to Radley. 'How long will it take you to decide what it is *you* feel about *me*?' she asked.

'No time at all,' he said, merrily. 'I'm in love with you. I've been in love with you from the very first evening we met. I love you as tenderly and completely as it is possible for a man to love a woman.'

She didn't dare look up at him.

'Shall I go on?' he asked.

She nodded, unable to form words.

'Once you've thought everything through scrupulously, and if you decide you want me, then there'll be no stopping us, Bernadette. We will live the happiest of happy-ever-afters! You will be Queen of Clarion. We are the same, you and I, capable of a genuinely equal and loving partnership.'

'Do you still think I'm selfish?'

He squinted at her, as if assessing. 'I think you still are a bit . . . yes, maybe a very little bit. But I think you've *had* to be selfish, to protect yourself. From now on, I intend to protect you. You will mellow with love and security, I know it. But no more childish behaviour from you. We're leaving your childhood far behind. You're a grown woman, accountable and intelligent. You don't need to be selfish any more.'

Radley was irresistibly happy, the corners of his mouth dancing with mirth, his eyes flaming with love and sentiment. Bernadette was awed by the sight of someone as ardent as herself. 'Why didn't you tell me you loved me before now?' she demanded.

'Couldn't you tell?'

'No! You're such a strange person. You use effusive language all the time; who could ever tell what you really think?'

'Would it have done me any good to tell you before now?'

'Probably not,' Bernadette admitted.

'You seem to have a habit of trampling on and despising any creature unlucky enough to have feelings for you.'

'What do you mean? I do not!' she gasped indignantly.

'What about David?'

'Oh, fuck David! David doesn't count for anything!'

Radley lifted a disapproving eyebrow, and she rushed to clarify. 'I mean, the reason David doesn't count is because his feelings aren't *true*. He doesn't know me at all, he doesn't see me, he just has a crush on this imaginary, projected person.'

'Now who does that sound like?' asked Radley, slyly.

'Oh well, let's not get philosophical!' she said carelessly, tossing her head in impatience. 'You were telling me that you loved me . . .'

'Yes. Would you like me to tell you again?'

'Yes please,' in a small voice.

'Bernadette, I love you.'

She quivered in his arms, almost unable to believe that the handsome, charismatic, powerful man in front of her was speaking with such sincerity and tenderness. The universe was good to Bernadette, but surely not *that* good? Was it all some horrible trick?

'Do you promise? How can I know you're telling the truth?' she asked quietly, fiddling with one of his shirt buttons.

'I suppose you can't, initially. But the passing of time will help. Despite my loquacity around you, I'm actually much more a man of action, rather than words. You will know by my actions, over time. Because I intend to show you what love is in everything I do, going forward.'

She closed her eyes and moved to kiss him, but felt his finger against her mouth, stopping her. 'Not yet, Bernadette. I want you to be sensible of the choice you are making. You can't kiss me to bide time; I won't be satisfied.'

She peeked at him from under dark, bristly lashes, looking so much like an inquisitive sparrow that he laughed out loud.

'I think I am yours,' she said carefully. 'I mean, I think you might be crazy, but everyone seems to think I'm crazy too, so I suppose that would make sense. There's certainly no one I can think of that I would rather kiss.'

He laughed again. 'I'll be content with that for now, though I'll deny you your kiss until you're on sure ground. Our first kiss was in the most unromantic environment possible – when we'd had plenty of prior opportunities to do it romantically. Trust you to kiss me in an ugly stairwell that stank of Chinese food! Next time, we do it right.'

'This is quite romantic,' she said, leaning in hopefully, gesturing vaguely to the moon and the ocean.

'Yes,' he said, getting to his feet and taking her with him. 'This is very romantic. But it's not our celebration.'

She let him lead her back inside, and they joined the party proper. It was a long evening for Bernadette, who did not like listening to speeches or conversing with strangers, and who was entirely overcome with her own particular affairs. Tim and Elizabeth sat enthroned at the centre of their adoring friends and families, like royalty at a banquet.

Radley and Bernadette did not speak much, but they sat next to one another, aware of the physical space between their bodies, and what little effort it would take to violate the gap. She was so confused by her new-found affection that it made her quite human, and she was very nice indeed to David, who sat on the other side of her. David recognised Radley as a romantic rival, but was too in awe of him to do much about it. Radley would occasionally address a few affable remarks in his direction, and David would stumble and stutter over his reply, breaking out in a sweat.

After a friend of Tim's had given a short speech, Lauren approached Bernadette, where she was sitting between her two gentlemen admirers.

'Well if it isn't the Man Whisperer,' she drawled drunkenly.

'Emphasis on the *Man*,' muttered Bernadette.

Lauren scowled, leaning in close. 'I know your little secret, you bitch.'

Bernadette turned in her chair to face her antagonist. 'Oh do go away. Don't be bitter, just because I don't want to be with you. You don't know anything.'

'I know you're a *bitch*,' Lauren sneered, backing away. 'You're a messed-up bitch.'

Bernadette turned angrily to Radley. 'Did you tell Lauren I was gay?'

Radley pretended to think about it, then shrugged. 'I might have done.'

'Idiot. You've caused me all kinds of trouble.'

'I may have contributed slightly, but I think I had honourable intent.' He pressed his lips to her ear in a way that made her shudder with desire. 'At the time, I was trying to distract Lauren from her theory that you were in love with Tim.'

Bernadette's heart sank to think of her so-called love for Tim. What a waste of years of concentrated longing. She felt shamed and slightly dirty; loving Tim no longer seemed like the honourable thing.

Once the party reached its conclusion, Elizabeth and Bernadette walked back to their room arm in arm. Elizabeth prattled happily about the evening, aglow with excitement and anticipation. Bernadette offered murmurs of approval and consent, but could hardly focus. The darkness around them seemed to be pressing against her, the tall trees were whispering unnaturally, and the only thing that could protect her from the engulfing dark, the terrifying unknown, was Elizabeth's mercy. She clutched harder at her friend's arm. It suddenly seemed so glaring and obvious: Radley Blake was a good man, and she was in love with him. She thought desperately of how stupid she had been, and how many times she could have lost his love and attention. Her foolish pursuit of Tim could have cost her everything. Why had she been so blind to the truth? It seemed as though she had been almost purposely damaging any chance of happiness. And how easily she had been willing to hurt Elizabeth! She felt sick with self-loathing.

When they entered the warmth of the bridal suite, Bernadette felt a sense of relief, as though a predator had been pursuing them on their night-time walk. The emotion coursed through her body, and made way for sudden tears.

'I'm . . . I'm in love with him!' she cried, clutching at her stomach as though she had been punched, gasping for air and leaning against the closed door for support.

Elizabeth turned in alarm. 'Who, my darling?' she asked breathlessly. 'Who are you in love with?'

'Radley!' wailed Bernadette. 'I'm in love with Radley!'

'Well of course you are!' Elizabeth said, with a laughing exhale. 'Of course you're in love with him.'

'But I'm frightened. I love him too much. It's not going to be. I can feel it! Something terrible is going to happen. How can he love me when I'm so dreadful? And he knows it all! He knows how bad I am!'

Elizabeth gently led Bernadette to the bed and sat with her, rubbing her back rhythmically. 'You're not bad,' she said lightly. 'You're a human being. And nothing terrible is going to happen. Radley's just the best. He's good, and kind, and so smart. He's not going to hurt you, I promise. I'm happy you've finally real-ised you love him. I could have told you that ages ago!'

Bernadette looked up though her tears. 'Really? You knew that I loved him?'

'Of course! You guys have this crazy energy around you whenever you're together. It's insane – practically visible sparks of love and chemistry. Tim and I talk about it all the time.'

'Tim thinks I'm in love with him too?'

'Yeah, it's been obvious from the beginning. And Radley told us he was in love with you immediately. He's crazy for you. He's honestly never been like this about anyone. He's a super-proud man, very reserved usually, private and sensitive – but with you, he just couldn't help himself. He said right away that he would do anything for you.'

Bernadette settled into snuffles, wiping away tears with the back of her hand and rubbing her face against Elizabeth's shoulder.

'Now you *can't* be unhappy.' Elizabeth smiled. 'You're in love with a man who loves you back. And I'm getting married tomorrow!'

The wedding day dawned clear, the sun shining brightly over the hued ocean. The sun was an immediate omen, Bernadette thought, promising actual gain, much more straightforward than wishing on stars. The sun was shining and so the wedding would be beautiful, and like everything involving Elizabeth, it was that simple.

The happy bride looked as pretty as ever that morning, as she ate a plain breakfast of toast and fruit and read messages from friends and relatives, missives that made her smile with delight and pronounce herself 'the luckiest creature alive'. Bernadette oversaw bridal operations with the skill and strategy of a veteran, running through checklists and answering phones, tracking down hair and make-up artists, and welcoming the other bridesmaids into the suite. She even gave Lauren a hospitable hug and kiss when she arrived.

Bernadette herself didn't like too much fuss with her hair and make-up, so she was finished before the other girls, who sat dotted around the room being worked on by talkative stylists. Everyone was already drinking champagne and celebrating, but Bernadette didn't want alcohol, and she was already restless from being cooped up in the room too long, pacing like a caged lioness, tripping over hairdryer wires, and upsetting trays of make-up.

'Bernie, love,' said Elizabeth finally, as Bernadette's elbow capsized a plate of curling irons. 'Why don't you get dressed, and then go and check on the church for me? I don't know if the orders of service are down there. There should be one in every seat.'

'Okay,' said Bernadette, glad to have an excuse to leave, and some definite action to occupy her. 'I'll go and check.'

'It should be nice and quiet at this time,' Elizabeth smiled. 'You can say a little prayer while you're there.'

Bernadette snorted a half-laugh, and went to the bathroom to change into her dress. The bridesmaids' dresses were of a soft peach chiffon, floor-length and with capped sleeves. She admired herself in the bathroom mirror, and wondered why she couldn't wear such an ensemble every day. She felt curiously detached from her reflection, as though the woman staring at her was some unknown person, a poised and beautiful stranger.

It was a pleasant walk to the little forest church, and Bernadette didn't see any other guests. She supposed they must all be getting ready for the grand event. She wondered which room Radley was staying in, and whether he had a tree house or a cliffside room. It was sad to imagine him waking up alone in a hotel room, and she felt an acute longing to be with him. He need never be lonely again.

The path to the church wound through the trees, and all around her were the perfect sounds of nature. Birds called to one another high in the treetops, the leaves rustled softly in the pleasant breeze, and her dainty footfalls did not impose.

Elizabeth had had the right idea in sending her out to the woods. Bernadette already felt calmer.

When the church came into sight in the clearing, it was as if the community of woodland creatures knew to show deference, as the sounds were less riotous there. The birds were quieter, and their chattering had a distinctly reverential air.

The church was very pretty: a simple construction of white wood, with a clean spire and a single bell. Bernadette found herself almost reluctant to approach, as though she would be turned to dust for setting foot in such a holy place. She walked hesitantly towards the building, filled with a sudden trepidation, but nothing supernatural stopped her from crossing the threshold, and it was easy to step from the bright sunlight into the cool and comparative gloom.

The church was empty and had been readied for the wedding. The aisle led to an uncomplicated altar, where flowers had already been placed. It was beautiful, and Bernadette was taken by the old jealousy, wanting the pretty scene to be her own destiny.

She shook herself sternly and looked at the pews, checking for the orders of service but seeing only the bare wooden seats. There was a noise at the front of the church, and looking up, she saw Tim entering from a side door.

Sound abated, time eased, and Bernadette suddenly felt trapped by destiny. It was too obvious what would happen next, and she had no strength to fight it. Despite her cold and pragmatic exterior, she was a superstitious person at heart. She had relied on signs from the universe to guide her in other things. She placed great emphasis on the metaphysical, because human nature was so unknown to her.

She walked down the aisle, a bride to a groom, the path so

conspicuous and easy. It was as if one of her childhood story-book dreams had at last become reality. The universe was condoning Tim, finally delivering her hero. Why would this strange scenario have been conceived otherwise?

Tim didn't say a word, and they stared at each other as her body carried her towards him. She stopped within arm's reach, gazing up at the face she knew so well, the face of the man she had wanted for years. He was wearing a grey morning suit, and it was not difficult to imagine that this version of Tim was *her* Tim. He looked as she had always imagined him, his blue eyes misty behind his glasses, his blonde hair kissed by the soft church light.

'You look beautiful,' he said, and she blushed like a maiden. 'Bernadette, I'm so sorry.'

'It's okay,' she said. 'I'm sorry too.'

He smiled at her and took her hand. She wondered if their encounter was over, but as she watched, a look of tender misgiving crossed his features, distorting them momentarily into an expression of pain. He tried harder with his smile, encouraging her sympathy, playing with her fingers in his, and she felt him tug her towards him slightly, with a quick laugh of nervous enquiry. Following the movement, she stepped forward so she was at his chin. He was looking down at her searchingly, as if trying to read her soul for absolution.

'Oh Tim! Tim!' she breathed, her body trembling with the surreal climax.

Reassured by her words, he bent his head and kissed her. Although it had seemed ordained, Bernadette was still taken off guard by the conflicting sensations. She was kissing Tim, her Tim, at last, and her thwarted passion had an outlet. But having imagined it so many times, it was strange that the kiss was nothing at all like she had pictured. His mouth was tight and firm against hers, and he held her to him with rigid determination. She moved against him, her lips searching for softness, for something that would feel like Radley's kiss. That kiss had been so instinctive that she had been lost in it, but kissing Tim was a performance exercise: she was working to try and make herself feel enchanted, but her mind was much more powerful than the physical sensation, and other than the thrill of a goal obtained, she felt nothing real.

It was Bernadette who realised they were being watched. She opened her eyes, discomfited, and in her peripheral vision saw a nightmare. She jumped back from Tim, leaving him gasping, and stared in horror at Lauren and David, who were carrying the wretched orders of service.

'You *bitch*,' spat Lauren, loudly.

Bernadette glanced at Tim, who looked like a man whose whole life was flashing before his eyes.

'Lauren—' he began, but David cut in hysterically.

'This is outrageous!' he said shrilly. David appeared to be having a revelation of his own, learning all of a sudden that he actually hated Bernadette. And indeed, Bernadette did seem to stand, at that moment, for everything a weak man must fear in a woman: she was selfish, vain, sly, conniving and vicious. She was dangerous, sinful and vulgar. David looked electrified by his hatred, a vision of love turning to repulsion.

'Lauren, David—' Tim tried again.

'You're both disgusting,' said Lauren. 'How could you do this?'

Bernadette went cold with dread. 'Please, Lauren,' she began. 'Please don't tell Elizabeth. I'll die.'

'Elizabeth? I'm going to tell everyone! I wonder what Radley Blake's going to say. What's *he* going to think about this?'

'Please,' Bernadette urged. 'I'm begging you, please don't tell Elizabeth.'

'You don't deserve our clemency,' David hissed. 'You're a crazy, oversexed harlot!'

Bernadette saw how much her two accusers despised her, and she could not blame them. Tim was useless by her side; a man she would never love again. She was drained of all feeling for him; all she cared about was Elizabeth.

She stumbled towards the exit, unable to stay any longer and face her punishment. She had to fend off Lauren, who clutched at her as she passed, spilling the orders of service in the process. David skipped out of her path as if she was poisonous.

'Coward!' Lauren called after her. 'You're a coward!'

Bernadette ran, Lauren's words ringing in her ears. She had never been called a coward before; she had always been praised for her fearlessness and daring. But it was true: she was a coward, an emotional adventure-seeker who couldn't face the reality of her own nature.

She dashed back through the woods as if her enemies would chase her, tears streaming down her face. She didn't know where to go. She couldn't return to the suite and face Elizabeth; she could never see Elizabeth again. She sobbed harder, out of breath and distraught, feeling as though her Judgement Day was at hand.

As the path widened and she reached the central resort, there were other people walking around, dressed in their wedding attire, enjoying the sunshine. Bernadette had nowhere to hide, but she slowed her pace to a fast walk and kept her head down, sensing the concerned glances but refusing to make eye contact.

She headed for the resort exit, down the hill towards the main road. She couldn't go back to collect her belongings and risk running into anyone. She would hitch-hike all the way to Los Angeles, and if she died on the journey, so much the better.

After an hour or so of walking, the hem of the peach chiffon bedraggled and dusty, Bernadette had stopped crying, exhausted from her frantic pace and the thoughts in her head. She was haunted by her own nature. She was terrified of what she had left behind.

Perhaps with her gone, Lauren and David wouldn't feel the need to tell anybody. It was *her* they hated, not Tim. Perhaps they had thought up some plausible excuse for her absence and the wedding was now under way, with Elizabeth blissfully unaware.

Or perhaps they had told Elizabeth of the betrayal, and she had been so devastated that she had jumped from the cliff in her wedding dress, falling to her death with a broken heart. But no – Radley was there. Radley would stop that from happening. He would be there to protect Elizabeth.

Radley was the only person Bernadette wanted to see. Radley would understand. Radley knew her faults and loved her still. Radley was the source of all goodness and sanity.

As if she had summoned him by magic, Bernadette realised that a car had slowed and was following her. Radley himself was in the back seat; Mick was driving. The windows were rolled down, and both men were staring at her. She stopped and looked at Radley, hoping to see some sign of comfort – but there was none. His glance was cold, and for the first time, she was frightened of him.

'Get in the car, Bernadette,' he said.

Bernadette shook her head, unable to move.

'Get in the car, or I will get out and drag you in here myself.'

Bernadette shook her head again, vigorously. 'I can't,' she said. 'Please don't make me.'

Unexpectedly, Mick spoke up from the front seat, his nasal voice fierce with emotion. 'Get in the car, Bernadette, or *I'll* come and get you.'

Shocked at hearing Mick say anything other than his customary 'Uh-huh', Bernadette made haste and got into the car, sliding along the back seat next to Radley.

'You're both unnecessarily violent,' she muttered nervously. 'Accosting a girl in the road, with threats of—'

'ENOUGH!' bellowed Radley, making her jump in alarm. 'None of your nonsense. Now there's a woman back there who needs you, and you're going to play your part.'

'What's happened?' she asked, terrified.

'What's happened? Well, after witnessing your little *encounter* in the church this morning, Lauren and David told Elizabeth all about it, sparing no detail. They also decided it would be a good idea to inform the whole congregation, and now the vile rumour mill is in full operation.'

'Lizzie!' Bernadette gasped.

Radley looked down at his hands and said quietly, 'Elizabeth wouldn't hear a word against you. Or Tim. She shut Lauren down pretty quickly. Tim and Elizabeth are going ahead with the wedding. But I won't have you disappearing from the service and adding fuel to the fire. You're going to go back there, and you're going to smile, and look beautiful, and face the damage you've wrought.'

Bernadette shrank back against the seat. 'I can't!' she said. 'I just can't! Please don't make me. Please, let's just take this car and keep driving – I've never needed protecting from anything more than this. You said you wanted to protect me!'

'Curb your manipulation, and don't remind me of the stupid things I said to you.'

Bernadette's heart went cold. 'They weren't stupid things.'

'Bernadette. Stop. This isn't about you. And it isn't about me. This is about Elizabeth.'

'She won't want to see me!'

'Of course she will. She loves you. You don't think I came to get you of my own accord? Elizabeth begged me to find you. She was worried that you'd do yourself a mischief.'

Realising that Radley's feelings for her had altered, Bernadette was quiet. Tears began streaming down her face, and she could do nothing to stop them.

'No more crying,' said Radley, harshly. 'You need to look presentable so that all these people can whisper nasty things about you. Here . . .'

With the help of a pack of tissues and a bottle of Evian, he wiped Bernadette's face clean of make-up. 'That's better,' he said, when he'd finished. 'You're so pretty you don't need that stuff anyway. But you mustn't look defeated, scarlet woman. You must play your part convincingly.'

While he was gently cleaning her face, Bernadette looked at him for some sign of relenting, but there was none. He had become a different person, the person that other people had described when she had interviewed him: his face an impenetrable, impersonal mask.

The car drove up as close to the church as possible. Radley jumped out and Bernadette followed him. He took her hand in his, not as a gesture of solidarity, but to stop her from taking flight.

The church clearing had a different atmosphere now that the building was filled with people. The common human energy was grounding, and the approach was not as sinister. Bernadette was tripping with adrenalin. She held her chin high, ready to accept her fate.

In the vestibule, Elizabeth stood waiting patiently with her bridesmaids. Lauren was there, sulking in her peach gown. Elizabeth looked beautiful, all in white, and when she saw her friends, her face lit up. She came towards them with a smile.

'Elizabeth, I . . .' Bernadette began, her heart in her throat.

'It's okay, sweetheart,' Elizabeth said. 'It's okay. Tim told me it was his fault. You don't have to explain anything. Thank you for coming back. That was a brave thing to do. I didn't want to get married without you.' She smiled up at Radley. 'We waited for you.'

Radley gave her a warm kiss and a reassuring smile, and entered the body of the church without a backwards glance. The organ struck up with Pachelbel's Canon in D, and it was time, literally, for Bernadette to face the music.

As they had rehearsed, the bridesmaids were to walk down the aisle before Elizabeth, with Bernadette leading the procession. Elizabeth gave her a nod of encouragement, and taking a deep breath, Bernadette entered the church for the second time that morning, her head spinning, dizzy and confused by it all: her lack of understanding, and her own passivity.

Her vision was not clear, and she didn't know where to focus her eyes. The little church was packed with guests, every pew crammed, people standing and staring at her. There was a general whisper at her entrance, and she could feel their dislike and confusion hitting her like a punch to the face.

She realised that Lauren, walking behind her, was also struggling. Lauren had been the unwelcome messenger, and now here she was, processing publicly with the woman she had shamed.

Tim was standing at the front of the church with his groomsmen, facing the bridal party. He gave Bernadette the briefest of nods, but Radley would not look at her. He was unbearably handsome in his suit, his chiselled features taut with suppressed emotion.

The ceremony passed in a blur of remorse. Elizabeth was calm and happy, looking up at her soon-to-be-husband with no reproach. Bernadette was thankful for her friend's swift forgiveness and genuine cheer, although she couldn't understand it.

The moment that the minister asked if anyone present had any objection to the marriage, a sort of thrill seemed to go through the crowd, and all attention was focused on Bernadette and Lauren. But both women stood statue-like, with downcast eyes, as the minister hurried on.

After the service, when the hymns had been sung, and the readings given, and the couple declared husband and wife in the eyes of God, they all emerged from the church to the bright woods, and walked the short distance to the reception.

Long tables had been arranged in a clearing overlooking the ocean, with a dance floor and a live band. There was a profusion of flowers, the pretty wedding colours looking well against the dark greens and blues of the natural setting.

The crowd, to a man, eschewed Bernadette, not venturing anywhere vaguely near her. Usually she worked hard to avoid the society of others, and it was a singular experience to have society shun *her*. During the wedding breakfast she sat with the other bridesmaids, none of whom felt inclined to communicate. She concentrated on eating the delicious food, which dried quickly in her mouth, and listened conscientiously to the numerous speeches, including Tim's lengthy and well-rehearsed declaration of devotion to Elizabeth.

When it came time for the first dance, she stood with the others gathered near the dance floor, going through the motions, as Tim and Elizabeth swayed to 'Fields of Gold', staring at one another contentedly. Bernadette looked for Radley, but couldn't see him.

Once Eva Cassidy had ceased singing about barley, others were encouraged to join the party, and several couples started dancing. Elizabeth came to Bernadette, smiling, and taking both her hands led her on to the floor.

'How are you doing?' she asked, pulling Bernadette into a hug.

'I'm just so sorry,' Bernadette gasped, hugging her back, hard.

Elizabeth smiled and shook her head. 'Hey! Shit happens! You couldn't have known he was going to be in the church. And you'd done so well up to that point.'

The two women looked at each other for a long beat, and then both of them started laughing, Bernadette somewhat hysterically. 'You *knew*?' she gasped. 'You knew all along that I was in love with him?'

'I suspected that you *thought* you were in love with him,' Elizabeth corrected her. 'Which was pretty funny. There you were, lusting after poor old Tim – and I mean, I love the man, so I'm not blind to his attractions, but he's *so* not the kind of guy that beautiful women usually run after; no wonder it turned his head – and all the time you had Radley, who's so obviously perfect for you, just dying to be with you. I knew you'd figure it out.'

Bernadette hadn't thought it possible she could love Elizabeth any more, but she looked at the other woman with an overwhelming rush of feeling. 'I just wish I'd figured it out before this morning.'

'Tim told me it was his fault. He's been stupid about this whole thing, but he's an okay guy at heart. I'm not saying I'm letting him off the hook that easily, but we're good. I couldn't have forgiven his behaviour over anyone but you.'

The two women hugged tightly, and Bernadette wanted to cry with relief at Elizabeth's charity. Suddenly Radley appeared beside them and tapped Elizabeth on the shoulder.

'Excuse me,' he said politely, 'but may I cut in?'

'Of course!' giggled Elizabeth, standing on tiptoes to give him a kiss on the cheek. 'Be my guest.'

Radley took Bernadette in his arms and they danced away, moving well together. Her response to his closeness was devastating, her whole body quaking with love and fascination.

'Thank you,' she said, staring up at him.

'I didn't do it for you,' he said, not meeting her gaze. 'I did it for Elizabeth. The last thing she needs to do on her wedding day is babysit *you*.'

His words were shards of crystal, falling and breaking. It pained her to hear him, so different to the man she knew.

'Please,' she said. 'I'm so sorry.'

'Who are you sorry for, Bernadette?'

'For Elizabeth. And – and you.' As she said it, she realised that Elizabeth was not the only casualty of her morning's activity. She had hurt Radley Blake, the gentle genius.

He gave a curt laugh. 'Please don't be sorry on my account. You have been the cause of your own suffering, as I have been mine.'

'Oh Radley!' she cried. 'Please, please don't!'

'Hush,' he said, leading her from the dance floor as her anguish attracted the attention of the people around them. He walked her quickly towards the woods, and she was so grateful to be in his company that she practically skipped at his side. Once they were far enough away to be out of sight, she turned to him and tried to embrace him, but he would not be held, and firmly moved her arms away.

'Please,' she whispered. 'It was just a kiss. It didn't mean anything, honestly. I don't care for Tim at all.'

'Just a kiss? You kissed my best friend's husband. On their wedding day, in the church where they were to exchange their vows. You befriended her, whilst pursuing him. You knew exactly what you were doing, and were given every opportunity to rein back. And you made me believe, truly believe, that you could love me! That you could do the decent thing. Idiot that I am.'

'It sounds bad when you put it like that,' she gulped, desperately scrolling through possible paths for the conversation. He was angry, angrier than she had ever seen him, but it must be possible to win him round. She just had to communicate how much she loved him.

'I don't love Tim,' she continued. 'The kiss was a terrible mistake – but it was an act of closure!'

'Closure?' he repeated, incredulous, as if every thought in her head was an abomination. 'You needed closure, did you? Well, tell me, how is Elizabeth ever to get closure from that act? How am I? Your behaviour affects more than just yourself.'

'Oh don't be hurt, my love! You can't be hurt that badly. I love you! *I love you*, Radley.'

He looked at her like she had slapped him in the face, and actually recoiled. 'And again!' he said. 'Unbelievable, woman! You choose to tell me that now? You have no skill at modelling other people's mindsets. You have no empathy.'

'Don't you want to know that I love you?'

'I don't want your sympathy, your cheap words. You think I can't be hurt? You think I'm not as vulnerable as you, just because I'm a man? Does it weaken me, in your eyes? You've done more harm than you could ever fathom, Bernadette, but best for you that you don't know it, if it will save you some of this pain.'

She was too distraught to move; she just stared at him, shaking. It was cold out of the sun. 'But . . . you said you loved me. Just last night, you said it. You can't have changed your mind. You must love me still.'

'My love is not unconditional, the love of a mother for a child,' he said, glowering at her. 'It's a possessive hunger, the jealous love of a man for a woman.'

'Well that doesn't sound quite right,' said Bernadette, scowling too. 'You might want to work on that.'

His eyes widened, like a horse about to shy, and she wasn't sure if he was going to smack her, or laugh. He did neither, but there was a shift in his expression, and his posture relaxed a little. He gave a rueful smile. 'Well, yes, we might both learn to love the way Elizabeth does. She has a refinement of feeling inaccessible to people like you and me.'

Bernadette sensed hope in his manner, and tried to move to him, reaching out her arms, but he held her off.

'I thought we could make each other happy,' he said. 'But perhaps we are too alike, too selfish, after all. You are not for me, and I won't think on it any more.'

'I am for you!' she sobbed, as he turned away and she realised he was beyond her. But he gave no answer to her cries, stalking back the way they had come through the dappled forest glow, the light and shade allowing him camouflage, so that he eventually disappeared from view in an organic haze, as if the memory of the man lingered a moment after his body was gone.

Epilogue

Bernadette resettled herself comfortably in the hard-backed chair, preparing for another few hours of meet-and-greet. It was arduous, but also fascinating, to meet the women who had been affected by her work. They always had their own stories to tell.

She sat in front of the large board that advertised her newly published novel, *A House of One's Own*. Across the table, a queue of women stretched back towards the entrance to the bookstore.

Looking up quickly, she thought she had seen him – a tall hulk of a man, dark and brooding. A figure that haunted her, day and night. She hadn't seen him since he had left her in the woods nearly two years ago. And not a single day passed when she didn't think of him. If love was to be proved by constancy, it was now quite evident that Bernadette was truly in love.

She knew that he was well, that he was working just as hard. Elizabeth was patient with her regular questioning when they met once a week for dinner, lingering over a home-cooked meal, Tim pouring them both drinks and entertaining them with stupid jokes but making himself scarce once they had eaten.

'How is he?' Bernadette would ask, immediately.

'He looks the same. He came round the other night and we played Cards Against Humanity. Clarion is kicking butt; they've just been awarded some huge military contract.'

'And is he . . .?'

'No. He's not dating anyone.'

Bernadette felt the hairs on the back of her neck tingle, and glanced up again. The line of women was growing longer. She tried to stop thinking about him and focus on the task in hand. Elizabeth and Tim had encouraged her to reach out to him, but she couldn't. She didn't know what to say.

She finished scrawling her name across a copy of her book and the reader left, satisfied. Her pen was running out of ink, and she bent down to her bag to find a new one. The next copy of her novel was banged down on the table impatiently.

'One moment,' she muttered, her head in her bag.

An unmistakable male voice, with that inimitable overconfident drawl, replied, 'Please make this one out to Radley, the love of my life, who I wronged most terribly.'

When she looked up, she found herself face to face with him. Elizabeth had been right: he looked no different. But she had forgotten how extreme his energy was, how it felt to be in his presence, to bask in his overpowering allure.

'Radley,' she breathed – and it was the most exciting sound to ever pass over her tongue.

'Bernadette. I read your book. It was quite readable, I thought, even though I'm not the target demographic.'

'Thank you.'

He smiled at her, and she was undone.

'How are you?' he asked, solicitously, as if they had no history, as if they were strangers meeting for the first time.

'I'm . . . okay. I'm trying not to think about myself too much right now. I've retired the Man Whisperer, you know.'

'Yes, I know. I've been following your work. And Elizabeth has kept me up to date on all the rest.'

'Yes. She has for me too. About you, I mean.'

'Then you know already that I enjoyed your book.' He picked it up, measured and thoughtful. 'How autobiographical is it?'

'Well, I, um . . .'

'Because I must say, I quite liked the genius botanist chap . . . what's his name?'

'Rodger Bentley.'

'Rodger. Right.'

'Right. He's the hero,' she said, feeling a little faint. 'Obviously.' She had forgotten how arousing it was to maintain eye contact with him, his dark gaze so completely overwhelming.

'*I* never saw you as a racy seductress, as you know,' he said, quietly. 'I saw a confused and lonely girl, far away from home and her mother's love.'

Bernadette gulped, and it was a moment before she could answer. 'Yes. I know.' She paused. 'The novel, it's really a sort of . . . love letter. An apology.'

He stared at her, deeply, as though looking for some sign of the old cynicism or coquetry, and she smiled at him, plainly, as a friend would.

'Well I thought it was about time I stopped by and offered my congratulations.' He kissed her hand theatrically, looking down at her with twinkling eyes, with that suppressed mirth that characterised him. Bernadette was so engrossed, she didn't even stop to complain to the woman behind Radley in the line, who was surreptitiously filming them both on her iPhone.

'Thank you,' she said again, at a loss for words. She had wanted this moment for so long.

He nodded and turned away, leaving her ravenous.

'Radley!' she called after him. 'Radley – will I see you again?'

He glanced back. 'Perhaps,' he said with a smile. 'If you're good . . .'

Acknowledgements

I would like to thank the team at United Agents: Dallas Smith for kicking things off and sending my unfinished manuscript to the literary folks downstairs. Millie Hoskins for reading and believing and encouraging Jon to take a look. Jon Elek for being the very best agent a person could possibly hope for, and much more besides. And a big thank you to Celine Kelly for all her help and encouragement.

Thank you to everyone at Hodder and Stoughton for making the process feel actually romantic. Carolyn Mays for being my champion. Emily Kitchin for being so lovely, clever and patient. Jane Selley for making the thing actually readable. Louise Swannell for filling my diary with exciting events, and Auriol Bishop for all of her incomparable magic touches – not just the roses and ribbons and cinnamon buns!

I would also like to thank Paulina Sandler, my best friend, who happens to be some kind of closet literary genius, the world's most prolific reader, and an incredible critic. Thank you for being the appraising eye, Paul. Ali Sudol, my dearest artistic inspiration and beautiful sister. DA Wallach and Liz Brinson Wallach, my family, thank you for letting me read you bits out loud, celebrating with me, and taking constant care of me. Stacey Ferreira for supporting my career as a novelist, and being a great girl-boss and an amazing friend. Raiyah Bint Al-Hussein, my brain twin and most beloved voice of the universe. Always love for Elon, Damian, Griffin, Kai, Saxon and Xavier.

And unending gratitude to my parents, for everything. You are my greatest blessing, and I love you more than . . .